The
HORROR
of
JULIE BATES

Fran Rizer

First Print Edition October, 2016

FranRizer.com
OdysseySouthPublishing.com
or OdysseySouthPublishing@gmail.com

Odyssey South Publishing and logo are trademarks of Odyssey South Publishing.

This book is presented as a work of fiction though the story was told to the author as fact. Some names have been changed, are products of the author's imagination, or are used fictitiously.

ISBN-13: 978-0692766170
ISBN- 10: 0692766170

Thanks to Adam Rizer for assistance in research on the city of Columbia and to Nathan Rizer and Aeden Rizer for use of their photos which begin on page 348. Special appreciation also to ghost hunter Richard D. Laudenslager for consultation on things paranormal and, most of all, to Julie Bates for sharing her story.

PREFACE
FROM FRAN RIZER

WHEN A red-haired woman approached me at a book-signing, I expected her to ask me to autograph one of my cozy mysteries. Instead, she asked me to *write* a book for her. I went into my usual spiel that she could do a better job of putting her story on paper than I, but we agreed to meet in the coffee shop after the signing. Writers are frequently approached to write or co-write someone else's story. Most of the time, we decline politely, but there was something about this mysterious stranger that made me hesitate to dismiss her so quickly.

The HORROR of JULIE BATES is that woman's story. I spent many, many hours recording Julie Bates' tale and many more days and nights scaring myself as I wrote her story from her point of view, changing only names. The occasional third-person chapters were added after I was fortunate enough to obtain Richard Arthur's journal.

1

MY HEART woke me—hammering so hard I could feel the *thump, thump, thump* inside as my body rocked with the pounding. Shrill shrieks assaulted my ears as every muscle spasmed in terror.

Then I realized the screams were coming from me.

Drenched with sweat, I dropped my sopping wet nightgown to the floor and pulled on yesterday's jeans, sweater, and tennis shoes in a hurry because though I was alone, I felt like someone was watching me. From the corner of my eye, I thought I caught a glimpse of a shadow on the wall—a grotesque, winged silhouette—but nothing was there. Like so many nights since returning to South Carolina, I'd suffered a terrible nightmare, but once again I couldn't remember what it was about.

The need to get away overwhelmed me, and I shoved my cell phone, house key, and the envelope

I'd addressed the night before into my pants pocket. Fresh air might slow down my desperate hyperventilation. I opened the door, but the early autumn air was colder than expected. Back inside, I added a jacket over my sweater and started out again. No need to take my purse. I'd be right back after a quick walk to the post office.

JERRY PATTERSON. No doubt about it. Even though ten years had passed since I last saw him at our high school graduation, and I'd never seen Jerry lying down nor wearing a high-dollar, three-piece suit before, I recognized him immediately. The surrounding pre-dawn darkness felt eerie, but Jerry's face was clearly visible beneath the city streetlight.

We'd exchanged a few emails after I sought him out on Facebook, and I'd looked forward to seeing him, but not this way.

Stunned, I stood staring at Jerry Patterson lying motionless on the sidewalk. *Act like an adult,* I told myself, *do something. Check his pulse.* Just as I stepped closer to Jerry, a street person shuffled up to me. Scruffy beard, faded shirt, torn jeans, and worn-out sandals — uniform of beatniks, hippies, and now in the twenty-first century — the homeless. He smelled like baths came few and far between, the unfortunate norm for those who live under bridges or in public parks and city cemeteries.

The homeless guy bent over Jerry and reached toward him. For a moment, I visualized a CNN film clip showing someone robbing an unconscious person on a city street, but this man's hand didn't reach for Jerry's pocket. Three fingers pressed against the side of my old classmate's neck.

"Lady," he said, "if you got a cell phone, call 911. He shore ain't breathing good, but I feel a little pulse."

Why didn't I do that the minute I saw Jerry? Lately, I don't act like myself. I'm in a fog a lot of the time.

"Whatcha think happen to him?" the vagrant asked after I lost my cool, screamed at the 911 dispatcher to send an ambulance to the corner of Taylor and Assembly Streets, and disconnected. *Calm down,* I told myself. *This kind of behavior isn't me. I don't scream at people.*

"I don't know," I said. "He doesn't look like he's bleeding anywhere. Could be a heart attack, but see how his left arm's bent. The bone in there is most likely fractured."

"Mebbe he fell and broke it after he had a stroke or sump'en."

Sirens sounded in the distance, rapidly increasing in volume until an emergency vehicle screeched to a stop at the curb. Two EMTs jumped from the ambulance and rushed over to Jerry. I moved out of their way.

A city police cruiser pulled in right after them. A

uniformed officer stepped from the car and pointed a flashlight, dang-near blinding me with the high-powered beam shining right into my eyes.

"What happened here?" he demanded after he'd asked and written down my name, address, and date of birth on the notepad he'd pulled from his pocket. His manner was official even with his rather extreme southern drawl. He was one of those big men whose dirty blond hair was shot with gray — probably a little prematurely. I guessed his age to be early to middle forties.

"I was walking to the post office and saw this man lying on the sidewalk," I said. "I thought he was dead, but this gentleman . . . " I turned toward where the guy had stood. He was gone.

"What gentleman?" the policeman asked.

"There was a homeless man here. He felt Jerry's carotid artery and said he was still breathing. He told me to call 911."

"What makes you call the man homeless?"

"Dirty, ragged — the way he was dressed and smelled." I watched as the policeman wrote these responses in the notebook.

"I'll want to talk to him." He looked up at me, and his eyes scolded me as though I were responsible for the homeless man slipping away.

"He was right here until you arrived." That wasn't a real defense, but I used it.

"You called the victim 'Jerry.' Were you together

before he collapsed?" He continued making notes.

"No, I just saw him lying here when I reached the corner. The homeless man showed up right after." I shoved my hands down deep into my pockets to warm them and to hide the fact they were shaking.

"Probably didn't want to chance my running his name and finding a warrant on him," the policeman said. "You saw the victim first? What did you do until the homeless man arrived?"

"I really didn't do anything. It was only a minute and I was in shock." I felt color rush to my face, and I added, "I went to high school with the man."

"The homeless guy?"

"No, the one on the ground. He's Jerry Patterson. I guess if the homeless man hadn't shown up so fast, I would've come to my senses and checked Jerry's pulse myself."

"I'll need you to go over to the police station and speak with our forensic artist. She'll do a composite portrait so we can find the man who disappeared when I arrived. He may have harmed Patterson before you came on the scene." The officer put the notepad back into his pocket. "I'll want a full statement, too, but I'll get that while you're at the station."

The policeman stared at me without a word for a minute.

"What were you doing out here before daylight?" he asked. "Were you coming to meet the man on the sidewalk?"

"I've been having trouble sleeping. When my dreams wake me, I like to get out of the house. Besides, I had something to mail, so I was headed to the post office." I pulled the addressed, stamped envelope from my pocket and waved it at him as though that proved what I'd said. "I have no idea why Jerry Patterson was here this time of morning."

"Don't you know you shouldn't be walking downtown before dawn? The homeless who refuse to spend the night in shelters hang out around this area. Certainly not all, but some of them are dangerous."

"Nobody's ever bothered me." I looked down at myself. Maybe no one had ever tried to rob me because I looked homeless myself, and I may have smelled as bad as some of them. My dad used to say, "Horses sweat, men perspire, and ladies glisten," but I had no doubt that I'd been blasted into wakefulness not perspiring, and certainly not glistening — definitely sweating.

The policeman turned to the EMTs and asked, "Where are you taking him, which hospital?"

"None," said the older attendant. "Need to call the coroner. This man's dead."

"Did he just die? Aren't you even going to *try* CPR?" I called to him, almost yelling.

"Lady, he's been a stiff at least two hours."

The policeman scowled at him before turning back toward me. "You called for an ambulance. Did you realize he was deceased?"

"No, but I didn't touch him. The homeless man told me to call 911 because he thought Jerry still had a pulse when he felt his neck."

"More likely he wanted to distract you while he got away."

I shivered. Not from cold.

"I'm Sergeant Nate Adams." He pointed to the badge and name tag he wore. "You can sit in my cruiser while I wrap this up with the coroner. If there are any signs it's a suspicious death, we'll need to call in a K-9 unit and try to track down the guy you think is homeless."

He opened the car door, and I sat inside.

It seemed like hours before the policeman returned.

"Are you calling in homicide detectives?" I asked.

"No. There are no signs of violence. He probably had a heart attack." He stared at me silently for a moment and his eyes narrowed. "What makes you think this is a murder? What are you keeping back from me?"

"Nothing. I told you exactly what happened."

"This doesn't make sense. Too much of a coincidence that the two of you are on the street this early unless it was planned." He waved his arm toward the body. "I think you came down here to meet this fellow."

"But I didn't," I insisted.

"And your disappearing homeless man doesn't make much sense either."

"I swear I'm not lying."

"Just tell the truth. What was going on?"

I didn't answer.

Dead silence in his car as he drove to the police station.

2

RICHARD CROUCHED behind the old tombstone. He felt lucky that this one block of Columbia had a mission shelter, a public park, and an old graveyard all within short walking distance of each other and an even shorter running distance. He'd darted to the cemetery because the police searched the park anytime something strange or illegal happened downtown, and authorities would think nothing of rousing up everyone sleeping at the mission if they decided to look for him there.

The cemetery seemed the safest bet to stay hidden, yet close enough to see what was happening. Richard had slept there part of the previous night. He opened the small bag of belongings he'd hidden behind that particular grave marker and carefully unwrapped his spare pair of skivvies from around his binoculars. He returned the underwear to the bag and added them to the socks, cushioning his hunting knife along with a couple of oatmeal-raisin cakes.

Hunkered down, Richard watched the policeman talk to the red-haired woman. He wondered if he should have stayed with her. No, that wouldn't work at all.

The EMTs had obviously just told the cop that the man was dead. Big deal! Richard had known that when he first saw the body. He'd lied to the woman to keep her from becoming hysterical before others arrived on the scene. He would've felt guilty as hell running away if she'd gone ape-shit. The policeman had assisted the redhead into the back of his patrol car. Surely they wouldn't arrest her for finding a body on the street. Then again, because his opinion of some local law enforcement had changed since he'd been living homeless, he wasn't sure of that.

Richard had watched this woman before. In fact, he'd been following her when she'd discovered the dead man. He liked the way her hair swung when she walked as well as the shapeliness of her legs and butt in the tight jeans she wore. She was a little heavier than the girls in magazines and on television these days. Round and gorgeous. Reubenesque. He'd tailed her several times previously when he'd noticed her walking down Assembly Street before daylight. Each of those times, she'd wound up at the post office, dropped an envelope or two in the blue box out front, and then headed back toward the direction she'd come from. He'd always abandoned her when the sun came up.

Now, as she sat in the cop's patrol car while the coroner and other officials performed their necessary duties to declare the man on the sidewalk officially dead, Richard couldn't see the woman.

He curled into a fetal position and went to sleep.

3

HEAD: WOBBLY and dizzy. Heart: thudding in my chest. I looked around the police station lobby, hoping for something to eat. Some people can't eat at all when they're stressed. I've always been the exact opposite. Being upset makes me hungry, and the proof was in the ten pounds I'd gained in the year since my mother was murdered.

I shivered, and my skin felt cold from the evaporation of sweat pouring out on my forehead and arms. I shook so hard that I might have tipped over the plastic chair I sat in if it hadn't been bolted to the floor. I'd been sweaty when I awoke, but this was different—anxiety, not fear.

Hard to believe I'd found a dead body on the sidewalk in front of the post office, much less that he was someone I knew. My mind flashed back a dozen years. As though I were a spectator, I saw myself: a shy teenaged girl in tenth-grade algebra. Jerry sat at the desk behind me. I stood and walked over to the pencil sharpener, fully aware that Jerry was not only watching, he would get up and follow me like he always did. When I turned to go back to my seat, he was standing so close that his elbow brushed against my breast.

"Scuze me," he said. I glared at him, but deep inside, I smiled. I liked the attention, I liked Jerry, and only years later did I realize that the elbow on my young boob had been a way of sneaking a feel — accidentally, on purpose.

That often-repeated tacky move back then should have been enough to keep me from seeking Jerry out on social media when I returned to South Carolina barely six weeks before, but my high school class had a ten-year reunion coming up, and I was feeling rejected at how my relationship in New York had ended. I'd messaged Jerry "This is Julie Bates. Do you plan to attend the reunion this fall?"

"Yes, will you be there? I heard you moved to New York," he'd answered, and for several weeks, we'd been emailing. He'd said he was a lawyer — never mentioned any reason he'd be downtown before daylight — and I certainly hadn't told him about my nightmares and how they sometimes forced me out of the house at dawn and earlier.

Maybe the policeman was right about my finding Jerry being too big a coincidence, but I knew for a fact that I'd had nothing to do with his being on that street, nor his death.

A young man in uniform came by and asked, "Can I get you a cup of coffee?"

"Yes," I answered, "that would be wonderful, and do you have any crackers or maybe a doughnut?" He frowned when I mentioned the doughnut. I guess he thought I was stereotyping him. Or maybe he thought I wasn't thin enough to be eating doughnuts. He motioned toward a machine across the room—a huge dispenser with glass doors. I could see nabs and honey buns and candy bars and bags of chips. I rummaged through my pockets, but all I found were the cell phone, my house key, and the envelope I'd planned to mail. I lusted for a handful of quarters or a couple of dollar bills.

"What do you want in the coffee?" the guy asked.

"A little cream and sugar," I said, then corrected myself, "no, better make that artificial sweetener," as he walked away.

He returned and held out a Styrofoam cup, but my hand jerked too much to take it.

"Are you okay, lady?" he asked.

I nodded yes, but I felt like I might pass out.

Just then Sergeant Adams came from the back and walked over to us. He stared for a moment, bent over me, and asked calmly, "Are you on any kind of medication or illegal drugs?" I answered by shaking my head back and forth, emphatically no.

"She asked me for a doughnut," the young cop

volunteered. "I showed her the machine."

"No money?" the older man asked me.

"I didn't think I'd need any."

"You should always carry enough cash to make a phone call," he said. He paused, obviously listening to the sirens passing by on the street outside the police headquarters.

I had no reason to laugh except that I tend to giggle like a twelve-year-old when I'm nervous, and he made me *very* nervous. "My mom always said to take enough money for a telephone call when I went on a date. These days, a girl wouldn't be able to find a pay phone if she needed to call home." I held up my cell phone in front of him. "This is usually what a woman carries these days."

A little smile on the sergeant's face calmed my nervousness just a bit as he sat down beside me, and asked, "Is there anyone you'd like to call?"

"What do you mean? Do I need a lawyer?"

His turn to laugh. "No, you don't need a lawyer. You're not a suspect, not even a person of interest. The coroner thinks Patterson's death was probably a coronary. His left arm appears broken, but that might have happened when he collapsed. I meant did you want to call a friend because you're obviously so upset."

That's when it hit me. I'd been back living in Mom's house — my house now — for over a month, and Jerry Patterson was the only person I'd sought out. I'd had dinner one night with Glory, my next-door neighbor, but I'd refused her other invitations by pleading too much work to do. I no longer had any friends in my hometown. Realization that I was all alone brought tears.

Sergeant Adams waited until I got myself under control before calmly saying, "Let me see your identification."

"It's back at my house in my purse."

"I'll drive you home to get it."

BRIGHT YELLOW and orange flames shot high into the smoke-blackened sky above the area where I lived. The sirens we'd heard must have been fire trucks. As Sergeant Adams turned the cruiser onto my street, the pit of my stomach felt like a cannonball had blasted into it. The inferno was my house.

The blaze licked under the wooden floor of the front porch to the dirt below — down where my daddy taught me how to dig for doodlebugs many years ago. The windows blew out with a loud *whoosh*. I couldn't bear to see it, but I stared, unable to tear my eyes away. Stopped at a safe distance, I saw the walls crash down and collapse over what remained of my home and the mementos of a lifetime — my lifetime.

Bedlam — flashing red and blue lights as sirens announced more fire trucks and police cars coming. Even with the car windows closed, the smell of smoke choked me.

I gasped.

Adams reached across the seat and patted my hand.

"Your house?" he asked softly.

I nodded and grabbed the car handle, but he'd locked the door.

My next-door neighbor ran up to the cruiser. The sergeant pushed a button and lowered my window. The smell of smoke was overpowering.

"Oh, thank you, Jesus!" Glory shouted into the window. "I thought you was asleep in there. I done told the firemen that there was a woman in that house. I called them the minute I saw flames through the windows."

"Thank you, Miss Glory," I mumbled.

Glory leaned into the window. A bright pink chenille bathrobe covered her short, chubby body, but her wispy gray hair didn't hide her matching pink scalp. The fire had brought her outside before she'd had time to plop on her curly white wig. She turned and ran toward the firefighters, shouting, "Julie's not in the house. There's no one in there! I was wrong. She's here."

The policeman closed my window from the driver's side of the car, but I could still hear the sounds. Chaos reigned. Neighbors and strangers clustered in groups while people screamed at each other to be heard over the noise.

The cheap clapboard houses on this street were built close together years before when the mill put them up for their workers, and several firefighters kept a steady stream of water on the homes on each side of mine. So far, the fire was contained to just my place.

"Isn't that the house that Mrs. Juliana Epps lived in?" Officer Adams asked.

"Yes, she was my mother," I said.

Sounding robotic, he said, "I'm so sorry for your loss," and then coughed. "I was one of the first policemen to respond to that case, but I didn't make the connection between Juliana Epps and Julia Bates. I guess Bates is your married name."

"Mom didn't like 'Juliana,' so she named me Julia and called me Julie. Bates is my maiden name, my daddy's name. Mom remarried after he died. She divorced Epps a few years back." I rattled off the explanation in short, staccato bits.

"Were you living in the house?" Adams asked.

"Yes, my friends in New York told me to rent some other place because Mom died there, but my mother was the sweetest, kindest woman I've ever known. If her ghost showed up, I would have welcomed her, but there've been no signs of her other than memories."

"What about the killer?" Adams said. "You didn't worry he might return?"

"No, I just wanted to come home."

"You looked familiar to me. I just couldn't place you. I went to your mother's funeral, probably saw you there, but I don't think I ever spoke with you."

"Since I was in New York City when it happened, a female detective cleared me fast. I went back North right after the service. I sold Mom's car real cheap because I didn't need it, but I couldn't sell the house then. I just ran away from it all. I guess I thought I could put off my grief and deal with mourning at a more convenient time."

"Is now a more convenient time? Did you come back to Columbia to clean out the house? Maybe get it ready to rent or sell?"

"No, I don't plan to rent or sell it. I'm living in the house." I stared at the fire—speechless for a moment, mesmerized by the flames.

"Well, I guess I should say I *was* living in it." I finally added.

"Why'd you really come back?"

"I lost my job when I got back to New York. The publisher I worked for decided to lay off the in-house proofreaders and hire independents. I started working from my apartment as a self-employed proof and copy reader. You know, doing the same thing I did before, but freelance. Working at home, I can do my job anywhere so long as I have a computer." I paused.

"And that brought you back here?"

"Kind of."

"Then what was the real reason you came home?"

"That's personal."

He smiled. "Don't you know nothing is personal when you're talking to law enforcement after finding a dead body?"

"I guess not. I'd been dating this guy, Greg, for almost five years, since I first moved to New York. We broke up . . . oh, what the heck! He dumped me." I felt my face screw into a frown. "Mom's house was just a little mill house, but it's paid for, and like I said, I wanted to come home. I've been back a little over a month." I burst into tears again. Sergeant Adams handed me a wad of tissues from a box on the console.

"Insurance!" I gasped with a sudden realization. "I don't even know if Mom had homeowners' insurance on the place."

Of course, even that wouldn't save my parents' wedding pictures and the boxes of my school papers and prom photos Mom had stacked in the middle room, my bedroom, after I moved.

Sergeant Adams had brought me to my house to pick up my identification, but there was no way we'd get *anything* out of it. The home I'd run from only a few hours earlier—totally gutted. The only thing standing was the chimney with black streaks of soot, and the fire wasn't even completely extinguished. Whatever in the house had been causing the nightmares that woke me in terror since I came home, it should be gone now. I looked up to see Glory headed toward us. Sergeant Adams opened my window again.

She leaned in and kissed me on the cheek with a loud smack. "Now, don't you worry about a place to sleep, Julie. You can stay at my house like you did when they had that awful yellow tape everywhere, last year, and . . . " She grinned. "My clothes won't fit you, but we can get you some things from the thrift store."

I opened my mouth to answer her, but a loud noise sounded—kind of like a cross between a big bang and a *whoosh*. An explosion rocked the air and a ball of bright yellow and orange blasted into the sky. Probably the hot water heater or the cook stove.

"There's no point in your watching this," Adams said. "We can go back to the station. I still need a formal statement from you."

"I assume they're going to want to talk to me when the fire is out," I said and motioned toward one of the fire trucks.

"I know. I'll leave word where you'll be."

I couldn't take my eyes off what had been my house. Firefighters had reduced the roaring flames to smoldering ashes with occasional orange flickers peeking through the smoking debris.

"I guess so," I sighed.

Glory leaned through my open window and said, "You look a mess." She looked across to Sergeant

Adams. "Why's Julie in a police car? Did you arrest her? What did she do?" Her questions tumbled out one after the other.

"She's not under arrest. She found something on the sidewalk, and I need a complete statement from her."

"Well, her house has burned to the ground, and she lost her mother just last year. Can't you see how upset she is?" Glory smiled. "Let her come in my house for a while and get herself together."

"I need her statement. I . . . "

The car radio interrupted him with a call about a convenience store robbery.

"That's right up the street from here," Sergeant Adams said. "If you promise not to leave, you can stay here with your friend. I'll come back to pick you up. Patterson appears to be a natural death anyway, so your statement is really just a formality." He pulled the small notepad from his pocket and read my cell phone number to me. I nodded.

"I'll call when I'm on the way back for you to make your statement and help with the sketch of the homeless man," he said. Another announcement on the radio blurted for all units near the robbed store to report to that location.

Sergeant Adams unlocked my door, and I stepped out of his patrol car. Glory put her arm around me and told the policeman, "We'll be inside my house over there." She pointed to the right side of what had been my home.

He didn't spin any tires, but Sergeant Adams left in a hurry.

Here I was a young, healthy adult, but I let the elderly Glory lead me into her house like I was a two-year-old. She gently pushed me down onto the couch in her living room and said, "You sit right here. I'll make us something to drink. Would you rather have hot tea or a cup of coffee? This fire is such a shock, such a terrible shock."

"Coffee," I answered.

She motioned for me to lie down. When my head was snuggled on a throw pillow, she slipped off my shoes, pulled her crocheted blue afghan off the back of the couch, covered me, and tucked me in just as Mom did years ago.

The memory came the same way I'd remembered being in school with Jerry Patterson at the police station. I didn't recall what happened as though I were a part of it, but more like an out-of-body experience. I was watching from above, perhaps from the upper levels where parents and friends sat for the graduation rituals.

I saw myself decked out in a University of South Carolina graduation cap and gown, seated with hundreds of senior students that filled the coliseum bottom level. I stumbled slightly as I filed across the stage with the others on my row for our diplomas.

My point of view changed when I saw Mom and

Glory seated in the balcony as though I were sitting behind them.

"She almost fell," my mother said to Glory.

"She's okay, Juliana," Glory assured Mom and patted her on the shoulder.

When the announcer called my name and I stepped forward to accept my diploma, Mom and Glory refrained from yelling. Some of the audience had screamed for their graduates, ignoring the request to hold all applause until the end. Instead, Mom grabbed Glory and embraced her while they both grinned.

They met me outside the coliseum when the ceremonies were ended, and Mom pulled the three of us into a group hug. "I'm treating you two to dinner," my mother said. "My smart, beautiful daughter for graduating *summa cum laude* and my best friend for a birthday treat. This is a very special day for me."

When we arrived at the restaurant, Mom presented Glory and me with presents—a blue crocheted afghan she'd made for Glory and a pink one for me. In the happy vision, I *saw* the delighted expression on my face when I opened my package.

"Sorry I can't give you something big like a car," my mother apologized to me.

"Mom, you couldn't give me anything I'd love more than something you made," I answered.

Now I lay on Glory's couch with her blue afghan

over me. My pink one had no doubt perished in the fire. The scenario from the past dimmed, and I heard footsteps. I opened my eyes, expecting to see Glory coming from the kitchen in the rear of the house with coffee for both of us.

Instead, I realized the sound had come from the porch. The front door opened, and a man stepped in and carefully pulled the door closed behind him with his gloved right hand. In the left, he carried a bouquet of white roses. He wasn't anyone I recognized, and he didn't look like he was from our neighborhood.

I sat up quickly and stared at him. He wasn't a big man, maybe five feet and eight or nine inches tall. His head turned as he looked all around the room, and I saw his handsome face from all angles. He appeared toned and trim in vintage clothing—old-fashioned black tails with a top hat and white gloves. I was too dumbfounded to speak or move.

He held the roses out toward me, but I sat motionless and didn't reach for them. Slowly he looked all around the room again and then stared straight into my eyes. That attractive face turned evil—twisted and malevolent—and his mouth contorted into rictus, a grotesque grin. His head began to move up and down, not just his chin, his entire face. When his head detached itself from his neck and moved up and down like a bobble head, I knew this was unreal—another dream. I shook myself, but before I could stand, the creature wrapped his arms around me and lifted me.

In only seconds, we were no longer in Glory's house. The man set me on my feet, and I saw that we were standing in the middle of a heavily overgrown field full of dense elder trees, briars, and vines. Remnants of broken grave stones revealed this was a cemetery—a very old one. Even covered with growth, I recognized that the clusters of large sunken rectangles in the ground could only be depressions of old graves containing remnants of caskets that had rotted and collapsed.

On a small incline near the railroad track that slashed off an edge of the field, broken bones were scattered about, but most disturbing to me was a small pine box lying on its side with the top missing. Inside I saw the tiny bones of an infant skeleton. The sky darkened, and rain began pelting the man and me like bullets of ice.

Looking back at the fiend who'd brought me here, I watched his clothing transform to a full-length gray robe with a hood falling over his forehead so low that it shadowed his face as though he didn't have one. He wasn't holding a scythe, but I knew who he was. I shouted one word—NO!

4

MY BODY shook, but neither the dream nor I caused the motion. Glory held me by both arms and jerked me from side to side while she shouted my name.

"Julie, Julie, what's wrong?"

I managed to mumble, "Bad dream," but that hadn't been like the other nightmares I'd been having. I always forgot the others when I awoke. Everything—each detail I'd seen and the terror I'd felt—remained with me, burning holes into my brain.

"Well, I certainly don't want to have any dreams like you must have had while I was making the coffee. The way you was screaming, I was afraid you'd fallen or hurt yourself some way. Do you want to tell me about it?"

"Oh, no," I answered. "I just want to forget it." I'd complained to myself about not remembering the nightmares. Now I just wanted this most recent one to go away. Forgetting would be a comfort.

Glory went to the kitchen and returned with two steaming mugs. She placed them on the end table beside the couch, sat down beside me, and propped her feet on the coffee table. I did the same thing and registered a moment of surprise. My tennis shoes were muddy. That shook me, but I didn't mention it to Glory. They had been clean when I set off down Assembly Street that morning, and I'd only walked on pavement until my nightmare.

I reached across her and picked up my coffee, but a quick sip told me it was too hot to drink. My cell phone rang as I set my cup on the table beside my soiled feet.

"Miss Bates, this is Sergeant Nate Adams with the Columbia Police Department. I'd like to pick you up and take you back to the station for your formal statement now."

"Sure," I answered, hoping that would distract me from the bad recollections. Adams must have called from right in front of the house because he knocked as soon as I disconnected the telephone. Glory let him in and graciously offered him coffee, but he declined and seemed eager to leave, so I didn't get to drink mine. Glory frowned as the policeman and I left.

"SO YOU left your ID and money at home and now it's all destroyed in the fire," the sergeant said as he drove to the police station.

"Yep." I knew that wasn't a very polite answer, but I wasn't in a polite mood. I've always been fairly easy going, but recently, my nerves stayed on edge, and I'd noticed my manners slipping at times as though I were someone else entirely.

"Don't tell me that you kept all your funds in cash hidden under your mattress," Adams said and gave me a slight smile.

I barely managed not to roll my eyes. "I may have been born and raised in the South, but I didn't fall off a turnip truck last night." I answered in a trite cliché. "Most of my money is in the bank, but with my purse burned, not only do I not have identification to show you, I don't know how I'll get any money from my account."

"I can help you get a duplicate driver's license."

"I don't have a license. I moved to New York City right after I finished my degree at USC. My South Carolina driver's license expired on my last birthday, and I haven't gotten a new one since I moved back here."

"What about New York? Didn't you have a license there?"

"Never bothered. I traveled by subway and foot like most everyone does in Manhattan. I had a New York non-driver photo ID, but it was in my purse."

"Tell you what. I'll lend you some money to hold you over until you get identification for here in South

Carolina."

"That's not part of your cop duties. Why would you do that for me?"

"I feel like I know you. As I said, I was one of the first responders to your mother. When I saw her, I wanted desperately to do something for her, but nothing could be done. I couldn't even cover her with a sheet because it would have destroyed evidence. Helping you will be like doing something for her."

"I'll accept your offer, and I'll pay back every penny as soon as I get into my bank account."

I held my hand out as though he would just hand me money. I must have been brain-dead with shock because I certainly wasn't thinking clearly. Finding a dead body, watching my house burn, and dreaming about death personified was enough to make me not act like my normal self, but I'd behaved like I was dense a lot lately.

"I'll drive you and use my debit card for what you need." He smiled. "Don't want you running down the street and finding another body."

I couldn't help it. My shoulders hunched and I sobbed.

"I apologize. This isn't the time to tease you," the policeman said. "I know you're upset about your friend and your house."

Adams reached into the tissue box. It was empty. He scrambled around in the glove compartment and handed me some paper napkins. I wiped my eyes, and then blew my nose—not a dainty sound, but a honk.

"I'm not scolding you, but you're acting like an idiot if you're out walking city streets before daylight with no ID on you."

He told the truth, but I didn't like being compared to an idiot.

"What difference it is to you?" I asked. "Will it be inconvenient to write your report without verifying my identification?" *I'm being ridiculous,* I thought. *Getting snarky with law enforcement is never a smart move.*

Sergeant Adams drove into the police parking lot and stopped the car, but sat there without making any move to get out and go inside.

"My wife went running one morning with no identification," he said. "She was struck by a car."

"I hardly think not having ID caused her to be hit," I snapped. "Besides, I'm on sidewalks all the way from the house to the post office. Bet your wife runs on a road."

"She doesn't run anywhere now, and the lack of ID didn't cause the accident. The absence of identification is why she died from her injuries before they ID'ed her and called me. I didn't get to see her, to be there with her, during her final moments."

The irritability that I'd been experiencing dissolved, and I felt like myself again. "I am *so* sorry," I said. "Sorry for your loss and for being snippy with you."

"You have a right to be tense," he said. "You've had a horrible day." He opened his car door and came around to my side. I didn't expect him to hold my door for me, but he did.

As we entered the building and went down the hall, I told him, "I've been having horrible nightmares for days, or should I say nights?" I smiled at him, and then added, "I even had one earlier before you came back while I was resting at Glory's."

"Tell me about it."

I described the man in the top hat as well as the field where he'd taken me. I didn't say anything about my shoes. That mud *couldn't* have come from that imaginary cemetery.

Sergeant Adams didn't laugh at me though I'd kind of expected him to think it was funny.

"I think I know that field you dreamed about. I'll take you there after we finish up here."

AT THE police station, I answered questions about Jerry Patterson. There wasn't much to tell. I'd known him as a teenager and had recently looked him up on Facebook, but we hadn't seen each other in ten years.

Jerry had volunteered that he was divorced and perhaps the reunion could lead to our getting to know each other. I didn't tell the officer that Jerry had confused me by seeming eager to see me, but wanting to wait until the reunion to meet. He'd seemed happy at the thought of getting together, but hesitant at the same time. Probably scared I'd gained fifty pounds in the past ten years, but I was nowhere near fluffy, just a little more pleasingly plump than I'd been back then.

After I signed the police statement, a fire marshal showed up and asked another round of questions about when I'd gone out of the house that morning and whether I'd left any appliances on. Like I'd admit it if I did, but I hadn't. Next, Adams took me to Officer Brenda Hodge, the sketch artist. I'd expected someone with pads of paper and drawing pencils. Instead, she worked with a computer. It didn't take long for her to create a reasonable likeness of the homeless man I'd seen that morning.

When she finished, she said, "Wow! Cut his hair and clean him up—he'd be hot as hell!" I took a close look at the computer-generated drawing. He was a fine specimen with eyes my mom always called Paul Newman blue, thick brown hair, and a face like a slightly unkempt David Beckham, one of my favorites.

Sergeant Adams congratulated us on such a good, quick job, and insisted he take me to lunch when I confessed I hadn't eaten all day. He refused my suggestion we simply pick up some hamburgers at a McDonald's drive-through. "I want you to eat a good meal," he insisted as we sat down in a booth at the

Waffle House.

"In that case, I'm eating breakfast," I said. He sipped orange juice while I had coffee. I placated his desire for me to eat a "real meal" by having scrambled eggs, cheese grits, and applesauce. He chowed down on some special that included eggs, sausage, hash browns (smothered and covered with onions, cheese, and chili), raisin toast, and a waffle.

"You said you worked on my mother's case," I said between bites of grits and eggs. "Are there any recent developments? When I went back to New York, the officer said they'd let me know if there was anything new. I've heard nothing."

"The case is still open, but there's no additional evidence. The lead investigator thinks it's a burglary that went bad." Adams added ketchup to all the stuff already on top of his hash browns, making them look even messier than when the server brought them.

"That's never made sense to me," I said between bites of egg. "You saw the house. Why would anybody think there was something there worth stealing?"

"Probably high on drugs *if* that's how it started. Wanted money to buy more and wasn't too discerning about where he stole it. If it had anything to do with burglary, the perp went there to steal, found your mother, and got other ideas."

"What do you mean? Other ideas?" I asked and then added, "Could the killer have been a female?" I pushed away my plate and motioned to the server for more coffee.

"Not likely. You know your mother died of blunt force trauma, don't you? Females don't usually kill that way, and your mother showed no signs of having fought back. She wasn't a tiny woman. It would have taken someone very strong to overpower her." He coughed and chewed on the rather big bite of hash browns he'd shoved into his mouth.

"No," I said, "Mom wasn't small. She was my size. We could wear each other's clothes."

He paused and stared at me. "No offense by my comment. She must have been a beautiful woman. In fact, probably looked almost exactly like you."

The fact he'd said he saw her body, but he had to guess what she'd looked like should have told me something, but I was clueless.

"She had me young at fifteen. She wasn't even forty-five yet when she died. People said we looked like sisters." Tears stung my eyes and I tried to blink them away. *I'm not a crybaby,* I thought, *but I can't control myself.*

He added, "But the results of the postmortem make me think it was never a robbery."

"Why?"

"You know that she'd either been raped or been involved in some very rough sex with a boyfriend, don't you?"

"I didn't know she'd been raped, and I don't

know anything about her having a boyfriend."

He'd shocked me, and though I wanted to know all there was about my mother, some part of me wanted to get even with him for hurting me with that information. "You're telling me my mother was raped and beaten to death?" The words shot from my mouth like venom.

"I thought you knew that."

The female officer hadn't told me any details, but the funeral director had advised me not to view my mother. "Just remember her as she was before this tragedy," was his suggestion. Had both the police officer and the mortician protected me from how heinous the crime had been?

"No, I didn't know that until now," I said and pushed my plate away.

Sergeant Adams looked embarrassed. "I thought you did or I wouldn't have been so blunt about it."

His use of the word 'blunt' brought 'blunt force trauma' and what that could have meant to mind. "Is there DNA?" I asked.

"No DNA. Apparently he used protection and either flushed it or took it with him. Even if we'd ID'ed him on DNA, a good defense attorney would argue that the invasion occurred after his defendant left following consensual sex."

"I don't even want to think about it if there's nothing to lead to an arrest," I said. *Denial!* my mind shouted at me. *If something hurts too much, just run away and ignore it. Grow up!*

"What about Jerry Patterson, the man I found dead in front of the post office this morning?"

"What about him?"

"Do you know anything more about that?"

"Less than you do. You knew him. All I know is he's dead now and there were no obvious signs of what killed him. He could have died of natural causes, maybe a heart attack, stroke, or aneurism, though he's awfully young for any of those. More curious to me is why he was out on the street before daylight all dressed up in a three-piece suit."

He wiped his mouth with his napkin and nodded toward the door.

As soon as we were back in his car, the sergeant insisted on taking me to Walmart.

"I know you've probably been buying your clothes in the better New York stores, but we can pick up a few things to tide you over," he said.

I've gone shopping with men before who hurried me and acted like I was a pain in the behind. Adams was patient, and after I'd picked out a pair of jeans, some pants and a couple of shirts, he suggested getting a back pack as well as other essentials such as a comb, toothbrush, mouthwash — pretty much what I usually put in my overnight case.

As we drove away, I asked, "Are you still taking me to where my dream was?"

"Let's make that another day," he replied. "I had

to check out some homeless folks who were starting fires in Potter's Field not long ago," he continued. "Your description matches that place exactly."

"I've heard of Potter's Field," I said. "It's over behind that big cemetery where I-126 comes into town, isn't it?"

"That's it. Technically, it was a city cemetery over two hundred years ago. Everyone thinks that only patients at the local asylum, prisoners at the penitentiary, and indigent or unidentified bodies were buried there. Records are incomplete, but they show that anyone who lived in the city could buy a plot. It's sad that the place is in such bad shape."

"Do they still bury unidentified people there?" I asked.

"No, now if a person is unidentified or the body isn't claimed, custody winds up going to the county coroner. After what's considered a decent interval, the coroner authorizes for the body to be cremated, and the cremains are buried in the new county cemetery. They couldn't bury unidentified people in this Potter's Field anyway. It's been full for years."

"I've always wondered why they call graveyards for poor people 'potter's' fields."

"It's in your Bible."

"I confess I'm not a Bible scholar. We went to church sometimes at Trinity Episcopal downtown, but not often."

"Well, I grew up participating in youth Bible

Drills, and I remember a lot of it. After Judas betrayed Jesus, he gave the thirty pieces of silver to the chief priests, but they didn't want to use the silver in their church because it was blood money. They used it to buy a potter's field to be a burying place for strangers."

"That doesn't explain why the word 'potter's'," I said.

"The word 'potter's' came from the fact that the site was strip-mined for potter's clay. That made it unsuitable for farming, but a fine graveyard for those who couldn't be buried in orthodox cemeteries. You can look it up in the Book of Matthew in the New Testament of the Bible."

"I'll get a Bible and read it," I said softly.

"You don't own a Bible?" he asked in disbelief before quickly adding, "I'm sorry. Yours would have been in the fire."

I didn't tell him that I didn't have one because I'd never owned a Bible, but I did say, "If you say I dreamed about Potter's Field, I'll take your word for it. Maybe we can check it out another day when I'm not so tired." The thought of visiting a cemetery after hearing so much about my mother's death no longer intrigued me.

When we returned to my street, my lot was surrounded with yellow tape with an attached sign stating the fire was being investigated.

The sergeant walked me to Glory's door, patted

me on the shoulder and said, "I'll check on you tomorrow. I'll be by around mid-day and take you to lunch, and we'll go get you some identification."

"Julie! I was getting worried about you!" Glory greeted me when she opened the door. She'd put on a blue and lavender flowered cotton house dress and her tightly curled wig. "The fireman wanted to talk to you, and I told him you'd gone off with a cop."

"I know," I answered. "He interviewed me at the police station."

We sat on the couch side by side in the front room. She slipped off her shoes and propped her feet on the coffee table. I did the same, still puzzled by the mud on my sneakers. I hadn't cleaned them before going off with Sergeant Adams. I didn't mention it to Glory.

"There isn't much I could tell them. You know more about the fire than I do," I continued talking about the fire marshal to avoid thinking about my feet and when or how they'd been soiled.

"I was worried because you were gone so long. "

"Officer Adams took me to lunch and then to Walmart. I bought some clothes, underwear, and a toothbrush." I held up the bag. "So at least, I have something to wear until I get my finances straightened out."

"Do you have money problems?"

"Oh, no. I just need identification to withdraw cash and get a new debit card. Sergeant Adams has offered to help me with that."

She harrumphed like an old man and changed the subject.

"I've got a pot of stew on the stove, and I been thinking. Lately, nine times out of ten, I fall asleep in my recliner while I'm watching television. I know you slept on the couch here in the living room when we lost Juliana, but this time, I think you should take the bedroom, and if I bother to get out of the chair, I'll sleep on the couch."

"Oh, no, I couldn't do that. I'll be fine on the sofa."

"You don't understand." Glory's tone went almost angry. "I want the front room! I'll be quiet if I need to go through to the kitchen, but I been sleeping harder and later recently, most of the time in here. You'll probably wake up before I do, and you can put the coffee on."

She laughed. "That's the advantage of this house. With the bedroom behind the living room and the kitchen behind the bedroom, first one up gets to cook breakfast."

I didn't comment that the disadvantages were that the rooms were directly behind each other with no halls and no closets. Homes like these old houses were sometimes called "shotgun houses" because if someone stood at the front door and fired a shotgun, the pellets would go straight through and out the back door. The ones in this part of town had been built before indoor plumbing, so bathrooms had been added at the rear taking up part of what had been back porches before the mill sold the houses.

That evening I sat on the couch while Glory lay back in her recliner. We watched television for a while before I asked her, "Miss Glory, did my mom have a boyfriend?"

"Not that I know of. I never understood that. Juliana was pretty—just like you, but she never did much but work. Didn't even go to the movies after you moved away. It's a shame she left us so young like she did."

"You found her, didn't you?"

"Yes, she'd promised she'd drive me to the grocery store because it was raining that day, but she never answered when I kept on calling. I got scared she was sick. We had keys to each other's houses, so I went over. I found her on her bed, all beat up and bloody."

"Did she . . ."

"I don't wanna talk about it," Glory interrupted. "I'm gonna get a bedtime snack. Would you like a couple of crackers with peanut butter before bed?"

"Yes, ma'am, I'll get them."

"No! You've had an awful day. Go on and get ready for bed. I'll bring 'em to you."

There was never much point in arguing with Glory. I went into the bedroom, and she passed through the room on her way to the kitchen in back.

"I'm gonna wash up before I get us some bedtime snacks. I don't want to keep you up by me goin' back and forth to the bathroom." She giggled. "I laid out an old gown of mine that should fit you. Sure ain't gonna ever be my size again."

A black piece of nylon and lace was spread out over the chenille bedspread. I picked it up and gasped. I couldn't imagine Glory ever being young enough to wear this sheer gown. Then I thought how sweet it was of her to take it out for me. There wasn't much living space in a shotgun house and even less for storage. This gown must have been special for her to save it so long.

"Julie! Julie!" Glory's voice came from the bathroom.

I hurried to her shouting, "Miss Glory, what's wrong?"

Through the door, she answered, "My arthritis is something fierce tonight. I can't reach my back. Will you wash it for me?"

"Sure," I answered, relieved that she hadn't fallen. I pushed the door open and, for the first time ever, saw Glory naked. She handed me the wash-cloth and soap. She leaned forward so I could reach her back, but not before I got a glimpse of her pathetic old body. Pendulum breasts like in *National Geographic* documentaries. A round stomach that fell in rolls to her — what shall I call it? — hoo-hah. That's as good a word as any and a whole lot nicer than some terms for that special female place. Despite her belly, her legs were spindly and ended in feet covered with varicose veins.

I mentally scolded myself for being so critical about the poor old lady's body. She'd been a friend to both Mom and me ever since she moved next door to us when I was in high school. Now she'd taken me in when I had nowhere to go. How dare I react negatively to what time and life had done to my friend? I gave her a good back scrub and finished with a neck massage.

While I rubbed the tension from her muscles, I wondered if age would have changed Mom as much as it had Glory. Mom wasn't thin, but she was smaller than Glory and her flesh had been firm. Would I, myself, someday have a body like Glory's? That thought ended my massage efforts.

"Thank you, Julie. That felt good." She grinned. "Now get out of here and let me put on my pajamas and make our snacks."

I lay across the bed and reached for *The Haunting of Hill House* by Shirley Jackson from the bedside table. I'd read it several times before, not as a proof-reader, but for my own entertainment through the years. I'll read anything the publishers send me as part of my job, but for pleasure, I like scary stories.

The main character, Eleanor, hadn't even reached Hill House before Glory came in with a tray.

"Oh, you haven't dressed for bed," she said. "I'd

hoped to tuck you in."

"I haven't showered yet," I reminded her, "and I'm a little old to be tucked in."

"You've forgotten. I don't have a shower, just a tub. Juliana had the shower added over the tub at your place, but I never did that here."

"Then I'll have a nice, soaking bath." I held up the book. "If I promise not to get it wet, is it all right to take this? I like to read in the tub."

"I remember that. It's why I put it by the bed. It's yours anyway. Juliana lent me some of your books after you moved away."

I flipped the pages to the back cover and saw my name and the date. As a girl, I'd signed and dated books at the end when I finished reading them. I'd been fourteen when I first read *The Haunting of Hill House*. No wonder it had terrified me.

Glory opened the cedar chest at the foot of the bed and pulled out a clean towel and washcloth. She tossed them to me and said, "Now, hurry before your milk cools off."

"Milk?" I questioned. "I'm sorry, but I don't drink milk. I'll just have water. You drink the warm milk."

"I made it special for you with a half teaspoon of honey."

"Mom loved hot milk and honey at bedtime, but I don't. You go ahead and drink it while it's still warm."

Glory looked unhappy, but she left the room, and in a few minutes, I heard her laughing either at or with the TV.

I filled the tub with hot water, soaked, and read until the water was cold. Putting on the black nightgown, I thought how much Greg would have loved it. In the bed, I tried to concentrate on anything except the fire, but a faint smell of smoke clung to the air around me. Then a noise distracted me. At first, I thought it was Glory moving around in the front room, but then I realized that I could hear her snoring.

Besides, the scratchy sound came from the side walls as well as the one between the kitchen and the room I'd be sleeping in. I'm not very religious, but I actually prayed, "Please, God, don't let there be rats or animals in the walls." I lay there, listening and praying, until the sound stopped. After what felt like an eternity, I accepted the silence, munched on the crackers, and sipped water that Glory had left on a bedside tray. I was asleep before I finished either.

5

"STOP IT, wake up!" The words were loud and shrill.

I heard Glory's voice, but I couldn't move. I was still asleep, and I couldn't awaken. My body was frozen, and yet I could feel sweat dripping from me, saturating the sheets.

"Wake up, wake up!" Glory shouted.

I finally managed to blink my eyes.

"Here, sit up," she said and put her arm around my shoulder. She lifted me to a sitting position, and that movement freed me to speak and move.

"Thank you, Jesus!" Glory exclaimed.

"What happened?" was the best I could get out.

"I don't know. You didn't wake up and I wanted coffee, so I decided to tiptoe to the kitchen. You were lying in bed, stiff as a board, eyes wide open, with an expression on your face like you was scared to death. I tried and tried, but you didn't respond."

"I *couldn't* wake up," I said.

"Are you okay now?" she asked.

"Gotta go to the bathroom," I answered. I didn't want to tell her that I felt like I would burst wide open if I didn't.

"Do you need help to get there?" Glory asked.

"No, I can do it. You make the coffee," I answered. When she went to the kitchen, I got out of bed and hobbled to the bathroom.

I shrieked. The few drops of urine that trickled out set my bottom on fire. Here I was with "honeymoon cystitis" when I hadn't had any intimacy in months. I wondered if Dr. Todd would see me. He'd been my doctor until I'd moved five years ago.

I didn't need this. What I needed was to buy a new computer, but I might purchase a gallon of cranberry juice first. I had to call Dr. Todd's office, but they wouldn't be open yet. Sleeping "late" by Glory's time was eight A.M.

I had to sit there a few minutes for the agony to ease. I washed my face, brushed my teeth, and went to the kitchen. I must have stayed in the bathroom even longer than I thought because Glory already sat at the table drinking coffee and reading *The State* newspaper. I limped through the kitchen to the bedroom and exchanged the black nightgown for a new shirt and jeans. I had to leave the pants unzipped because the pressure was unbearable on my stomach and below.

A bowl of oatmeal, a platter of turkey sausage, and a bowl of red apples centered the table. My coffee was already poured and I felt like I did long ago when Mom set the table just like this on school mornings. She'd adopted what she considered "healthy eating" when I was a child.

"Want a piece of the newspaper?" Glory asked and offered me the sports section.

"No, if you don't mind, I'm going for a walk. Maybe I can eat when I get back, but I don't think I can sit still or eat until I see Dr. Todd. I need to call him as soon as his office opens."

"Why do you need the doctor?"

"I think I have an infection," I answered.

"What kind?"

"UTI," I answered.

"Urinary tract infection?" she questioned. I nodded yes and she said, "Oh, you don't need to go to the doctor for that. I've got a potion here that will cure you right up." She went to the cabinet and pulled out a jar about half full of something thick and brown like a muddy molasses. Glory insisted I take two giant tablespoons of the concoction. It was *some* kind of bitter and nasty!

She frowned at the grimace I made when I swallowed. "I know it doesn't taste good, but it will get rid of that pain." She hesitated, and then added, "I want you to have a dose every morning."

At first, I'd hurt so bad that I couldn't eat, and

then, miraculously, after taking Glory's medicine, my bottom stopped burning. After breakfast, I headed to the post office to take the envelope I'd planned to mail yesterday morning. The day was cold, but sunny. A walk would give me time to think.

Adams had offered to pick me up at lunchtime and take me to the Department of Transportation to get a non-driver ID to use until I felt ready to take the test for a S.C. driver's license. A picture identification would give me access to my money.

"TCB." I actually *heard* Mom say those words in my mind along with the Elvis Presley recordings she always played and even danced to when she was alone. Then I saw her. She wore a light blue cotton dress, what she used to call a "house dress." She'd been wearing that dress the day I'd come home from middle school crying. I saw myself, a twelve-year-old with a red ponytail, come in the back door and sit in the kitchen before putting my head down on the table and sobbing.

"What's wrong, Julie?" Mom asked.

"Nothing," I lied. I waited a few minutes before asking, "What 'cha doing, Mom?" though I could see perfectly well that she was washing pots and pans.

"TCB," she said. "You know what that means, don't you?"

I laughed through my tears. "I know. It's what Elvis Presley always said, and it means 'taking care of business.' What business are you taking care of today?"

"Taking care of cleaning up the cooking pots before your daddy gets home. Everything's ready and in the oven." She dried her hands on the dishcloth and stepped over to me. Gently smoothing my hair, she asked, "What's got you crying?"

"It's okay," I answered.

"No, it's not," my mother said. "What is it?"

"The music teacher said that boys have to wear black pants and white shirts and girls have to wear black skirts and white blouses or we can't sing in the program at school tomorrow."

"Is that something to cry about?" she asked in a soothing tone.

"I didn't know until today. I don't have a black skirt, and I heard you and Daddy talking about being short of money this month."

"You weren't supposed to hear that," she said. "Who am I?" she added.

"My mama."

"Then leave it to me. I'll take care of it after supper."

I watched as she hugged my daddy when he came in. Saw myself go to bed and Mom get out her best dress and sewing box. She cut, she basted, and then she sewed on the machine.

Though the vision ended, I remembered the next day. Mom had gotten off work and come to the school for the choral performance. I'd stood proudly wearing my black skirt made from my mother's best dress, and I'd cherished that skirt way after it was too small. I'd taken it to New York with me after I graduated from college, planned to keep it forever, but it had burned in my house.

I needed to get started TCB. Make a list of things to do: Find out if the house was insured. Buy a new computer. See if I could afford a car and a place to live. Glory was nice, but I couldn't stay there indefinitely for several reasons.

My work required quiet, and I'd already seen that Glory would be a constant presence talking *to* me or *at* me most of the time. She'd gotten on my nerves sometimes since she moved next door, but the fact remained that she was an elderly lady who shouldn't be forfeiting what few comforts she had. I didn't want her feeling she had to cook for me and take care of me.

Another problem was the sleeping situation. I couldn't blame the dream and sweats that morning on Glory or her house because that kind of thing had begun at my house before the fire. I'd hoped moving in with Glory next door might put an end to the nightmares, but the Potter's Field dream the day before while lying on Glory's couch squashed that thought. Also, something had caused me to be paralyzed when I awoke this morning, and I didn't think it was the pain.

I'd had a hard time getting to sleep when I stayed

with Glory right after Mom's death. The house was noisy. It squeaked, and there were sounds in the walls at night—scratching and occasional banging. Sometimes I heard them in the daytime, too. Thinking of the sleeping problems made me realize that I'd grown drowsy walking in the sunlight.

When I reached the house, Glory had gone somewhere, so I would be by myself until Sergeant Adams picked me up. I didn't bother to change clothes, just lay down on the bed. No noises in the walls. Surprisingly, I went to sleep immediately.

The nap was strange from the beginning. I was aware that I was sleeping, but I consciously thought how nice it was that nothing was distressing me. I felt no apprehension or fright and considered myself lucky, knowing I would not wake up crying, trembling, or dripping wet.

Later, the clock would show that I didn't sleep more than fifteen minutes, but I had no knowledge of time passing until I heard the footsteps. When I'd heard the noises the day before, I'd been on the couch in the front room. Now I lay on the bed in the middle room, but I heard someone on the front porch. The sounds weren't loud thuds, just regular steps. Was it that strange creature who'd taken me to Potter's Field?

My first instinct was to get up and check the front door, be sure it was locked, but a stronger compulsion told me to lie still. *Don't acknowledge these figments of imagination,* I told myself. *It's not real. Fantasies — only wild thoughts.* I rolled over to the side of the bed and kept my eyes closed. Silence.

Perhaps I went back to sleep. I'm not certain, but the next footsteps were in Glory's front room and then in the middle room with me. I squeezed my eyes shut like a little child, hoping that refusal to look would make whatever it was go away and that if I couldn't see it, I would be invisible also.

The bedsprings squeaked. The mattress sank a bit as though someone had sat on the other side of the bed. Should I scream? Jump up? What should I do? When I felt an arm thrown across my shoulders, I did both. I leapt from the bed shouting as loud as possible, looking at the other side of the bed expecting to see the man with the top hat. He wasn't there. No one lay on the bed. No one was in the room with me. Was it all imagination? Had I been unable to stop my mind from creating such fear?

A glance at the bedcovers disproved those speculations. The covers were rumpled as though someone had lain there. I reached out and touched the spare pillow that clearly showed the imprint of a head. The pillowcase was freezing cold. I raced out the back door, around the house and to the street.

6

RICHARD ARTHUR had planned to watch Assembly Street beginning before dawn. He'd hoped to see the beautiful red-haired girl with the firm, tight butt that had attracted him since the first time he saw her weeks earlier.

He'd spent the night in the Columbia Men's Mission shelter. Tired of the cemetery's lumpy ground, he'd wanted a hot meal and a warm bed. Sometimes the shelter was miserable, with old men coughing and bumping around, but last night had been fine. He'd slept soundly and felt rested, so rested that he'd slept late. He hadn't seen the redhead after he left the mission to patrol the streets looking for his prey.

Since the red-haired woman was usually out a lot earlier, Richard was thinking about heading down to the caves to hang out with friends, and then he saw her headed toward the post office. She wasn't really walking, more like a slow run. Richard fell in behind her and smiled when she crossed the street a block before the intersection where she'd found the body yesterday. She must have been headed to the post office as she frequently did, but she obviously didn't want to stand on the spot where a corpse had been the day before.

Richard crossed the street and closed in on the woman. He reached out and touched her shoulder.

7

THE MINUTE I felt a hand on me, I whirled around. The homeless man was touching me.

"What the . . . " I shouted. "You scared the life out of me."

"Didn't mean to," he said in a calm tone. I looked more closely at him. Beneath his homelessness, he *was* hot. I hadn't noticed that when we stood by Jerry Patterson's body. Guess when someone you know lies dead at your feet, you aren't too aware of some ragged stranger's good looks, especially one who's disheveled and looked homeless. I also realized that when you've recently had something invisible in your bed, you're happy to see a real face, especially one that looks delighted to see you.

"Just wanted to know if you're okay after yesterday." Genuine concern filled those blue eyes.

"I'm okay, but why did you just disappear like that? I had to go to the police station and help them make a sketch of you."

"Even more reason for me to lie low for a while."
He fell into step beside me and we walked together.

"Are you in trouble with the law?"

"No, not at all. I'm a writer. Doing research on
the homeless in America for the book I'm writing."

"I don't believe you."

"Why not?"

"I just don't believe you. You may smell better
than you did yesterday, but I think you're genuinely
what you appear to be. By the way, where'd you
shower?"

"Right over there at the mission." He pointed
across the street to the Columbia Men's Mission
shelter. "If you spend the night there, they'll feed you
and let you shower."

"I knew people could eat and sleep there, but I
never considered bathing, too." I thought for a
moment. "Are you really a writer? I'm a proof-
reader. What's your name?"

"Richard Arthur."

"Do you write under a pen name? Most of what I
proof is fiction. Maybe I've worked with one of your
books."

"This will be nonfiction, but maybe it will wind
up with you if I can get it in with a major publisher."

"Let's hope so."

"Yep, and then come the interviews on the *Today*
show and piles of money so I can shower every day

and drive around in a big Mercedes."

I couldn't help it. Authors intrigued me. Other women might want to be rock 'n' roll groupies. I just wanted to know writers.

"Have you had anything published already?"

"Yes, but this will be my first best seller."

We'd reached the post office, and I dropped my envelope in the blue box.

"There's an IHOP up the street, and I've got a few dollars in my pocket. Could I talk you into a cup of coffee?"

What the heck? My life sucked, and this man wasn't really homeless, he was an author. Not that I'm too good to have conversations with people whose misfortunes have left them on the streets. I'm just fascinated with writers. I wanted to talk to him, so I agreed. Soon we were sitting opposite each other with two cups of coffee in a back booth at IHOP.

"What's your name?" Richard asked.

"Julia Bates, but everyone calls me Julie."

"I looked for you earlier, but you weren't out," he said. "I'd almost gone to the caves when I saw you."

"The caves?" I asked and sipped daintily.

"You probably don't know about them. There are tunnels and caves down by the canal behind the old cemetery. A lot of homeless people live in those caves. Keep all their belongings in there safe and sound unless it ever floods."

"That's fascinating," I commented. "I've lived

here all of my life until five years ago, and I never heard about any caves. When you say 'old cemetery,' are you talking about Potter's Field?"

"That's where I'm talking about. The caves are behind Potter's Field, down below it. I've researched the place at the library. It was the city cemetery in the eighteen hundreds, but even in legal papers, it's called Potter's Field." He looked around cautiously, and I wondered if he were hiding from someone.

"Several citizens' groups have tried to get the city to clean it up for years, but nothing ever comes of it," he continued. "It's too messy for me, but some of my friends like it just the way it is. So long as it's neglected, they don't get bothered by the cops."

"The policeman who came about the man on the sidewalk said he'd been there because some homeless people had started fires in the graveyard."

"Let some folks have too much wine and they get careless. Sometimes a campfire gets out of control."

"How can I get there?" I asked and nodded yes to the server who stood beside us.

"It's not easy. You have to turn off of Huger Street and go through a tunnel under a bridge." He laughed. "The bridge is guarded by a staff-wielding hobo who calls himself Merlin the Mystic. He wouldn't mind letting a pretty woman like you go through, but that's not a place for you. Don't go there."

"I may have already been there," I said.

"Then you know the cemetery itself has been neglected for years, but it was treated horribly even when it was in use. Some of the graves weren't dug very deep. Some of the bodies were buried naked. Some of the caskets held more than one corpse. I visit the caves to talk with people, but I avoid the cemetery itself." He laughed. "Research isn't all done on the Internet and in the library, but there are places even I don't want to go."

"Do you do much at the library?"

"Sure. It's warm, it's pleasant, and the people who work there are polite to everyone. The library is a good place to be."

"I saw a man who looked homeless coming out the front door of the downtown library cussing and carrying on that they had no right to make him leave a public place."

"He'd done something wrong. Our county libraries don't put anyone out unless they're drunk or doing something illegal." He grinned and added, "Or they're sleeping. Can't sleep in the library, not even waiting for your turn on one of the computers."

I didn't say it, but I thought, *It's getting so I can't sleep anywhere.*

We both stopped talking and drank our coffee. After several minutes, I said, "I'm glad I got out in time to see you before you went to those caves this morning."

He said, "You probably needed to sleep late after

finding a dead man yesterday."

So he knew Jerry was dead, I thought, but I didn't mention it. *Had he caused my old friend's death? Was this man dangerous and I didn't see it because he was good-looking and claimed to be a writer?* "That's not the worst of it! The body we found was someone I knew from high school, and after that, my house burned down," I said.

"What? That house on fire was yours? What are you going to do? I'd offer you use of my place, but I don't have one." I faked a little laugh because he obviously meant to be funny. "I don't live in the caves nor under the bridge like a troll. I sometimes go to the shelter, but unless the weather's horrible, I sleep in another little cemetery near the post office." He smiled, which made him look even better. "Here I am talking about me when we should talk about you. Where will you live now that your house is gone?"

The thought of his sleeping in a cemetery, even if it wasn't Potter's Field, sent chills through me. I wasn't certain it made me feel sorry for him or fear him. I'd never known anyone who slept in a graveyard, but I pulled my thoughts away from that and answered him.

"I'm staying at my next-door neighbor's for a while. The house that burned was my mom's home. Well, it's been mine since Mama died. I've got to check today to see if it was insured. The mortgage is paid off, and I hope she kept insurance." I babbled.

"I'd think all of that would make you sleepless, not make you sleep late."

"It was really strange. I don't know if I was still asleep or awake, but I was paralyzed. Sometimes I wake up screaming, but this morning, I was frozen. Couldn't move, couldn't speak. The lady who's letting me stay with her was finally able to break the spell or whatever it was."

"Spell may be right. You need to see if that lady has a Ouija board in the house. If so, get it out of there. It sounds like you had sleep paralysis."

"What's that?"

"Exactly what it sounds like. It's when a healthy person is paralyzed for a few moments or minutes either at the beginning of sleep or at the end when waking up." He motioned to a different server for refills, but she ignored us, probably because of his appearance.

"What causes it?" I asked.

"There are some medical reasons considered in most cases, but lots of people think it's associated with demonic visitation."

"Is that why you asked about the Ouija board?"

"Yes, paranormalists believe Ouija boards serve as portals allowing demons to enter our world." I must have looked horribly frightened because he smiled and added, "But chances are you just reacted to a really stressful day yesterday and weren't quite out of REM sleep when you began to awaken. Some stages of REM sleep are very similar to sleep paralysis."

"How do you know so much about all this?"

"Research. I spend a lot of time seeking facts. I'd started a book on the paranormal before I got this idea to write about the homeless." He looked into his empty cup and waved at our first server again. She came right over and refilled our cups.

"Is that why you talk so differently today?" I asked.

"Yes, since I told you who I am, I don't have to pretend with you."

"Will you excuse me? I'll be right back."

He nodded and I went to the ladies' room. No pain. The cystitis was completely gone. If Glory had medicine to cure that, maybe she could cure my sleep problems.

When we left IHOP, Richard asked if he could walk me home. "Yes, but after that, you should go to the police department and give a statement so they won't be looking for you."

"I'll think about it," he replied. "I don't guess the lady you're staying with wants any company?" Richard asked as we reached Glory's door.

"Not hardly."

He turned, waved goodbye, and called, "See you later."

I wondered what name he wrote under and if I'd ever proofed any of his material. Then the doubts entered my mind — was he lying? He was certainly one of the strangest men I'd ever met.

The door was locked, so I knocked until Glory came to let me in. The room felt like a meat locker when I stepped inside. I exaggerated a shiver and said, "It's freezing in here."

Immediately, my thoughts went to paranormal television shows I'd seen. *Aren't cold spots signs of ghosts?*

"The weatherman on TV said it's going to get hot today. That little window air conditioner won't cool off all three rooms if I wait until it's hot outside to turn it on. Gotta get it started early, afore it's sweltering outside." Glory smiled.

I confess that relieved me. Richard's talk about Ouija boards and demons had spooked me. I wasn't frightened at the thought of a ghost, but evil beings scared me. If ever Glory or I had a ghost, it would probably be Mom, and like I've said over and over, I wasn't afraid of my mother — living or dead. Rationally, I knew this, but I was still happy to know there was an actual reason for the cold.

Glory reached out and dropped something into my hand. "Here's your key to the house. I got it back after . . . " She sniffled. "When there was so many cops over there at your ma's house every day, I sneaked under that yellow tape one night and got my key I'd given to Juliana and brought some of your things out. Didn't want anyone messing with your boxes. Now this key is yours."

"Thank you, Miss Glory," I told her and slipped the key into my jeans pocket. That's when I realized my cell phone was missing. I couldn't remember the last time I'd taken it from my pocket or if I'd had it at all since I called 911 about Jerry's body. Then I recalled showing it to Sergeant Adams when we talked about a woman needing to always have enough money to make a phone call. Not wanting to make Glory think I was accusing her of taking the phone, I didn't mention it. Instead, I asked, "What kind of stuff of mine?"

"Packages of your belongings Juliana boxed up and saved when you left town. We'll go through them together tonight. Right now, you better go do your hair and put on some makeup. That cop stopped by and said he'd be a little early to pick you up. Said something about his work shift being changed. I found your birth certificate and social security number in one of the boxes. They're on the coffee table here. You'll probably need 'em to get ID."

I grabbed Glory and gave her a big hug. She was the best friend I'd ever had, and she'd been a good companion to my mother, too. She was obviously lonely, and I hadn't spent much time with her since I'd come back to South Carolina. I still knew I wouldn't live with her a lot longer, but I felt guilty about my earlier thoughts and irritability.

Sergeant Adams arrived early. He treated me to

lunch and insisted I call him Nate.

We wound up in a long line at the Department of Motor Vehicles, but it moved quickly and when our turn came, they issued me a picture ID.

AS WE left the bank, Nate said, "I know you want to buy a computer, and I'll be glad to take you shopping tomorrow afternoon, but I've got to go on duty now."

I was disappointed. My livelihood depended on a good computer. Frequently UPS delivered hard copies of manuscripts from publishers, but some emailed the books to me, and I used "track changes" on my computer to mark corrections before returning the work by email.

Back at the house, Glory and I spent several hours talking about my mother and good times they'd shared. Then we went through a cardboard box full of snapshots and pictures, including my school photos from kindergarten through college. Finding several prints of my mom when she was young thrilled me. I pulled those out and set them aside to put in my new wallet.

Glory told me she'd posted a note on the yellow tape next door for mail and packages to be delivered to her house. The mailman had brought change of address cards for her to give to me.

"I need a nap now," Glory eventually said. "Why don't you lie down across the bed while I rest on the couch?"

I tried, but it was impossible for me to go to sleep. Every time I closed my eyes, I saw that creature at Potter's Field. I finally gave up. I was *afraid* to sleep.

Was I simply stressed by all that had happened with finding Jerry Patterson's body and seeing my house burn or was I over-reacting to whatever nightmare I'd had the night before and that horrible cystitis? There was no sound coming from the walls right then. Was I subconsciously staying awake listening for unexplained noises?

Escape? I needed to run away, and I did — in my favorite way, fiction. Until Glory woke, I read stories from *The H. P. Lovecraft Collection.*

After Glory's nap, we spent the rest of the afternoon looking at more of the things my mother had boxed up and Glory had rescued from my house before the fire. All of my report cards back to kindergarten were there along with curly red locks of my hair and my baby book. I even found a diary I'd kept in my early teens.

The evening meal was a big salad and pizza in front of the television set. I didn't have the heart to tell Glory that pizza was no longer as big a favorite of mine as it was in my teens nor that pizza in New York was a whole lot better than what she'd bought at the grocery store. *Don't even be thinking thoughts like that. Should thank my lucky stars that my mother had Glory as a friend when I was in New York and that she's my friend now.*

At ten o'clock, Glory said, "I'm an old lady, Julie. I need to rest. This is my bedtime."

As a guest in her home, I couldn't very well say I wanted to watch more TV when she was sleeping in the room with the television set. After her bath, I went to the bedroom and closed the door to the front room.

"Good night, Julie," Glory called. "Sleep tight."

I lay down just to rest, vowing not to close my eyes. Every time my eyelids drooped. I forced them open while straining to hear any sounds from the walls. The later it got, the more sleep terrified me. I couldn't bear being frozen in slumber again. Coffee! Maybe that would help. Not wanting to wake Glory, I checked to be sure the door to the living room was securely closed.

I'd filled the coffee carafe with water when I realized that the smell of hot coffee would probably wake Glory even faster than noise. She seemed to sleep fine through the house noises—bangs and crunching sounds—in the walls, but she was used to those. I dressed quickly and stuffed some money in one hip pocket and mints on the other side. There was an all-night diner between the house and the post office. I'd go there. I slipped out onto the back porch and walked around the house to the street.

Turning right to cross in front of the house and head toward the diner, I stopped abruptly. Someone was sitting on our front stoop. At first, I thought perhaps Glory had come out the front door, but this person was bigger than she was. Could it be Richard? The silhouette was all wrong. Did I dare just walk casually in front of the house? There was no sidewalk. The steps ended at the street. What if the person grabbed me?

The head turned toward me, and the shape stood. I caught a quick glimpse of a wicked, hateful face glaring at me but not the man who'd taken me to Potter's Field. Filled with fear, I turned to the left and took off running down the street as fast as I could — away from the diner and post office, toward the fairgrounds I hadn't been to since I was a child. I glanced over my shoulder. The form was right behind me, and even in the shadowed darkness of no street lights, I saw a black cape.

The faster I sprinted, the closer the footsteps pounded the pavement behind me. My legs hurt like they were on fire. My heart pounded, and my chest burned. It seemed like miles while my legs, my entire body, weakened with every step. Hair on the back of my neck rose with fear when a quick look over my shoulder showed the man, if that's what it was, gaining on me.

Just as I realized I was about to collapse, I saw a light ahead. Post lamps illuminated a stairway up to double doors with a warm glow shining through red Tiffany glass. An ornate sign above the door spelled out Owens Hotel. I looked up at the windows. The building appeared to be five or six stories high. I raced up the steps and reached for the door. It swung open before I touched it, and a grinning man dressed in a burgundy doorman's uniform with gold braid held the door open wide.

One sweeping glance took in the room. Deep, plush crimson carpet surrounded a round fountain bubbling sparkling water in the middle of the lobby beneath a tremendous brass chandelier. Maroon brocade cloth covered the walls, and the registration desk was marble. An antique elevator faced me, and pots of luxurious palms sat on each end of lavish gold velvet settees. Beautiful to the eyes, but offensive to the nose. The room smelled like cigar smoke—both fresh and stale.

I ducked behind a palm and was happy to see the doors close without admitting anyone. Perhaps my pursuer hadn't seen me enter the hotel or, more likely, he only wanted to catch me alone in the dark.

As I cringed behind the plant, I saw another woman near the palm by the far wall. Her draped gray silk dress was hemmed at mid-calf—very retro.

The elevator opened and out stepped a man and woman. She wore a purple fringed flapper miniskirted dress, draping loops of pearls, and a feather cloche hat. His pin-striped suit with pleated pants and double-breasted jacket was accented with a gold watch chain and spats on his shoes.

What was happening? Were they having some gigantic costume ball upstairs, maybe a roaring twenties party? Speculation stopped when the lady in gray stepped around the palm. Arms extended, the woman clutched a gun—both hands wrapped around the handle. *Keerack!* She fired, and the man crumpled to the floor, grabbing his right knee. The flapper woman ran back into the elevator, and the doors closed. The doorman rushed to the fallen victim.

Sweat popped out on my face and neck. My legs collapsed beneath me. Helpless, I fell face first into darkness.

8

I DON'T remember returning from that hotel to Glory's house. Nor do I recall going to bed. What I do know is that I awoke easily the next morning all tucked under the covers and feeling a gentle touch on my cheek.

"Lullaby and good night, go to sleep now, my darling . . . " The melody was "Brahms' Lullaby" and the words were my mother's own version of that song. The touch was hers, and the voice was hers. I opened my eyes fully expecting to see my mother's face leaning over me. Instead I saw myself, a four-year-old with bright red curls lying in the bed I slept in as a child. It was white with pink rosebuds painted on the headboard. Beside me stood my beautiful mother, stroking my forehead and singing to me as she often did back then.

My heart wasn't pounding out of my chest. I wasn't screaming, and I wasn't frozen in fear. I felt completely safe and loved as the vision faded. Just those brief moments with my mom left me feeling at peace. *Was it all in my mind? Was Mom really here or did it all happen in a dream — a wonderful dream instead of a nightmare?*

What about earlier? Why can I remember it? The entire waking, going out, and seeking refuge in the hotel had to have been a bad dream, but not the kind of nightmare that left me devastated.

The aroma of fresh coffee invited me to join my roommate in the kitchen.

"Morning, sleepyhead," Glory said. "You were snoring when I slipped through your room to go to the bathroom and came in here to start breakfast. We both slept in this morning. Are you still going off with that cop today?"

"Yes, but he's on duty right now. I don't expect him here until after he finishes working at three."

Breakfast was a cottage cheese omelet. I'd finished eating that and an apple when Glory brought out the nasty brown medicine again. I didn't argue this time. Just took it to make her happy because I had no signs of irritation.

The morning passed pleasantly with only one problem: I couldn't find my cell phone. Glory and I looked all over for it before we gave up and went through another of the boxes she'd saved from my house, this one full of pictures. I took out several more snapshots of my mother, one of them the way she'd looked when I was about four years old and when I'd awakened. We talked about Mom for a long time and then ate lunch. I stood from the table and began putting our dishes in the sink.

"I'll do those," Glory offered.

"No, thanks. I'm going to wash these and then bathe. Officer Adams is taking me to buy a computer when he gets off duty. Why don't you watch television or take a nap?"

"I'll do both while you get ready for your date." She put a sarcastic tone on the word "date." *Is Glory jealous that I won't be spending the afternoon with her or does she resent my wanting a computer? I need it to maintain my income.*

Those concerns washed away while I bathed. The water felt warm and slippery on my body. I admit that a lot of the time, I'd let my hair air dry and just pull it back into a ponytail that varied from a burst of silky curls on some days to a frizzy red mop during humid weather. This time, with the aid of a blow dryer and curling iron I found in the cabinet beneath the sink, I actually created a hairstyle before taking the time to do full makeup and put on my prettiest Walmart outfit—khaki pants with a rust-colored blouse.

My mind kept slipping back to my mother singing "Brahms' Lullaby." Since her death, I'd begun to realize how truly blessed I'd been to have a mom like her, even when she made me do things I didn't want, like wearing earth tones, which I hated. I loved red and pink. I wanted dresses the color of the roses painted on my bed, but she always said, "Julie, the browns and rusts are so pretty with your hair." In New York, I bought lots of red clothes, but after a while, I realized that I always received compliments when I went to work in orangier tones—the rusts and gingers. Gradually, I'd come to realize that Mama had been right.

If only I'd realized how often she'd been right, especially in my late teens. Losing my mother before I was thirty had been difficult, but the fact she'd been murdered intensified the loss. I couldn't stand to think how brutal her death had been. The little house that I'd resented and despised living in to the point that I never brought friends home after school because I felt we were poor had been filled with love until I left. *Maybe I should never have left home. Maybe if I'd still been living there, Mom wouldn't have been attacked.* Now the house had burned to the ground and was gone—like my mother and father. I lay across the bed and sobbed.

When I'd regained control of myself, I thought about touching up my makeup, but that was a lost cause. I went to the bathroom and stood at the lavatory, planning to scrub everything off and start over.

The face that looked back at me from the mirror wasn't mine.

I stood in shock staring at someone who looked a lot like me, but was *not* me. My hair was the color of Mom's. The biggest difference between my mother and me was that she had green eyes while I'd inherited my dad's dark blue. There were no bruises or marks on the face reflected in the mirror, but the expression of pain in those emerald eyes broke my heart.

I reached out to touch her cheek, but my fingers met only the hard surface of the mirror, and the image melted into mine. For just a moment, I thought I saw a shadowy dark figure behind me, but when I turned, no one was there.

Imagination, I told myself. *But, oh, what I'd give to see her, speak to her, hug her again.*

THE GRIN on my face couldn't have been wiped off with a beach towel. While at the computer store, I'd checked my email and found notification of two manuscripts being sent for me to proofread. Now, with my new MacBook computer in my lap, I believed that getting back to work would help my life return to slightly normal.

"Sergeant Adams, thank you so much for running me around while I was taking care of business," I said.

"I've told you already—call me Nate. I consider myself your friend and want to help you get your life as close to normal as possible," he said.

"I really do appreciate that," I answered.

"Let's get something to eat," he suggested.

"I'm so excited over this computer that I'm not even hungry. I can't wait to set it up."

"Do you have Internet access at Glory's?" he asked.

"No," I said as reality set in. "Like Mom would say, I have to take care of business before I can check out the Mac."

"Call Miss Glory and tell her we'll be late."

"I'll need to use your cell. I couldn't find mine this morning."

"Then we need to get you a new cell phone so you can take care of business and so I can contact you without going through Miss Glory. Who's your contract with?"

Dealing with the cell phone was fairly simple when we reached the franchise. I'd carried insurance, and the company replaced my phone with the exact same model without a whole lot of hassle. I didn't doubt that telling them my house had burned but not mentioning that the phone hadn't been in it had helped hurry up the process. Nate offering his police ID along with mine was probably a factor in speeding up the process, too.

As soon as we were settled in Nate's car, I called Glory.

"Hello?" She spoke the word like a question.

"Miss Glory? This is Julie. I just got a new cell phone, and I called to give you the number."

"I see it here on caller ID. When will you be home?"

I turned toward Adams. "When will I be home?"

"After dinner," he said, and I repeated his answer to Glory.

"Oh, then I'll put the chicken back in the freezer. I just wanted to know when to put it in the oven." Her words oozed disappointment.

"Go ahead and cook it," I suggested, thinking she could eat some for dinner and we'd probably have enough left over for tomorrow.

I switched the phone to speaker mode so Nate could hear her.

"I'm not worth the bother." Glory sounded pitiful. "I'm not going to cook it just for me." Clearly, she was trying to lay a guilt trip on me, but I wasn't taking this one. She'd managed by herself before the fire sent me to stay at her house. She could get through one evening without me.

"Don't say that, Miss Glory. You're . . ."

Nate interrupted me, "Tell her not to cook. We'll take her a meal when you go home."

"I heard him," Glory said. "Tell him this poor old lady will accept his kind offer with appreciation."

Nate and I grinned at each other.

Glory's sad, oh-poor-me tone remained when she added, "Then you won't be *real* late?"

"No," I answered trying not to show exasperation in my tone.

"Is she getting on your nerves?" Nate asked after I disconnected the call.

"Kind of, but I think the problem is me, not her. She thinks of me like I'm still the teenager I was when she moved next door. I'm almost thirty years old and spent five years living alone in New York. I'm not used to answering to anyone." I paused, and then added, "I don't know why, but I've been a lot more irritable than usual since I moved back to South Carolina."

"Of course you are. Being here makes you think of losing your mother. Miss Glory just worries about you. It's not such a bad thing to have someone care enough about you to be concerned about you. I feel a need to watch out for you myself."

"I appreciate all you've done for me, but I seriously doubt that anyone who took care of herself in New York City needs to be watched over in South Carolina."

"Different situation. Anything that happened to you in New York would have been random. That's not true here. Your mother was murdered and though Jerry Patterson's death hasn't been ruled homicide, that's because the coroner can't find the cause of death and is holding off until he gets toxicology results." He frowned. "I haven't wanted to tell you, but the fire marshal's report is that your house fire was probably arson."

"What's your point?" I asked.

"I don't want to scare you, but do you have any enemies in this town? Could all of this misfortune be intentionally aimed at you?"

"Not that I know of, but when you name everything like that, I can understand why my nerves are shot. Getting ready today, I looked in the mirror and saw my mom's face instead of mine. This wasn't a dream. I was wide awake."

"Stress could do that to you, and you know it can affect your condition."

"My *condition*? I'm round, not pregnant."

"I meant your nerves. You're not *round*, you're perfect."

"Well, thank you, but I know I could stand to lose some weight. Greg, my boyfriend in New York, said he liked a woman with some meat on her bones."

"Lots of men do. It's like a vehicle. Some guys want to drive a Hyundai; I'm a Cadillac man myself."

"Are you flirting with me?"

"Certainly not! You're young enough to be my daughter." He paused and then added, "Well, *almost* young enough. About thirteen years, to be exact."

Assuming we'd go to the IHOP or Waffle House, I was surprised when Nate parked near an exclusive Mediterranean restaurant. I'd never been there before and was immediately impressed with the décor.

The entry was paved with old terra-cotta tiles

leading into the dining room where the flooring changed to inlaid brick. Dark wooden furniture, including heavy chairs upholstered in sensuous fabric, combined with earth-tone stucco walls could have resulted in gloominess, but they were offset by ornate carpets in bold jewel tones. The decorative candles, lavish urns, and gigantic elaborate mirrors established an elegant mood while soft illumination from Moroccan pendant lights over the bar and tables created an intimate ambiance.

When we were seated, I noticed the bright flowers on the tables were fresh. On each table, oil and balsamic vinegar were supplied in spray bottles. I'd been in many dining places in New York, some quite expensive, but this was the most exquisite dining room I'd ever seen.

A dark-haired man filled our water glasses and presented us with six-page menus.

"Do you know what you'd like?" Nate asked me.

"Not really. Do you have a recommendation?"

"Everything I've ever tried here was excellent," he said and opened his menu to the centerfold. "Their homemade hummus is far above average and so are the dolmas."

"Dolmas?" I asked and then realized that question may have made me sound like a country bumpkin.

"Stuffed grape leaves," Nate answered.

"I ate falafel in New York and that's on this

menu. I'll have falafel."

"Some ladies don't like suggestions on what to order in a restaurant," Nate said, "but if I won't sound bossy, may I suggest we have this appetizer combination with the hummus and pita bread, falafel, and dolmas? For the entrée, maybe the lamb shish kebabs with rice and grilled vegetables?"

I agreed and Nate placed our order.

"Tell me about your life in New York," Nate said after he'd told the server what we wanted.

"Not a lot to tell. I loved living in the big city, but since things have turned out the way they did, I wish I'd stayed in South Carolina and spent more time with Mama."

"If you enjoyed life there, she was probably happy for you."

"She seemed to be, but I regret leaving her. She was excited when I got engaged, and when Greg and I came down here to see her, she seemed to like him a lot."

"You're engaged?" He looked as sad as I felt.

"Not anymore." I hesitated. "I told you my boyfriend dumped me, but I'd rather talk about something else."

"Still hurting?"

For a moment, I thought he was asking about the cystitis, but I hadn't mentioned that to him. It wasn't something to tell a man unless he was your lover or your doctor. Then I realized he was talking about the break-up.

"More like ticked off than hurting," I said.

"In that case, we'd best change the subject."

"What about you? What made you become a cop?"

"My dad was a policeman."

"Are your parents dead?"

"My father was killed in the line of duty. My mother lives with me now, but before you start thinking I'm a mama's boy, I didn't move back home after my wife died. My mother lives with me in my house."

"This food is really delicious," I said, not wanting to talk about mothers although I knew that a woman should encourage a man to talk about himself on a date. That didn't count because this wasn't a date. What he'd said made me jealous. I wished my mother could live with me now.

Nate ordered a take-out dinner with herbed chicken, rice, and grilled vegetables for Glory. While we waited for the to-go order, we ate some delicious little pastries. An older woman came in with a gray-haired man. They caught my eye because she was very tall and thin with short white hair that matched her dress. He spoke softly to her when they were seated across the room from Nate and me. They were both looking at menus when she sat up straight in her chair and peered around the room as though searching for something.

When the lady stood, I assumed she was going to the ladies' room, but she headed in the opposite direction—toward Nate and me. She stopped at our table and looked down at us. I put the pastry I'd just bitten into on the plate and looked at her, wondering if she were someone who'd known me in the past.

"I'm a medium," was the first thing she said to me. Nate looked irritated.

"Yes?" I said politely.

"I didn't come here intending to deliver a message, but since I'm here and my spirit guide won't leave me alone until I do this, I came over. I have a message from beyond for you." She looked directly at me. I glanced past her and saw that her gentleman friend was ordering.

"Excuse me," Nate said. The term was polite, but his tone wasn't. "I believe there's a sign on the door that warns against solicitation in here." He cleared his throat. "We're not giving you any money for a message."

"Oh, no," the woman replied. "There's no charge. I only came over because I won't be able to enjoy my dinner until after I tell this young woman what my spirit guide is saying."

"If you don't leave our table, I'll have to call the manager." Nate reached toward his pocket and I wondered if he were going to show her his badge.

"I'll go, but you need to know someone is trying to contact you, to reach you." She rushed the words and turned away saying, "You need to let that person touch you."

"From the beyond?" Nate called behind her sarcastically.

She stopped and turned back toward us. "No, my spirit guide says the being trying to contact her is not from beyond, has not yet passed over." She walked back to her table and sat.

"There are kooks all over this town," Nate said. As we left, he stopped at a rack by the door and picked up several brochures. After we were in the car, he held out a magazine the size of *Reader's Digest*.

"This is the local *Apartment Finder*. If you see a few that appeal to you, I'll take you to look at them tomorrow."

"I'd rather you take me to buy a car tomorrow."

"Are you sure you're ready to do that?"

"I'm positive, and I have enough left from Mom's life insurance to get something reasonable. I'm neither a Hyundai nor a Cadillac person. I just want dependable transportation, and I guess I'll have to take the driver's test again to get a license."

"So long as we can schedule around my work, I'll help anyway I can, but I think you'd be happier not living next door to where your mother died."

"Don't forget that I was living in that house until the fire. Living next door to it is not a problem. Do you know if the police have any more leads about my mother?"

"No new clues that I know of. It's not good for you to dwell on it, and I think you'd be better off in a different neighborhood. Someplace where you wouldn't think about your childhood, your loss, and the fire every day."

"You know those mill houses were built out of town, but now the city has grown out beyond them. I'll probably move to the suburbs, and when I do, I'll need a car. I'll look for a place after I have my own transportation."

9

"I'M HOME," I called to Glory as I passed through the front room where she was watching television. "I brought you dinner. We ate at a Mediterranean place and Nate ordered chicken for you. I hope you like it. Do you want it here or at the kitchen table?" I jabbered on like I always did when I was nervous. That woman in white had upset me even though Nate and I hadn't mentioned it on the way home.

"I'll eat it here on my tray." She giggled. "After all, it *is* a TV tray. Wanna watch this program with me?"

"Not right now. I'm going to make iced tea. Would you like some?"

"Sure. Will you bring it in here to me? I don't feel too well tonight." When she said that, I couldn't help wondering if she was ill or just seeking sympathy. *Stop it, Julie!* I scolded myself. *Why am I acting and feeling so mean and cynical?*

I put the tea bags and water into the coffeemaker, which was how I liked to make tea, and sat down at the kitchen table to read *Apartment Finder*, turning down the corners of pages that listed units I might be interested in. When the brew was ready, I filled a big glass with ice, poured tea over it, and carried it to Glory.

She mumbled, "Thanks," while chewing chicken and watching one of her shows.

Back at the table with my own tea and my magazine, I was surprised when Glory came to the kitchen and sat down, placing her dinner tray and glass in front of her.

"I changed my mind," she said as she speared a piece of tomato with her fork. "There's some news special on instead of my show, so I decided to join you." She chewed as she played around with the grilled eggplant on her plate. "What's that you're reading?"

"It's *Apartment Finder*. Nate picked it up for me. It lists available rentals by location, which I guess is most important to lots of people, but not to me. Since I can work anywhere there's Internet connection now that I've bought a computer, I'm just looking for a good deal."

"Oh, so now the cop is Nate instead of Officer Adams?" Glory sounded like she was teasing, but she didn't smile.

"Well, he's turned into a friend who's helping me

a lot."

Now Glory's expression changed from "not smiling" to a definite frown. I realized that face probably meant a touch of jealousy and added, "But he's not as good a friend as you, Miss Glory."

"I don't see why you'd be looking for a place to live when you're more than welcome here forever." She stabbed her fork into a mushroom.

"It's not that I don't like being with you or don't appreciate your hospitality, but I don't want to impose on you any longer than necessary." I grinned and continued, "And I'm buying a car. It probably won't be new because I want to save enough to eventually make a down payment to buy a house, but I'll get dependable transportation, so even after I move, we'll see each other. In fact, since I'll have a car, we can do things together. I'll take you to the zoo. I've heard they've expanded it even more while I was gone. We can make a day of it." I ended with almost a begging tone, "Just be patient with me."

Instead of placating her like I'd hoped, I'd made her angry. She set her glass on the table so hard that tea slopped out of it. I jumped up for a towel and wiped away the spill.

Now Glory's look wasn't just a frown, it was angry. "What makes you think I want to go to the zoo? I don't like animals. They smell bad. That's why I've never had a pet, and if having a car makes you a big shot, I could have a nice new one anytime I want." She spat the words out so violently that saliva flew from her mouth.

I leaned across and hugged Glory. I knew that elderly ladies living in old mill houses didn't have enough money for fancy cars. I'd hurt her feelings and offended her, too. She'd probably never been to the zoo because she couldn't afford it and didn't have anyone to take her.

"Please don't be upset," I said, "I just mean that even when I move, I'll be in Columbia, not far away like when I was in New York. I'll take you anywhere you want. We can go to the movies or a mall if you like."

"You mean we can do something together when you're not too busy with that cop?"

"He's a friend, too, Miss Glory."

"Friend? Friend? Don't even consider that I don't know what that man wants with you and why he wants you to move out of here into your own place." She spoke so violently that spit *and* chicken flew from her mouth.

"Miss Glory! He's too old for me."

"Yeah, that's the worst kind. He's friending you to groom you and then he'll have you in bed the minute you're not staying here." She paused, then huffed, "He'll have to wait until you're out of here though. I'm not having you and that man together in my bed."

"Miss Glory, I promise you I'd never think of

doing such a thing." That's what I said, but I thought, *After that cystitis, I have no interest in anyone touching me there, and if I did, I'd wait for my own place, somewhere you couldn't listen through the door.*

"Just remember that promise." She spat out the words. "I'm going back to the television."

"Yes, ma'am."

Glory slammed the door between our rooms. I finished my tea and put the glass in the sink before going to the bedroom. A framed portrait of my mother now stood beside the stack of books on the bedside table. It was so life-like that it took my breath away. I picked it up and gazed into those bright green eyes. I knew I should go to the front room and thank Glory for putting the photo there, but I didn't want to deal with her right then. I lay across the bed and read Stephen King's *Salem's Lot*. That was one of my favorites, and having my old books by my bed was great, but I was ready for something new. I might even read something besides horror paperbacks.

I was totally unprepared for what happened next.

"Don't think you're going to be a whore now that your Mom's gone! That man just wants in your pants."

Glory didn't scream; she screeched. She ran into the room, grabbed *Salem's Lot* from my hand, and threw it across the room.

I stomped out the front of the house and slammed

the door. Glory's unbelievable anger and rage had been far more open than her usual passive-aggressive acts when she was angry. A moment later, she ran up behind me and hit me on the shoulder with the book.

"Here," she demanded in a hateful tone, "don't go off without this."

"Thanks," I mumbled, shoved the paperback into my pocket, and walked away. Glory didn't follow me. We both needed time to cool off.

I headed down Assembly Street toward the post office—the opposite direction I'd gone during what I now called the hotel dream. Glory removing my important items from Mama's house before the fire seemed fortunate, but I couldn't help thinking that she'd had no right to take my things, and if these mood swings became more common, I'd need to get out of her house even sooner than I'd planned.

Besides, Glory's place was too small for both of us. I felt guilty sleeping in her bed while she slept on the couch, and there wasn't much privacy since she had to go through the room I occupied to reach the bathroom or kitchen. I admitted she was gracious to let me stay at her home when the house was surrounded by yellow crime tape after Mama died, and it was kind of her to welcome me in after the fire. But why was she so determined to keep me there? Was it just the way of a lonely old woman who craved company since her best friend, my mom, was murdered? I decided to go back and apologize.

When I turned around, someone was following me, and it wasn't Glory. This couldn't be happening again. He was tall, seemed to be a male dressed in black, and wore a cape that draped around him and over his arms. His shadow on the wall of a pawn shop brought vampires to mind but worse than that, I thought it was the same one who'd followed me to the hotel in my nightmare.

I'd proofed a few books about vampires — those creatures of the night — but I didn't really believe in all that gobbledy-goop. It wasn't Halloween. Perhaps one of the bookstores was having a midnight paranormal book release party with a costume contest. Yes, that was more reasonable than a roaring twenties party at the hotel had been.

The hotel incident sprang into my thoughts. Maybe it had been a hallucination, a horrible dream, but then again, what if it hadn't been? Could Assembly Street be haunted? At the next intersection, I turned left beside the county library onto Hampton Street. I ran. If this thing wasn't after me, it would continue walking at the same pace right past where I'd turned off of Assembly. I hurried faster and looked back. He followed me, picking up speed, also. I hooked a right onto an unfamiliar street and sprinted as fast as I could — scared this was a vampire who would catch me.

A block later, I saw a sign: Gates Street. I grew up in Columbia and never heard of Gates Street.

Loud music—not rock 'n' roll, but still a hard-driving sound with a solid beat—erupted from a big yellow church-looking building.

Another look over my shoulder. The man was even closer. My legs stung from running. My chest burned like fire, and I was terrified. I'd escaped whoever chased me before by going into the hotel. I was right by the church door. I ran inside.

An African American man stopped me. "Whoa, Missy," he said with a pronounced South Carolina drawl. "You gotta pay twenty-five cents to get in. Doan matter if it's change or a case quarter. You gotta pay before you go any farther."

I pulled a quarter from my pocket and handed it to him. He examined it carefully and bit it between his front teeth.

"No, ma'am, no slugs or tokens. Gotta be real money." He handed it back to me. I looked at the coin. It was a perfectly good collectible New Jersey state quarter,

"It's real," I protested. He shook his head no.

I handed him another quarter. He bit this one, looked at it, and shook his head no again. I dug around in my pocket and pulled out two dimes and a nickel. He motioned me inside.

The interior was full of young black people dancing. I stepped forward to get a better look.

The man motioned me toward a stairway. "This is a colored club," he said. "You gotta go up to the balcony."

What had happened to integration? I didn't know, but I didn't mind sitting upstairs. If the vampire-looking man followed me into the club, maybe he wouldn't see me there.

Breathing deeply, almost gasping, I climbed the steps. Downstairs was packed, but only five people sat there — all male, all white, and all sitting on the front row side by side, leaning across the railing.

"Come over here with us," the one closest to me said. I sat down in the seat beside him, hoping I'd be less noticeable seated than standing.

"My name's Clyde. Isn't that the greatest dance you've ever seen?" the young man asked me. He looked like a member of a barbershop quartet with his vest and bow tie. I noticed the other dudes wore similar clothing except for one who had on suspenders.

"I'm Julie," I said, and then, ignoring his question, I asked, "Is this a church?"

"I've been told it used to be the House of Peace Synagogue, but now it's a juke joint called The Big Apple. My friends and I come here to see the dancing. It's fun and we're trying to learn how to do it by watching them."

Some of the people downstairs had partners while others danced in a circle. Their vigorous movements included lots of booty-slapping and twisting. Many held their hands on their stomachs, but instead of rubbing circles against their abdomens, their middles rotated against their hands. Those who weren't grinding wagged their fingers at each other or waved both arms toward the ceiling like I'd seen people in clubs dancing to the old song "Shout!"

When the music stopped, everyone on the bottom level stood still. I'd been so wrapped up in escaping the vampire and watching them dance, I hadn't noticed their clothing. None of the women wore slacks or jeans. Each had on a dress or skirt, and some wore socks with high heeled dance shoes. They all grinned, and sweat glistened off their foreheads.

"Got any nickels?" Clyde asked. I dug around in my jeans and pulled out what change I found. He picked out the nickels and added them to a handful that the other guys had given him. Then he tossed the coins to the lower level. The dancers scrambled around for them, looked up, and yelled, 'Thanks!"

"Each song costs a nickel," Clyde said. "We're all students at the University of South Carolina, so we're not flush, but we try to help out so they'll keep dancing."

"This doesn't seem real," I said.

"It's real, all right," Clyde answered.

"What year is it?" I asked.

"1937, of course. What year do you think it is?"

I looked over Clyde's shoulder and didn't care what year it was. The vampire man stood behind him and stared at me. He didn't fit the classic Count

Dracula description. He had no dark hair slicked down on his bald head. His mottled skin stretched over a lean, bony face. Clean-shaven except for a very scraggly, ugly, reddish brown mustache, his most frightening feature was his eyes. He stared directly at me with large, dark brown pupils surrounded by bloodshot yellow where white should have been. He winked at me.

That creeped me out even more than his looks.

I couldn't believe it. The college kids didn't seem aware of the creature standing right there behind them. He winked again and grinned. Two fangs slowly descended from his upper jaw down below his bottom teeth. They leaked liquid, but I could see it wasn't dark-colored blood. The drops were clear, like saliva. He slowly raised his arms, and I saw that the drapery wasn't sleeves of a cape. He had wings — big leathery wings.

I shot out of there straight to the stairway. Only a few steps down, I tripped, tumbled head over heels into darkness.

COOL AIR and a gentle touch on my forehead awoke me. I immediately realized this was not my mother's touch. "Where am I?" My words were full of fear.

I opened my eyes and gasped in surprise. The sun had risen.

"I'm here. You're okay. I just don't know why

you're here."

I recognized the voice. My favorite man in uniform—Nate.

"Just lie here a few more minutes," he said.

"But where am I?" I questioned again.

"I found you collapsed here on the sidewalk," he answered. "I went by the house, and Glory said you'd rushed off after an argument last night."

"Yes, but I wound up at The Big Apple."

"That's where you are, on the sidewalk in front of The Big Apple."

I glanced away from the street. The building behind me had the same arched doors and windows as the yellow building, but it was a neatly painted gray with white trim.

"I've been here before. One of my friends had her wedding reception in this place right after college, but this isn't where I was last night."

"Where were you?" Nate asked in a serious tone.

"I was at a Big Apple Club on Gates Street. It looked like this building, but it was shabby and painted yellow. Everyone in there was dancing except a few students from the University of South Carolina."

"We need to get you to a doctor. You're confusing real life with things you've read."

"No! It happened, and a vampire was there, too."

"You must have hit your head when you collapsed," Nate said and lifted me to a sitting position. "I'm taking you to the emergency room."

"No," I protested. "I'm fine."

He leaned close to my face and stared into my eyes. "Your pupils look okay," he said. "Follow my finger." He waved his hand back and forth, then made circles. I followed his movements with my eyes.

"You seem all right, but if you start feeling dizzy or nauseated, tell me." I nodded yes enthusiastically.

Nate patted my hand, a fatherly touch that increased my resolve that his interest in me wasn't carnal. "Let's go eat a healthy breakfast and plan our day," he said.

"Aren't you on duty?" I asked, looking at his uniform.

"I just got off when I found you," he said.

At IHOP, I chose scrambled Egg Beaters, turkey sausage, and whole wheat toast. Nate devoured a stack of pancakes and a side of bacon. His bacon smelled good, but I usually ate turkey bacon like my mother fed me during high school and college. I'm not sure if that was because of habit or it made me feel like I was a "good girl."

As I glanced around, I saw Richard come in. I waved at him, but he didn't respond. Just turned and quickly left.

"Now, tell me what kind of car you want," Nate said while drinking a third cup of coffee. "Will financing be difficult since you're unemployed?"

"I'm not unemployed; I'm self-employed, but I don't plan to buy on credit. Most of the money from my mother's life insurance is in the bank. I want safe transportation at a reasonable price."

"That's good, but I suggest you get a driver's license before you buy a car. Otherwise, we have to find someone to drive it home for you and you can't register a car in your name if you're not a licensed driver. Why don't we go to the Department of Motor Vehicles and get a driver's handbook so you can get a permit? That way I can legally take you out to practice driving before you test for your license."

"Okay, but if we're going to do that, can we stop at a florist's and then go by my mother's grave? It's not too far from the DMV."

"Of course," Nate said.

Why can't all men be so agreeable? I thought as I slid in the passenger seat of his Honda.

10

DAMN! THAT cop came by Julie's every day, and usually when he showed up, Julie went off with him. Richard didn't think it had anything to do with law enforcement. If the police officer was so concerned, why didn't he investigate something, solve her mother's murder, find out who set her house on fire or who killed her friend and left him on the sidewalk by the post office?

Richard had slept in the cemetery the night before, and he'd developed a crick in his neck, making him wish he'd finished with his research and could go back to living his normal life. He'd felt the same way one day the previous week, even wondered if he should change to a different subject for the book, but then he'd met an interesting couple who claimed they lived homeless by choice. They weren't kids who liked camping out either. These two were middle-aged and had raised a family. After sending the kids to college, there hadn't been much left in savings. According to the husband, they'd sold their house, banked the money, and decided to adopt a homeless lifestyle to make their funds last as long as possible for absolute necessities.

The longer Richard delved into the life of the homeless for his next book by living in their world, the greater compassion he felt for those who found themselves in that situation regardless of the cause. He couldn't believe anyone would intentionally take to the streets.

Richard checked his pockets. Still had a few bucks from his most recent trip to the ATM. Sometimes he thought he wasn't really "living" street life because he had some money available while most of the homeless didn't. Then again, a few of them received government checks and treated themselves to motel rooms and decent meals for a few days each month.

With some money and the woman he liked to watch gone off in the cop's car, he might as well start the day with coffee and pancakes. He walked to the IHOP, but the first thing he saw when he went inside was Julie and the policeman sitting in the back, talking and laughing.

Oh, shit! That was the last thing he wanted. Of course, Richard could leave or he could sit near them and listen to their conversation. Oh, hell, no! Julie had supplied law enforcement with a sketch of him.

Damn! Julie had seen him. She smiled and waved. He left as though he hadn't seen her.

His enthusiasm for breakfast ruined, Richard went to the laundromat across the street from the burned house. Coffee from their dispenser wasn't great, but it would do, and the place had chairs and lots of windows. He could watch Glory's house from there. When the cop brought Julie home, he wanted to talk to her.

Richard was daydreaming about Julie when he recognized Doug Kappa handing over a basket full of clothing to the woman at the dry-clean window. Richard had met Doug when he'd been working on the paranormal book. Doug's hat covered his baldness and he looked warm in his wool overcoat. With its neatly trimmed mustache and beard, Doug's face was as lean as his body was lanky, and his wire-rimmed glasses sat a little too low on his nose. He was putting the receipt in his wallet when he turned and saw Richard. A troubled look crossed his face.

"Doug," Richard said as he approached the man. He extended his hand, but Doug ignored it.

"What happened?" Doug asked with an expression of genuine concern.

"Oh," Richard said, relieved to realize that Doug Kappa recognized him but was confused by his shabby appearance.

"Writing a new book," Richard continued. "This one's about the homeless living in the city."

"I'd planned to buy your paranormal book, but I didn't realize it was finished. I'll check Amazon for it."

"No need. I didn't complete it. Decided the homeless might be more marketable."

The tall man laughed—a roar that seemed too enormous for such a slender person. "You don't fool me. You got scared when we went down to that asylum in Charleston, didn't you?"

Richard faked a chuckle. "Could have been that. Are you still hunting ghosts?"

"Don't say *ghost hunting*, man. I'm an apparition investigator, even started my own company though it's not full-time yet."

Richard's chuckle at that was genuine. "What's your day job now?"

"Exterminator." Doug unbuttoned his overcoat and showed Richard that his white shirt had an embroidered logo and the words "Infestation Extermination" on the pocket. "I've got to be going. Give me your number and I'll call you sometime."

"I don't carry a cell phone. You give me yours. I have a friend who may want to talk with you."

Doug handed Richard a business card before leaving with a long-legged brisk walk. Richard put the card in his pocket and sat back down in front of the window.

11

MAMA LOVED flowers. Standing in the florist's shop made me feel like I was with her. I could picture her tending to the large pots of flowers she grew on the porch and in our tiny backyard. I'd help her cut the bountiful dahlias, zinnias, and other blossoms she grew and she'd let me place some in jelly glasses while she made arrangements in vases on our kitchen table. When I moved to New York and tried growing those plants on my patio, I realized how green my mother's thumbs had been.

The chubby blond clerk waited patiently for me to return to the present.

"I want some flowers for my mother's grave," I told her.

"Do you prefer a basket, a wreath, a spray, or a pot plant?" she asked with a pronounced lisp.

"None of the above." I smiled. "There's a vase attached to the marker. I want flowers to put in it, but

I can't decide what kind or color."

When Mom died, I'd wanted to have a stand-up monument, something like a big granite angel, but I knew she'd want to be buried next to Daddy. That cemetery allowed only flat markers, and Mom's name and date of birth had already been on the bronze double at Daddy's grave, so I'd just added her date of death and laid her to rest beside my father.

"How about this pretty pink bouquet?" the clerk asked and lifted a beautiful arrangement of artificial blossoms.

"That would be fine for my mother, but not especially for my father. The vase is between their names. Besides, I'd really rather have fresh flowers."

"No problem. Let's do a mix with lots of red, purple, and yellow. That makes up nice and is suitable for a woman or man."

While Nate and I waited, I began telling him where Mom was buried and how to get there.

"I know exactly where she is," he answered.

"That's right. You said you were at the funeral."

"I attend a lot of funerals, and I can't relate all of the victims to their locations, but I remember your Mom's because I've been back there several times."

"Why?"

"I've stopped by to promise her that if the lead detective closes her case without an arrest, I'll keep investigating on my own. I made that vow before I met you, and now I'm even more determined that monster who killed her won't go free."

"Was the rape horribly atrocious? Not that rape and murder themselves aren't hideous." I was afraid of the answer to that question, but I asked it anyway.

"Brutal is all I can say. You didn't see her, did you?"

"No, the coroner advised me to remember her as she was before."

"Good advice."

"Here you go," the florist said, and handed me a stunning array made on a Styrofoam cone that would fit into the vase.

I couldn't stop staring at the gorgeous flowers during the short, pleasant drive to the cemetery. One thing I liked about the place was that the entire area, several acres divided into sections called gardens, was surrounded by a fence with a double-wide gate at the main entrance. An arch over the top of the entry was lettered RESTING IN PEACE.

As we approached the gate, clouds rolled in and darkened the sky. Even in the absence of sunlight, the cemetery was a pretty place with benches and walkways throughout each section. Mama and Daddy were buried in the Garden of Gethsemane, which was a section on a small hill with a large white statue of Jesus praying.

Nate parked as close as possible, which was about fifty feet from Mom and Dad. Turning off the car's ignition seemed to be the signal for the sky to turn almost as black as night and the clouds to release a downpour of cold rain.

"I've got umbrellas in the backseat, but let's wait this out until the storm lets up," Nate suggested.

He didn't get any argument from me. We sat in his car, surrounded by the storm, trying to listen to the radio between deep, rolling claps of thunder that accompanied sharp flashes of lightning.

The storm seemed to be stuck right over us instead of moving on. Finally, Nate retrieved two umbrellas from the backseat, and we began sloshing toward my family's marker.

Through the torrential rain, I thought I was seeing a distortion caused by the cloudiness. The wind battered a bunch of flowers in the metal vase between Mom's and Dad's names on their marker. Back and forth they whipped like most of the other floral arrangements across the graveyard. But the other flowers still appeared colorful through the wind and rain. The ones where we were headed didn't.

Someone had put black flowers on my mother's and father's graves.

I thought of nothing but getting those gruesome mementos of death off that grave. I began running, clutching the fresh flowers against my chest with one hand, reaching out to grab that hideous bouquet with the other. Of course, I fell.

Nate reached down and helped me stand. "Let's go back to the car," he said. "We'll come back later today or tomorrow."

"No!" I snapped. "I want those things out of there *now*."

When I was upright with my umbrella over my soaking wet head, Nate said, "You go back to the car and I'll get those flowers. Keep the fresh ones in the car, and we'll come back and put them on after the storm."

He may as well not have said a word. I would have crawled to my mother's grave to remove that mockery. I carefully walked the remainder of the way and then stood in shock over the marker that identified where my mother and father rested. Nate pulled the black-painted plastic flowers from the vase before leaning over and rubbing the bronze surface. His finger didn't make any change in the black that covered my mother's name and dates of birth and death — not that I expected it to because the rain had no effect on it.

"What is it?" I asked through tears.

"Paint. Just black paint. Vandalism happens in cemeteries."

"But why Mama's grave?" I tried to look around through the constant pouring rain. No other markers looked black or any color except bronze.

"Let's get back in the car and go to the office. We need to report this and ask if they've been having problems here."

The manager on duty wasn't the one I'd dealt

with when I made Mom's arrangements. He was short and stocky with wire-rimmed glasses and a gray ponytail that hung below his waist in the back. A few more inches and it would have to be tucked under his butt when he sat down.

"Desecration? Desecration of one of our graves? I can't believe that. Are you positive this storm didn't blow dirt over the marker?"

I thrust the black plastic flowers at him, dripping water on his desk. "Do you think I would put these on my mother's grave?" I demanded.

"No, of course not." He reached for a raincoat from the hat rack and picked up an umbrella from a stand. "Let's go look at it."

The rain slacked off as we rode back to the Garden of Gethsemane in the cemetery's golf cart. Either Ponytail deserved an Academy Award or this was, as he said, the first incident like this he'd seen while working at this cemetery.

"This is awful, this vandalism," he kept repeating all the way back to his office and again as he returned his raincoat to the rack.

"I thought this place was locked up at night and someone was on duty during daytime." My tone was accusatory, as though I thought this little man had gone out with a bucket of black paint and brushed it all over my mother's marker and flowers himself.

"We'll fill out a police report," the manager offered.

"I'll take it," Nate said. "There are some forms in my car."

The man looked out through the window, apparently checking to see if we were traveling in a police vehicle.

"Is that your car?" he asked.

"Yes, that's my personal vehicle, but I'm a policeman and can take the report for you."

Ponytail turned his attention to me. "Ms. Bates, I'm so sorry this happened. As soon as the weather dries out, I'll have some of our people clean the marker and retouch it if necessary."

"What if that black stuff doesn't come off?" I asked.

"It appears to be paint which should come off easily with the proper remover, but if it doesn't, we'll file on our insurance to replace the marker at no charge to you. I assure you that we're sorry this happened and will do everything we can to make it right."

WE RODE in total quiet from the cemetery to the Department of Motor Vehicles. Nate sensed that I didn't want to talk about the vandalism of my mother's grave and drove silently, leaving me to deal with my feelings.

I'd never felt so confused and abused in my life. The crazy dreams were bad enough, and now *this*.

We'd almost reached the DMV when an idea surfaced that I wanted to discuss with Nate, not as my friend, but as a cop.

"Nate, do you think whoever killed my mother messed up her marker? Don't murderers sometimes attend their victims' funerals and go back to their graves?"

"Yes, I thought of that, and I'll be sure the lead investigators in your mother's case know all about what has happened here."

When I went for my driver's permit back as a teenager, we had to wait forever. The same for my first driver's license. Things were certainly different this time. Nate insisted we just get a handbook, but I decided to try the exam so I'd know what to study. We signed up and only had to wait a few minutes.

When a hip young man called me up and assigned me to a computer, Nate wanted to sit with me, but the employee told him that wasn't allowed.

Even as distraught as I was over what had happened at the cemetery, my score was above passing. I insisted on taking the actual driving part of the test and was lucky enough to go out during a break in the rain. I passed! We left the DMV during another round of rain and thunder, but since I could now drive legally, Nate let me drive his Honda. Either he was one accommodating cop or he wanted to see for himself how well I could drive after a five-year absence from behind the wheel.

I wanted to go by Glory's and change clothes, but when Nate and I walked in, that was the last thing on my mind.

Surrounded by boxes and packing materials, Glory sat at the kitchen table fooling with my brand-new Mac.

"What are you doing?" I admit I screamed.

"Checking out your computer. The cable guy just left. We have WiFi now, so you can do your work here."

"You had WiFi installed?" I asked in surprise.

Glory grinned and nodded her head yes, apparently expecting praise and/or appreciation.

She got neither.

"Miss Glory, *please* leave my things alone. I know you think you're helping, but I don't like anyone trying to take over my life," I said in a nasty tone.

"Don't be so selfish. I didn't hurt this machine. The cable man set it up and checked it out. He said to give you this."

I looked down at the paper she'd handed me. On it was my WiFi password with a note to use the one he supplied to get into WiFi and then reset the password to something personal.

Nate stood—silent and still—not wanting to get into the disagreement. I began picking up all the packing materials and stuffing them into the box.

"I'll throw those away," Glory offered in a meek tone.

"I don't want to throw them away," I snapped, "I'll save them until I've checked out the damn thing and know I don't want to return it to the fucking store." It was all I could do not to spout every word I'd ever heard my father use.

Both Nate and Glory stared at me with bugged eyes and shocked expressions.

"I'm going to lie down," Glory mumbled. "I'm sorry I upset you."

She was hardly out of the room with the door closed before Nate asked, "Why don't you rest some, too? You've had too much stress today. We can run more errands tomorrow."

I sat at the computer and began checking it as I muttered, "Okay, please lock the door on your way out." *That tirade wasn't necessary,* I told myself. *What's wrong with me?*

Glory may have said she was going to take a nap, but soon the television was blaring a game show. I felt a lot of embarrassment about my explosive reaction to what in Glory's mind was kindness, especially in front of Nate, but I was happy to find the computer worked perfectly.

A Google search would probably show numerous articles about the history of The Big Apple building, but to make it quicker, I went straight to Wikipedia. I was shocked, but somehow not so surprised.

There was no mention of Gates Street. The original House of Peace Synagogue on Park Street burned in 1915. It was rebuilt and used as a Jewish synagogue until 1936 when it was sold with the provision that it never again be used as a house of worship. For the next two years, the building was a black nightclub called The Big Apple which closed in 1938, but in 1937, some USC students discovered the club and went there frequently to watch African Americans boogie. They called the dance the "Big Apple" for the club, and wound up introducing it to the public. Like so many fads, it took off and became the rage in New York, leading to national fame and performances in movies.

Another website showed a picture of The Big Apple building in 1937. It matched the shabby yellow building where I'd sought refuge from the vampire. After the nightclub closed in 1938, the structure went through several uses, but by 1979, it was abandoned. In 1993, the Historic Columbia Foundation took it over. It was moved to the corner of Hampton Street and Park Street, and turned to face Hampton.

I sat in shock for several minutes, and then I knew what I had to do. I wanted to go back into that building. I called The Big Apple.

"Hello, this is Amy at The Big Apple. How may I help you?"

"Well, I'm engaged and looking for a place to hold my wedding reception. I've heard about The Big Apple and want to get some information and to see the inside," I lied.

"Yes, I'll be happy to help you. Our capacity is one hundred and fifty people. We host meetings, dinners, receptions—and can handle all arrangements including catering, flowers, and decorations. Why don't you stop by and let me show you our facility?"

"I'd love to."

"Do you know where we are?" she asked.

"Yes, ma'am." *You bet I do!*

"When is convenient for you? I can see you at four o'clock if you want to come today or we can set a different appointment."

"My name is Julie Bates, and I'll be there at four."

Next I called Nate and informed him about what I'd read. I intentionally avoided telling him about my plan to go to The Big Apple. I was afraid he'd either try to stop me from going or insist on driving me there and going in with me. From Glory's house to Hampton Street was within walking distance, but I called a cab. First stop was at the bank where I used my driver's license to withdraw more cash.

I HADN'T paid much attention to the building when Nate found me on the sidewalk, but now I got a good look. The shape of the banquet facility with its arched windows was the same, but this crisply painted pale gray façade with white trim bore little resemblance to the shabby yellow place where I'd sought shelter. A historical plaque in front told about the past, including the dance.

Amy met me at the door. She looked about the same age as the college students seen around the USC campus, but she wasn't dressed like them. Her outfit was definitely in the "dress for success" category with a navy blue skirt suit, cream-colored silk blouse, and pearl stud earrings.

"Welcome to The Big Apple!" she said, and then added, "Are you Miss Bates?"

"Yes, I am."

"What is the date of your wedding?"

It took a moment for me to remember that she thought I was there to plan a wedding reception, but I finally did and answered, "We haven't set the date yet."

That's when I noticed she was writing in a little notebook, much like the one I'd seen cops with on television—just exactly like the one that Nate had used when I found Jerry Patterson.

"Oh, you don't need to make notes," I told Amy. "I'm just looking. Before I make official plans, we need to set the date and my fiancé will want to see everything."

"It will be important for you to choose a date soon. Weddings take a lot of preparation, and our calendar fills up quickly, but, of course, you're welcome to check us out and ask any questions you like."

I commented on how beautiful the interior was

and assured her that as soon as "John" and I set a date, we'd be back to see her.

She assured me that they could handle all of my reception needs. Then she asked, "Do you have any questions?"

"Is the building haunted?" I asked in complete sincerity.

"Pardon me, what did you say?"

"Is The Big Apple haunted? Does it have any ghosts?"

"No one who works here has ever reported seeing shadows or doors opening and closing by themselves if that's what you mean."

"What about in the past?"

"I've never heard of anything like that, but if you're considering a themed reception, we can certainly accommodate your needs. I notice you have a slight northern accent. If you've just moved here and are interested in local ghosts, you might want to visit the Vista area and the South Carolina State Museum. There are lots of tales about ghosts in those places."

I thanked her and left. I hadn't learned anything, but I'd been impressed with how beautiful the Historical Society had made that old nightclub, and I was surprised that Amy heard something slightly different about my accent.

When I left, I couldn't resist calling Nate and telling him about my visit to the modern-day Big

Apple.

"I don't think you should have done that," he said. "I think you're under too much tension. Reading scary books isn't helping you sleep peacefully, and researching the places in your dreams isn't a good idea."

"You don't understand. I feel better now that I've seen that the real place isn't like where I was in my dream."

"The problem is that you're sleepwalking during these delusions. I found you lying on the sidewalk. You weren't dreaming in your bed. People can do totally ridiculous things while sleeping. We arrested a man last week who shot his wife in bed and claims he was asleep when he did it. I worry about what you might do or about you getting hit by a car. You're totally defenseless when you're in that condition."

"I got away from a vampire, didn't I?"

"Did you? Do you believe you actually were chased into a building almost eighty years ago by a vampire? Last night? If so, I'm more worried than ever. I think you're having nightmares or delusions, maybe you're even psychic—have extrasensory perception—but I doubt that. I think these are stress reactions." He paused and then added, "I talked to my mother about you after you told me what you learned from Wikipedia."

"You what? Why?"

"She's very knowledgeable about local history.

She said that although what you read about The Big Apple says it was on Park Street before the Historical Society moved it to Hampton, the name of the street was originally Gates Street. She wasn't quite sure when, but she was positive that Park Street used to be Gates Street."

"Wow! How would my subconscious or maybe my dreaming mind know that?"

"I don't know, but even your visit today was a dream or vision. The building is no longer being rented out for receptions. It was bought in 2015 by two dancers who converted it to an arts venue and concerts. Vow to me you won't go back investigating until I can go with you?"

"Why? Do you think that vampire might still be hanging around in The Big Apple?" I shouldn't have, but I snickered.

"No, I just want to look out for you. Do you promise?"

"I won't promise not to, but I'll promise to try."

That conversation could have turned into a disagreement, but my telephone beeped another caller. I quickly said goodbye and tried to take the other call. No one was there.

12

THE HOUSE was silent when I entered through the back. Glory's door was closed, but I opened it just a crack to see if she were sleeping. She wasn't home. I turned the Mac on and began checking emails I'd received since the fire. I responded to a few, but my mind wasn't really into it. Glory had put a couple of boxes of Mom's papers and pictures in my room. I took them out and set them on the bed.

The noise began faintly — just soft knockings from the wall. I tried to ignore them and continued looking at the photos, pretending I didn't hear the sounds. They grew and grew until it became deafening booming. *Bang, bang, bang* followed by silence and then repeating itself over and over. Anxiety filled me with an overwhelming oppressed feeling. I felt sick to my stomach.

I've got to get out of here. As I headed for the kitchen, the pictures on the bed flew into the air swirling around like a miniature tornado. I ran. Through the kitchen. Out the back door. To the front yard.

Where can I go? I need wheels, a car, but Nate can't take me shopping right now. I laughed, perhaps it was almost a maniacal laugh—I'm not sure. I knew what I had to do. When I went off to New York, I was alone with a limited amount of funds. I'd found myself a job and an apartment by myself. Well, the apartment was just a one-room efficiency, but it had been mine. I didn't need a man, any man, to take me to buy a car. I had my phone in my pocket and I had money in my savings account.

I called another cab and went by the nearest branch bank and then to a car dealership carrying an ad that Mr. Scott, the bank manager, had shown me and then printed out for me. The advertised vehicle was brand-new, and I could purchase it and still have enough money to make a small down payment on a home later. *Who knows? If Mom had insurance, maybe a substantial down payment. That's another thing to do—find out about insurance. Wonder if Glory would know?*

When I stepped from the taxi, the cabbie asked, "Do you want me to wait for you or maybe come back at a certain time?"

"No, thank you," I answered and tipped him generously. I noticed several salesmen standing around the door talking. Some of them were smoking. Naively, I expected one of them to rush over and ask if he could help me. When no one bothered to approach me, I walked up to the group and said, "I've come to buy a car."

"Yes, ma'am," the youngest-looking man said. "Just look around and see what you'd like. We'll be here until nine tonight if you want to bring your husband back with you."

"I want to buy this car," I said and pulled out the ad my banker had printed off the computer for me. "This exact car at this price."

"Well, ma'am, that's a pretty cheap car and it's white. You'd probably like something in a prettier color, maybe a nicer interior, and more luxury items." The men standing around him smirked.

"It says on the ad that this Focus has automatic transmission, a radio, CD player, and air-conditioning as well as Bluetooth and Sirius. Those are the only luxuries I want." The men's expressions turned surprised. Were they not used to women speaking for themselves? If I hadn't learned to stand up for myself when I lived in New York, I would have been walked all over almost every day.

"Now," I said, "may I see the Focus in the ad?"

"Show her the car," one of the older men said to the first one who'd spoken to me. He walked with the younger salesman and me to the back of the lot.

Mr. Scott at the bank had warned me that "bait and switch" still existed. He'd cautioned me that the salesman would try to talk me into a more expensive model, but he said that if I stood my ground, they had to sell me the car at the advertised price.

Actually, I loved the looks of that little car. Yes, it was white, but I like white cars. My daddy always chose white vehicles. The interior was cream and tan—colors Mama repeatedly told me went well with red hair. Not that I had to match my car to my hair, but it made me feel good that the car interior was one Mama would have liked.

"I'll take this one," I said.

"Don't you want to take it for a test drive?" the young man asked.

"She needs to show you her driver's license if she's going to drive it," the older one said. "She came here in a cab. Always be sure anyone test-driving a vehicle has a valid license."

I showed them my license, and the three of us got into the car with the older man in the front passenger seat and the younger one sitting behind him. I started the engine and put the Focus in gear. To my ears, it purred. As we pulled out onto the street, the older man said, "Now, if you want more power, you may want to buy something with a bigger engine."

"I want this car, this exact car," I stated again, "and I want it at the price you advertised."

When we returned to the car lot, the young salesman again mentioned a husband. "Will your husband be coming by to fill out the finance papers?" he asked.

"I don't have a husband. If I did, he might have brought me over here, but I doubt it. I can make a purchase without anyone telling me what to do." My tone was snippy and I didn't care. These men were taking the pleasure of buying the car away from me.

We went into a tiny office where the younger man plopped down in the chair beside mine facing the older man behind the desk. "Now, you know we need verification of auto insurance before you leave."

"Mr. Scott at the bank said for you to call him and he'll give you all of that information," I answered. "He called and arranged insurance with his company for me. Here's the number." I handed him Mr. Scott's business card.

I didn't pay much attention as the salesman filled in insurance info on the paperwork while talking to Mr. Scott. After that, he said, "Will the bank be financing this or shall we apply to our own resources for financing?"

Apparently Mr. Scott didn't give him any details because he disconnected the telephone quickly after that question. "Miss Bates, your banker says that the bank will not finance this car for you. I'll fill out a loan application with one of the companies we deal with. Their interest rate is a little higher, but sometimes they're more willing to deal with customers whose credit rating isn't as high as the bank prefers." He took out another clipboard and lifted his pen above the papers on it. "Now, let's begin," he said.

"Sir," I said, "I didn't ask you to finance the car. I'm going to pay you right now." I opened my purse and began counting out the cost of the car in bank-banded hundred-dollar bills. I'm sure there are other people who don't have to finance their cars, but they probably don't pull that amount out in cash and I doubt they grew up in a mill house. Everyone should have paying for a new car with cash on their "bucket list."

SOMEONE ALWAYS comes along to burst a person's bubble. Happy as a pig in a poke, I'd been singing all the way back to Glory's house—singing those old Elvis songs my mother loved and sang. It wasn't just the car. Though I loved it, part of my happiness came from taking things into my own hands, dealing with a need on my own. This was a proactive decision like I used to make, not behaving as though I were in a trance half the time. I called Nate and asked him to come by the house after he got off duty.

When I showed off the car to Glory, she complained that it would be inconvenient to have it parked right in front of her house. She didn't think the mailman or the paper boy would like that. "And it's so small," she went on. "Why didn't you get something bigger that we could use to haul things in—something like those SUV things?"

Next, she thought the color was wrong. "I like black cars," she insisted. "That white will be dirty in no time, and I don't want you using up so much water washing it."

My defense to Glory not wanting the car parked in front of her house was, "I'll park it in front of Mom's house. I mean *my* house. The building may be gone, but it still belongs to me. I'll just park it on the street right in front of the yellow tape." Personally, I'd wanted to pay someone to remove the charred remains of the house as soon as the ashes cooled off, but Nate had told me they were still investigating.

"You'll still be dragging my hose over there to wash it," Glory protested.

"No, I'll be taking it to the car wash."

Expecting Nate to be happy for me, I met him at the door when he knocked. I pointed toward the car parked on the street. "What do you think?" I asked and tugged his arm, leading him to walk over to my new car.

"Think about what?" he asked.

"My car! This white Focus is mine." I patted the hood.

"I told you I'd take you to shop for a car. I probably could have gotten you a better deal."

"Mr. Scott at the bank said it was an excellent deal."

"I didn't realize you were so independent and

impulsive," Nate said, and I didn't like his tone of voice.

"But I am," I answered and rubbed my hand across the shiny white fender of the Focus. Then I added, "At least most of the time. So far as impulsive is concerned, this wasn't impulse. I knew when I moved back to South Carolina that I'd need a car sooner or later. Now is later."

Nate asked if I needed to go anywhere, but I declined. Anywhere I wanted to go now, I'd take myself. We didn't part in anger, but he still seemed miffed when he left.

After dinner with Glory, I bathed, and then snuggled into my bed to read. She told me good night and went to the front room to watch TV.

13

I AWOKE screaming—again. This time I knew why. It wasn't because of some bad dream I couldn't remember.

Howling in pain, I tossed and turned. My stomach felt like a boulder had dropped on it, and below that, my abdomen was on fire. I felt a desperate need to go to the bathroom, but just the thought of urinating made the burning worse.

"What's wrong, Julie?" Glory cried as she ran in from her room without her wig. I was glad to see her, didn't resent her at all. She could scold me for buying a car, boss me around, and irritate me, but I was glad to have her come to help me.

"It's the cystitis," I gasped and pressed my hands against my middle, but I couldn't bear any additional pressure. "It's back. Worse than ever. It hurts so bad I can't move, but I've got to go to the bathroom or I'm going to wet the bed."

I moved my hands below my stomach and clamped them hard against the part of me that seared. I pressed as hard as I could, but that didn't help at all.

"Move your hands away," Glory instructed.

I did.

"You're bleeding. There's blood on the sheets," she said. "Is it your time of the month?"

"No, ma'am," I answered, "and that might give me a few cramps, but it doesn't cause this." I struggled, trying to sit up. The agony intensified as I strained to move.

"Lay back down," Glory said. "I'll get something to help you." She went to the kitchen.

I couldn't imagine what she thought would help. *An ice pack? A heating pad?*

Glory was back by my bedside in no time. "Lay flat," she said, "and then spread your legs a little bit."

I slept commando, wearing a nightgown but no panties. Everything from my bosom down ached and blazed too much for me to feel any modesty when she lifted the hem of my garment.

First, Glory placed several towels under me. She sponged me off with a warm washcloth, and then she gently rubbed some kind of thick, ugly ointment all over me, including in the girl-part cracks and crevices. Immediately, the pain began to subside.

"We can wash this off in an hour or so," she said. "I want you to lie here and rest while the medicine works. I'll cook us a nice breakfast and by then you should be ready for a bath. We do need to double your tonic though. I must not have been giving you enough." She looked down at me with warm affection. "How does it feel now?"

"Much better. Much, much better," I managed to say. "Thank you, Miss Glory."

"Thank you, Jesus!" Glory shouted and headed for the kitchen. She was at the door when she turned around and came back. She pulled a clean blanket from the cedar chest at the foot of the bed, placed it across me, and tucked it in under my chin.

"When you feel like getting up and taking a bath, just pile all these bedclothes and your nightgown into one of the laundry baskets. I'll wash them after we eat."

"Oh, no," I whispered a protest. "I'll take care of them."

"You should probably rest for a while after breakfast. I'll take them across the street to the laundromat." I smiled at the thought. For as long as I could remember, Glory had carried her wash back and forth across the street in an old grocery cart that made her look as homeless as Richard. She used the same cart when she went to the grocery store.

I would have sworn I'd stay in bed all day, but like the tonic, Glory's ointment worked magic. By mid-morning, I felt fine and decided to go out. I needed to think, and I did that best out of the house.

The reality of The Big Apple building and its

history made me question whether my recent experiences were dreams or part of some bizarre other dimension. The noises in the house and the swirling of Mom's pictures over my bed creeped me out, and they *weren't* dreams. Thinking about them sent shivers down my spine.

I headed toward the business end of Assembly Street, but I didn't dwell on my thoughts long because I saw Richard Arthur headed toward me. He'd changed clothes since the last time I saw him. Looking raggedy, but clean, he grinned.

"Julie! I was hoping to run into you," he said.

"How are you today?" I asked.

"Going to the post office?" he asked without answering.

"No, just out for a walk."

"Has all the craziness in your life slowed down?" He fell into step with me.

I told him all about the Owens Hotel, The Big Apple, my mother's face in the mirror, and the pictures swirling up off the bed, and then I told him everything—banging in the walls, the feeling I was being watched, and that I'd felt sick and wasn't behaving normally lately. I told him about the desecration of my mother's grave, though that might have been simple vandalism.

Richard said, "I want you to call my friend Doug Kappa." He handed me a business card from his pocket. "Well," he added, "he's really more of an acquaintance than a friend. I met him when I was working on the paranormal book. He's a ghost hunter, and I think he might be able to help you."

It was hard to comprehend that there were some people who actually *wanted* to have contact with the creatures and ghosts that haunted my midnights. I'd seen television shows devoted to people seeking paranormal beings, but I hadn't thought of finding someone like that to help me. Just another example of the apathy that seemed to have overtaken me, but I was desperate for help. I looked at the tiny rectangle in my hand.

"This must be the wrong card," I said. "It's for a different business — some exterminator operating as Infestation Annihilation."

"Turn it over."

I did and found info on Doug Kappa, Apparition Investigations, with a telephone number.

"Thank you, thank you so much, Richard," I gushed. "I'm going home now and call him." Richard walked me back to Glory's house. I was happy she wasn't there. She'd already been to the laundromat and back because my bed linens and gown were neatly folded on the kitchen table, but she and her cart were gone.

Before calling the number, I checked the Internet for Apparition Investigations. According to their webpage, whether the client's problem was the manifestation of ghosts, poltergeists, or other supernatural beings, Apparition Investigations would discreetly explore the situation with the most modern equipment. Set off in a black border was a warning: DON'T BE DECEIVED BY PHONIES WHO CHARGE FOR THEIR SERVICES AND PLANT FAKE EVIDENCE. Below that was contact info including a telephone number, email address, and "Ask for Doug Kappa."

No better time to call than right then while Glory was still out of the house. The phone number took me to a recording of a female who told me that no one was available at the moment, but that if I left a message and number, someone would be in touch ASAP.

"This is Julie Bates. I think I'm being haunted. Please call me." I left my number and disconnected. Then I remembered that I hadn't asked for Doug Kappa, so I called back and said, "I just called and left my number. This is Julie Bates. If possible, I want to talk to Doug Kappa."

I lay across the bed and read R.L. Stine's adult horror novel, *Red Rain,* again, thinking I needed to buy some new books and hoping the call would come soon. At 5:05 P.M., my ringtone sounded.

"Hello," I answered on the first ring, but there was no one on the line.

When the phone rang again in five minutes, I answered but didn't expect to hear anyone.

"Yes, may I speak to Julie Bates?" The voice was

deep, soothing, and male.

"This is Julie."

"I'm Doug Kappa with Apparition Investigations returning your call."

"All kinds of weird stuff's happening here. Can you help me?"

"I won't know until you tell me what's going on. May I come by and talk to you?"

I thought about the fact that Glory might come in at any moment. She wouldn't like my having a man in the house. Come to think of it, inviting a strange man to the house wasn't a smart idea anyway.

"Could I meet you somewhere?" I questioned.

"What part of town are you in?" he asked.

I hesitated, once more considering how much information to give a stranger on the telephone. He sensed my indecision and asked, "Can you name somewhere you'd be comfortable meeting me?"

"How about the downtown IHOP on Assembly Street?"

"Fine. I'm in town right now myself. How long will it take you to get there?"

"Is ten minutes too soon?"

"Not at all. Describe yourself."

"Five feet, five inches. Not thin. Red ponytail. Wearing jeans and a pink shirt." I paused. "Now, you."

"I beg your pardon?"

"Now you tell me what to look for."

"Over five feet, seventeen inches tall with a hat covering my very bald head. Brown beard and mustache. The best way to recognize me is that I'll be wearing an Infestation Annihilation uniform." I smiled at his last sentence. I doubted there would be too many bald-headed men who stood six feet, five inches tall in IHOP.

I left a note for Glory telling her I'd be back soon. Didn't say where I was going. I knew that would irritate her and she'd been a lifesaver that morning, but at that moment, I was like Clark Gable in *Gone with the Wind* when he said, "Frankly, my dear, I don't give a damn."

Although the IHOP was in walking distance, I drove there. As I pulled into the parking lot, I saw a white van with an Infestation Annihilation logo on the door. It was a half circle with IA on the top half and reflected upside down at the bottom. Unlike some exterminators' vehicles I'd seen, it didn't have pictures of bugs or other creatures painted on it.

Doug Kappa was sitting at the counter when I came in, but he stood and greeted me. I noticed that the logo on his shirt was the same as the one on the truck except that it read Apparition Investigations. He was very slim and stood straight and tall, not hunched over like some towering people do.

"Julie, I presume," he said in a bogus British voice.

"Indeed," I replied in my own false accent.

"Let's sit over at that table." He dropped the extreme English inflection and motioned toward an empty space at the back. "We'll have more privacy." When we were seated, he said in a dragged-out drawl, "I hope you're southern enough to eat dinner at five-thirty. I missed lunch today and I'm starving." That southern accent sounded as false as the British one had.

The tonic that Glory gave me must have been an appetite stimulant as well as a cure for UTIs. "Sure," I answered him, "I'm in the mood for their fish and chips meal."

Our server arrived just as Doug said, "I'm going to have pancakes, a big stack of pancakes." She smiled and took our orders. She'd already written my request for fish when I realized I didn't really want the fish.

"Change mine, please," I said.

"Certainly," she said and poised the pen over her order pad.

"Make it a double cheeseburger with fries, lots of fries," I said.

When she'd moved away from the table, Doug asked in a serious tone, "Now, what's going on that made you call me?"

"First, I'm having nightmares that scare the devil out of me."

Kappa laughed. "Hope the things going on *do* scare the devil out of you because sometimes the devil is who causes scary events."

"Besides the dreams, there are strange things happening in our house," I said.

"Our? Are you married?"

"No, I've been living with an elderly friend named Glory since my place burned, but I'm hoping to move soon. The house we live in is old, and I hear things in the walls at night."

"If that's all, you may need my extermination services instead of my investigative ones. You could have rats or bats in the walls, maybe even a family of possums."

"That's not all of it. Things move around in the house, from one place to another. I know I'm not doing it, and Glory swears she isn't."

"I'll be glad to check it out for you. If it's animal infestation, there'll be a charge for it. Infestation Annihilation is my day job and how I support my ghost activities. If it's paranormal, I'll help you deal with it at no charge. So far, I don't charge for Apparition Investigations." He laughed. "Get good enough at it, maybe I'll have my own TV show."

"What could be going on at my house and how would you deal with it?" I was eager to learn how he could help me, and honestly, I could have cared less about the man's dreams.

"So far, it sounds like it could be a poltergeist or ghost. If it's a poltergeist, we'll try to banish it by putting a specific mixture of herbs in all four corners of the house as well as trying to identify who or what is triggering the activity. Frequently poltergeists feed off the energy of a developing adolescent, but occasionally their energy seems to come from an object instead of a person. If it's a ghost, it's here because it can't go past the light. We'll help it move on."

"If it's my mother's ghost, I don't want her harmed in any way, but I don't think Mom would do anything to harm me or cause me to have horrible nightmares about a vampire."

"A vampire? Have you seen one in your house?"

"No, not yet. I saw one in my hallucinations or whatever they are."

"Probably delusions or dreams." He laughed. "There are ways to defeat those paranormal creatures as well as demons, but true vampires are extremely rare."

"How do you investigate them?"

"We examine locations that are reported to be haunted, usually by ghosts, but beings like vampires and werewolves aren't ghosts. Some investigators like to go in without knowing what's been happening, so they won't be influenced or prejudiced before they begin, but I prefer to know as much as possible. I interview people and research the history of a place before I try to collect evidence that supports the paranormal activity. That's essentially what ghost-hunting is — seeking proof of paranormal activity, and to do that, we rule out normal causes of the events."

"I'm not able to give you much history on where I'm living now," I said. "I've only been there since my house burned a few days ago. I'm staying with an elderly lady who moved in next door to my mom and me when I was a teenager. It's just an average little mill house and I've never known anything unusual about it, but I hear noises, and things move around and disappear."

"These dreams about vampires—did they begin after you moved?"

"Yes, but I had terrifying dreams before that."

"What happened in those nightmares?"

"I can't remember, but I woke up screaming and shaking."

"And this was before your house burned?"

"Yes, but I might as well tell you. Where I lived had more history than where I stay now. My mother was murdered violently in my house." I paused while I stirred my coffee. "Do you think you can help me?"

"I hope so. I'm willing to give it a try."

"Do you believe vampires even exist?" I asked. "I've read *Dracula* and all those recent books where girls fall in love with them, and I've seen lots of movies. I even read all about Vlad the Impaler, the one some people think vampire legends were based on, but until I saw one in my nightmares, I never doubted that all of that was fiction. Do *you* personally believe they're real?"

"The more research I do, the more I believe in almost all of those horror legends." He smiled self-consciously and then added solemnly, "Evil is real."

"If they exist, can you get rid of them? I'm not so sure what happened to me was a dream."

"Everyone thinks vampires can be warded off by holy water and crosses, but my studies show that some of them are so powerful that religious artifacts have little effect on them. They're the ones who won't die from a wooden stake through the heart. Supposedly, the only way to destroy a strong vampire is to behead it." He'd finished his pancakes and pushed the plate out to the edge of the table.

"Have you ever seen a vampire?" The minute I said it, I realized it was a ridiculous question. If he'd ever seen one, he would have already told me.

"No, but I've studied about them extensively. A lot of what people see in movies is wrong. Now, in the case of werewolves, the fables are correct, they can be killed by a silver bullet to the heart." He finished his last bite and grinned before continuing, "But we have no reason to think that a vampire is in your walls or is causing you any problems other than a bad night's sleep. When can I come over?"

"As soon as possible, but Glory won't like it. I'll have to get her out of the house some way." I left the last fry on the plate. My mother's eating habits during my childhood were firmly ingrained. I just didn't feel right about eating a whole order of fries, much less the cheeseburger, but it'd sure tasted good.

"Tell the lady you're having the house exterminated for bugs and critters and that I told you the chemical is dangerous for older people. Show her the exterminating side of my card."

"How long will it take? Could you come first thing in the morning?"

"We'll need at least a few hours. It would be better if we have no time limit, like maybe all night."

"You say 'we.' Who'll be with you?"

"We work in pairs, and we prefer to work after dark. Besides, I take care of most of my exterminating business during the daylight hours. Is tonight okay?"

"I guess I could rent a motel room for Glory and me."

"I'll want you in the house."

"Okay, I'll get her settled somewhere else and then go back to the house to meet you. What time should I look for you and your partner?"

"How about nine o'clock?"

We set the time at nine-thirty instead, and I gave him directions to the house. When we went outside, Doug removed the magnetic logo sign off his truck, flipped it over, and drove away with it upside down. Clever — Ai for Apparition Investigations with iA for Infestation Annihilation. It was really ingenious for the two businesses even if I did think the names were too long to be memorable to most people.

When I arrived home, Glory was there. I told her I was having the house exterminated and she would need to spend the night in a rented room.

"You want me to spend the night in a motel?" Glory asked as though she'd heard me wrong.

"That's right, Miss Glory. I hear things moving in the walls here at night. Sometimes it sounds like they're beating against the wall. I talked to an exterminator today, and he said the best time to get rid of them is after dark. He also told me that the chemicals are very bad for an older person's lungs." I leaned over and hugged her. "You know I'd never forgive myself if I did anything that made you ill."

"What if you get sick again during the night? What if your UTI returns?"

"I'll take an extra dose of tonic before we go, and if I have any problems, I'll call you."

Glory looked a little confused, but she packed an overnight case and didn't balk at riding to the Crown Motel with me. It was one of those places with the rooms all in a row, only one level, with parking in front of each unit. The lobby, at the far end of the building, was separated from the rental rooms by a small area with an ice machine and other dispensers. Glory said, "This place looks old. Now, you're sure they're going to have a big color television and cable, right?"

"I guarantee it." I didn't dare tell her that I'd been there once before on the night of my senior prom. Of course, I'm sure she remembered that I'd been through a wild streak my last year of high school and then settled back down the first year of college, studying hard to keep my grades high enough not to spoil my scholarships. Small and economical that night ten years ago, the Crown Motel looked old and shabby now. I considered taking Glory somewhere else, but I was running late to meet Doug Kappa.

"You'll be fine here," I assured Glory after I filled out the registration and paid for one night. "I have to get back to the house before the exterminator arrives."

The night clerk, a short man who looked like Santa Claus wearing khaki shorts and an orange T-shirt even though summer had ended, charmed Glory with his assurances he'd look out for her.

"I'm putting you in Room 101 right on the other side of the registration office. I'll be here all night. If you need anything, just dial zero on the phone."

Glory grinned at him and said, "I want a bucket of ice and an orange soda out of that machine I saw next door."

"I'll get you those before I leave," I said.

"I'll do it," Santa told me. "You're in a hurry. We got the ice machine fixed last week. I'll fill her bucket with ice and get whatever this little lady wants from the soda and snack machines. Just give me a few dollars to cover the cost." I handed over a ten-dollar bill. At times, Glory could put away a substantial amount of snacks.

"I'll be happy to take care of her while you're gone," he said and shoved the ten into his pocket.

Glory grinned at him and said, "Please get me that ice and soda as soon as possible, and I want some of those little square cheese crackers and a candy bar." She stepped toward the door and then turned back and added, "I like those treats made out of cereal and marshmallows, too."

"I'll walk you to your room and you can pick out whatever you want when we pass the machines on the way," Santa assured her with a big smile.

"Well, let's go now." Glory's happy face showed she enjoyed the man's attention. "We need to get a lot of snacks so I don't need to call you for more. I'm going to put on my nightgown as soon as I get in the room. Don't know what I'd do if a good-looking man like you showed up at my door when I was ready for bed."

I was surprised at that, but he winked at her, and she winked back. I assumed that was just how older people tease each other.

Traffic was bad on my way back to town, and I

was barely to the house when Doug knocked at the front entrance. I opened the door and there he stood with a brown leather case and a blue backpack. He had on a black jumpsuit with the Apparition Investigations logo on his chest. *Is this wise?* I thought. *I wouldn't let him come to the house earlier today and now the two of us are here alone.*

"Hello," he said and brought his belongings inside.

"Where's your partner?" I asked.

"Aeden couldn't come. Got some kind of nasty stomach virus. I figured you'd probably already taken your roommate somewhere before I knew he couldn't make it, so I'm appointing you as tonight's assistant."

A shiver went from my head to the base of my spine. *Me? Help summon ghosts or other supernatural beings?*

"Don't look so frightened. I know what I'm doing." He closed the front door and began taking equipment out of the cases.

"What is all that stuff?" I asked.

He patiently held up and explained each item as he unpacked it. "This is a full spectrum digital video camera that can 'see' and record light spectrums invisible to the human eye." He put the camera down and took out another device. "This is an EMF detector. You've probably seen it used on television."

"I have no idea what you're talking about."

"EMF stands for 'electromagnetic frequency.' It

picks up high energy signatures."

He held up something that looked like a recorder. "Have you seen shows where they record empty rooms and hear voices?"

"Yes."

"This is a voice recorder that records EVP, which are audio frequencies undetectable to human ears."

"What does EVP stand for?"

"Electro Voice Phenomena."

He set the recorder down. "This is a shadow detector, basically a very sensitive motion detector. I also have thermographic, infrared, and night vision cameras."

"You need all this to tell if there's a ghost here?"

"Oh, if I could afford it, I'd have a lot more equipment. I'm taking it one step at a time. Seeking apparitions is a sophisticated business. Someday I hope to do it full-time."

When Doug finished unpacking, he set up equipment in various parts of the house, and then . . . he turned off the lights.

For some reason, with all those devices around the room, I wasn't frightened even in the darkness. "What do you want me to do?" I asked.

"For now, just sit down and stay still while I get everything adjusted."

I sat on the edge of the bed and tried to see what he was doing, but I couldn't tell anything more than that he was moving around, fiddling with instruments.

"Damn!" Doug exclaimed.

"What's wrong?" I asked.

"Everything. I'm going to turn the lights back on to check out my tools of the trade."

He spent two hours setting up equipment, finding out it wasn't working, fiddling with it, and then setting it up again. Nothing worked like it should have.

Finally, Doug began packing up his belongings. When everything was back in the case and backpack, he said, "Let's sit in the kitchen."

I thought maybe he would talk about ghosts and supernatural events, but I was wrong. "I'm going to have Aeden check this stuff out with me, but I think the problem may have something to do with the electricity in this house. I want you to have a professional electrician check out the wiring. Call and tell me what he says. If repairs are needed, have them made, and then call me. We'll try again after that's checked out and when the equipment is working properly."

"Before you leave," I said, "I've been wondering. Would you advise me to contact someone to do a séance."

"I've sat in on a few and I know someone who's probably legit, but I don't think I'd do that until we know more about what is going on. You have your wiring checked and I'll get Aeden to check out my equipment with me."

"Okay. Thanks," I said as he stepped out onto the steps.

"Lock your doors," he replied and pulled the door closed.

I went to bed without showering. Crawled between the clean sheets Glory and I had put on the bed when she came back after she'd washed them at the laundromat. I didn't attempt to answer the telephone after I tried several times and whoever was calling hung up on me after one ring.

I hope that's not Glory calling me. I thought about calling her, but I was so sleepy that I dozed off without trying.

14

I AWOKE behind the wheel of a car, but not my Focus, driving slowly along a two-lane road that was packed with vehicles headed in both directions — surrounded by car horns blasting and people hanging out of their vehicle windows yelling and screaming. I'd never before seen so much orange and purple or garnet and black dangling from radio antennas on big cars with fins. Traffic headed away from me was bumper to bumper, but so was movement on my side. The cars in both lanes, coming and going, made it impossible to drive off the road left or right to turn around and head back toward Glory's house.

When the traffic veered over to the right, I found myself with no choice except to stay in the line and drive into a parking lot. I was relieved to realize that I knew where I was. I could see the high bleachers of the University of South Carolina Football Stadium to my left and the circle of bright lights of a Ferris wheel looping slowly around against the dusky sky in front of me. The parking lot was between the Carolina Football Stadium and the State Fairgrounds.

"Park in the next open place," a teenager with a fifties haircut combed to a point in the back said and waved me down a row of vintage fifties cars.

I pulled into a space, turned off the ignition, and looked around. Families laughed as they headed across the parking lot, and like the automobiles they walked between, the people looked like a past time — the fifties, too. Few of the ladies wore slacks and none wore jeans. They had on dresses, and I spotted a few beehive hairdos.

Clothing on the men and children were equally dated. I should have been surprised or even scared, but I wasn't. That absence of emotion showed what my life had become — a series of unexplainable events that felt real though my mind told me they were impossible and refused to accept them enough for me to react as I should.

Stepping from the car, I looked at its exterior. I'd seen that vehicle in magazines and in movies. It was a turquoise '57 Chevy. I shoved the keys into my pocket and felt folded money. Following the crowd, I wound up at a turnstile gate where a toothless old man in overalls asked for a dollar — what he called "one greenback dollar." I handed it to him.

The exhibit buildings, merry-go-round, and other kiddie rides ahead of the walkway didn't interest me.

A left turn pointed me toward adult rides like the Round-Up, Tilt-a-Whirl, and Ferris wheel, their lights shining even brighter against the darkening sky as the sun sank in the west. I moved through the crowd with rides and games clustered inside that end of the grounds and sideshows surrounding the exterior of the area.

Two beautiful women, a blonde and a brunette, sat on the steps of the first tent. Each of them wore bathrobes. As I drew closer, their heavy makeup became obvious, and the unbuttoned top of the blonde's robe provided a peek at firm round breasts wearing only silver sequined pasties. She was eating fried potatoes. The smell of vinegar wafted up from them. I paused just close enough to overhear them without making it obvious that I was dipping into their conversation.

"Why do you eat those things?" the brunette asked. "They'll make you fat."

"I like them."

"I'm so tired of fair food I can't stand it. I'll be glad when this season is over and I go home. I want some of my mama's cooking."

The sign over the steps had been dark when I first approached, but now it began flashing in red neon: GIRLS, GIRLS, GIRLS!

The blonde looked up. "Oh, crap, we must be opening early tonight. Where did all these people come from anyway? We haven't had this kind of crowd any other day."

The brunette reached across and swiped one of the other girl's potato fries. "It's because of a football game." She waved her arm in the general direction of the stadium. "The boss told me we might start earlier tonight because today's some kind of big college rivalry here. University of South Carolina Gamecocks versus the Clemson Tigers, I believe he said. They call it 'Big Thursday' because the game is always played here on Thursday of State Fair week."

"Then we'd better go get dressed," the blonde said as she stood. She laughed, "Or maybe I should say get undressed." Both of them went into the tent.

I'd heard about Big Thursday, but the game between Clemson and Carolina stopped being played on Thursdays back in the fifties, long before I was born.

With the night fully dark now, the fairgrounds filled with lights and sounds as well as the smell of food. My stomach told me it was time to eat. I bought a Coke and a Polish sausage dog with peppers and onions. The low cost surprised me. There were a few picnic tables beside the food stand, but I continued wandering as I ate.

"Gentlemen, and this show is for gentlemen only, these are just two of the beautiful dancing girls you'll see in our presentation." The voice boomed out over speakers, and I looked up to see the two women who'd been sitting on the steps earlier. This couldn't possibly be a strip show, because the females were already stripped down to G-strings and pasties.

"Let me introduce you to Raven." The dark-haired woman stepped forward and did a little wiggle. "And here's Miss Blondie." The blonde pressed her arms together on the sides of her breasts and made them jiggle, and then she made the tassels on her pasties begin to rotate.

"When you come inside," the man on the speakers continued, "these girls and their friends are going to do the hootchy-cootchy for you. They'll show you everything you want to see while they wiggle and waggle and shake and shimmy. These girls have some muscle movements you won't believe."

I moved on around the midway.

"See ten of the wonders of the world." More words blared out over amplifiers, but they came from a male barker in a red and white striped jacket, red bow tie, and white straw hat. He stood behind a podium at the edge of another stage. Square canvas signs—big ones with brightly colored paintings of the attractions of the sideshow—hung on each side. I'd heard about these shows before, but I'd never seen them at the State Fair when I was growing up.

My mother had told me about how people were exhibited as "freaks" at the fair when she was a child, so when I proofread a book about P. T. Barnum and his "curiosities" after I moved to New York, I went to a similar show at Coney Island. Billed as "Nature's Mistakes," some of the performers, like the tiny Hispanic woman who was only twenty-nine inches tall, were victims of birth differences. Some of the exhibits were people who had intentionally changed themselves to appear in the show by having numerous tattoos cover their bodies or learning to do things like swallow swords or breathe fire.

I remembered that show, but now I realized that I was in one of those bizarre time-warps I'd recently experienced. Could this be one of the shows from the past that my mother had told me about? Was I actually traveling in time? While the front talker described all the interesting sights inside, I was drawn to the brightly colored canvas signs. Painted in the center of the one on the left was a picture of a very fat lady wearing a short pink dress with ruffles and a pink and white baby bonnet on top of her short golden curls. Lace trimmed her socks, and she wore white Mary Jane shoes. "BEAUTIFUL BABY BELLA, OVER FOUR HUNDRED POUNDS" read the words beneath her picture. *Four hundred pounds? This must be from the past*, I thought. *The obesity on television these days is six hundred pounds.*

One act was named in each large circle in the four corners of the banner: WORLD'S TALLEST MAN; HOTTIE, THE HOTTEST WOMAN ON EARTH; TOTALLY TATTOOED TOM; and THE TWO-HEADED PIG.

The canvas on the right side was designed the same but featured different attractions. The picture in the middle was labeled SAMANTHA SAMUEL — HALF WOMAN/HALF MAN. The right side of the person in the colorful drawing showed feminine characteristics including long, flowing blond hair, makeup, half of a blue satin dress, and one ballet slipper. The left side was masculine with short brown hair, and a mustache. He wore a strongman's fake leopard skin leotard on that side.

This sign also had a circle in each corner, advertising: DONALD THE DOG-FACED BOY; SONNY THE SWORD SWALLOWER; AMAZING SIAMESE TWINS; and THE ORIGINAL WOLF MAN.

"Step right up," the barker called. "See the wonders of the world. We can't show you all of them out here, but I'm going to give you a special treat and bring out the hottest woman in the world. One of her kisses would melt your lips."

The woman who stepped through the canvas flaps was just as pretty and just as made-up as the girls on the steps at the girlie show had been. Her red hair was slicked back into a bun. She wore a halter top with silver sequins and a matching bikini-type bottom cut high on the sides but not as skimpy as a thong. The temperature had dropped along with the sun, and I wondered if the audience closer to the front could see goose bumps on her skin. Her fish-net stockings had several holes and runs in them, and her silver-sequined high-heeled shoes looked worn.

She strutted across the stage, waving and smiling at the gathering crowd before she stopped at the left side of the platform and lit a torch on a stand the MC had placed on the stage. She faked blowing kisses across it, and big bursts of flame shot across the stage to the right. This woman was good.

I knew a little bit about that because after proofing the book about Barnum and going to the Coney Island show, I'd read a lot about circus acts and anomalies. Fire breathing was one of the most dangerous acts. It was accomplished by the performer spewing a fine mist of flammable fuel across a flame. The fuel ignited and made a fireball.

The freebie was over. I paid my money and followed the crowd into the tent, which was partitioned into separate rooms. The first stage was empty except for two jars—big ones, several gallons each—of clear liquid. Inside one was what appeared to be a piglet with two heads growing from the same neck. The faces were turned away from one another at about forty-five degree angles. Each had one eye of its own, but shared a single eye between them in the middle.

Although the barker had followed us inside and was talking about this two-headed pig being born several years ago in some foreign land, the animal looked fake to me. The skin appeared too pink, as bright as Porky Pig in the old cartoons. If this was real, that was some amazing preservative. I'd bet the piglet was made of plastic or rubber.

"This two-headed pig is just one example of polycephaly," the barker continued in an instructional tone. "This is rare but has been known to occur in almost all animals, including humans." He pointed toward the other jar.

"How many of you have ever heard of Chang and Eng, the original Siamese twins?" he asked. A lot of hands shot up.

"Here we have the preserved bodies of conjoined brothers connected at their chests, just as Chang and Eng were. Though Chang and Eng lived before medical science advanced enough to separate them, these boys could probably have been surgically separated if they weren't born far too premature to survive."

I pressed forward and took a close look. The boys appeared more real than the pig did. Their flesh was wrinkled and almost gray in color. Tiny particles floated in the liquid. To me, they looked like little pieces of skin flaking off.

"Come right along through here and meet the Beautiful Baby Bella," the man said as he led us into a separate room with an elevated stage closed off by dark green velvet drapes. I wondered if they had a jar large enough to hold Baby Bella, but he opened the curtain revealing a living woman decked out in giant pink baby clothes and holding a grossly oversized infant's bottle with a nipple as a prop.

"Say hello to Baby Bella," the MC continued.

"Hello," the crowd responded in unison.

"Hello," the woman answered in a high-pitched, tinkling voice that combined a childlike tone with a breathlessness reminiscent of Marilyn Monroe in films of her famous birthday wish to JFK.

"If you saw the sign outside, you read that Baby Bella weighs four hundred pounds." The man interrupted my thoughts. "That was before this season. She's gained almost a hundred and weighs about five hundred pounds now." While he spoke, Baby Bella mimed smiles and touched her fingertips to her cheeks like those little girls on the *Toddlers and Tiaras* shows—but her eyes were sad—so sad. "And now," the announcer continued, "Baby Bella will sing for you."

The itsy bitsy spider climbed up the water spout. Her singing voice was even higher than her speaking tone. She made spider-climbing gestures, wiggling fingers that were tiny for her size, though they looked like miniature overstuffed sausages.

Down came the rain and washed the spider out. She flapped her arms in a whooshing gesture.

Out came the sun and dried up all rain. Those flabby arms made a big circle over Baby Bella's head.

And the itsy bitsy spider climbed up the spout again. Baby Bella continued singing about six verses that I'd never heard before and then made a curtsying motion lifting up the sides of her ruffled skirt and bowing her head though she didn't attempt to stand.

I wanted to ask Bella how old she was because she had to be at least thirty, but there was no Q and A session. The curtain closed in front of the stage. We stayed where we were while the barker talked about sword swallowing. After a few minutes, the curtain opened again. Baby Bella was gone, and in her place stood a man as tall and thin as Doug Kappa, holding a scabbard with handles protruding from it.

"Meet Sonny," the man in the striped coat said. "Sonny wanted to be a part of our show, but he was blessed to be born normal unlike most of the people we present, so Sonny trained under the Great Sebastian, who is one of the world's best-known sword swallowers. Sonny can swallow anything, and if you've read about sword swallowers who have a hollow sheath down their throats to protect them from blades, that's not Sonny. He's not an illusionist or trickster. He has learned the muscle control necessary for his act with no deception needed."

Sonny stepped toward the front of the stage and said, "I'm going to need one of you to help me. Can I get a volunteer?"

Several men raised their hands, but he pointed at *me.* I shook my head no, but everyone around me screamed, "Go up there," until I gave in and climbed up the steps to the stage. Sonny pulled a knife from the holder.

I was apprehensive, a little scared he was going to want me to try to swallow that knife, but all he wanted his "volunteer" to do was examine the blade and assure the audience that it was sharp and solid metal, not collapsible. We demonstrated the first characteristic by my holding up a square of paper which he sliced in half with one swipe of the knife.

After that, he arched his head back and carefully slid the knife down his throat. Sonny and I repeated the routine with increasingly larger knives, then swords. He finished with the biggest one, thanked me, and walked away through curtains at the back of the stage.

Donnie the Dog-Faced Boy stepped from behind the curtain next. I couldn't tell if the hair growing from his face, including his forehead, was false or not, but he gave a pretty good performance telling us what it was like to be born covered in hair and how people reacted by laughing at him or being scared of him until he joined the sideshow.

I'd been excited about seeing the World's Tallest Man, but it turned out to be a black and white standup cardboard cutout that Totally Tattooed Tom brought out. Tom wore a trench coat, but it didn't hide his inked hands and face. After placing the cutout in the center of the stage, he stepped behind it. The man pictured was unbelievably long-legged and wore a suit complete with necktie and vest. He had the face of a young man, and he wore glasses.

"Before you is a life-sized image of the World's Tallest Man, Robert Wadlow," the MC said. "Others have been tall and others have been small, but according to the Guinness records, no adult has yet outgrown Robert. Born in Illinois, he died of an infected wound from a leg brace when he was only twenty-two years old. His growth was caused by a malfunction of his pituitary gland and continued throughout his life. Eighteen days before his death, he measured eight feet, eleven and one-tenth inches tall. This measurement was verified by two doctors, and this representation is exactly that tall. Robert Wadlow was known as 'The Gentle Giant' by many of his fans."

The speaker paused and then called out, "Come on out, Tom, and bring your Polaroid camera in case any of these fine folks want to have a picture made with Robert Wadlow, the tallest man ever."

Several spectators paid and were photographed with the cardboard giant.

"Now, Totally Tattooed Tom, please remove your coat and let us all see your personal art collection."

The trench coat fell to the floor, and Tom walked from side to side pointing to each tat while the MC described different drawings from his first heart with "Mom" on his arm to a detailed depiction of The Lord's Supper on his back. I noticed that Tom shivered and realized the temperature had dropped so much that I was cold even wearing a jacket. When Tattooed Tom disappeared through the back curtains, the MC began to pitch an extra pay attraction.

"Sometimes Mother Nature makes a mistake, and that's what happened with Samantha Samuel. Sam was born with the genitalia of both male and female. For just seventy-five cents, three thin quarters, you can meet Sam, ask questions, and *see* what makes Sam a genuine hermaphrodite." I wasn't interested in seeing Sam's privates. I'd read a lot about this act, too, and while there are people born who are intersexed with both male and female characteristics, my circus research had told me that most of the ones in freak shows were drag queens who hadn't yet had bottom surgery. They tucked and taped their male package toward the back, appearing female with neatly trimmed curls. Then, at the end of the performance, he brought his penis out for the audience to view.

I'd seen enough of the show. I stepped back, turned, and made my way toward the red EXIT sign while everyone else pulled out quarters and lined up to go to another part of the tent.

As I stepped through the canvas into a hall-like enclosure, a loud howl met me, followed by a low, guttural growl. Straight ahead was a large glass or plastic cube, several feet taller than I was. Inside, a man jumped around and pounded against the front wall of the box. He snarled and bared his teeth at me.

I almost laughed at him.

I assumed he was the Original Wolf Man shown on the sign out front and would appear before the audience in makeup with fake fur when his turn came. The creature stepped back to the center of the transparent cage, and right before my eyes, his face sprouted hair. His nose and ears grew larger at the same time. From a decent-looking man, he changed to a gruesome wolf and dropped down to all fours. He tipped his head back and howled again.

I wasn't scared. He'd positioned himself directly in the center of the cube before changing. This told me that the transformation was illusion accomplished by mirrors and projection. I slipped through the canvas flap beside the caged Wolf Man and found myself back on the midway.

But time was unreal. I'd entered the fairgrounds just as the sun went down, but when I stepped from the tent, the sky was black and lights on the rides were off. The red flashing GIRLS, GIRLS, GIRLS! sign was dark and there were no people in sight. I ran back the way I'd come, puzzled by the unreasonable lapse of time and absence of individuals and lights.

A low growl followed me. I turned and looked back. The Wolf Man loped along on four feet, gaining on me. The snarling grew louder, and I took off as fast as I could, but the sound told me the wolf was catching up with me.

No one stood at the turnstile, and the parking lot

was empty except for one car — a '57 Chevy.

The sky grew lighter. I reached the Chevrolet, opened the door on the driver's side and climbed in. Slammed the door and locked it. The wolf jumped onto the hood of the car, pressing its saliva-dripping mouth against the windshield.

My heart pounded like it might blast out of my body. Adrenaline exploded through me. The wolf raised a paw and beat against the glass. At that moment, the sun peeked over the eastern side of the fairgrounds. The wolf yanked his paw back and slid off my car. He turned and ran back toward the turnstile as the gray hair covering his body disappeared, and all I saw was the bare backside of a young man sprinting away.

15

HAD IT all been a dream? I awoke in bed at the house with the telephone ringing over and over.

Please, no more one rings, I thought, but I answered, "Hello," and heard Glory through the receiver.

"Julie, come get me. There's something wrong. I looked outside. There's police all over the place. Come get me." She sounded very old and very tired.

THE PARKING lot at the motel was blocked off, surrounded by police cars, fire trucks, and an ambulance. I parked a block away and walked to the lot. A police officer in uniform stopped me. "Sorry, sweetie, you can't go any closer. It's not safe. We've got a major problem here."

"What happened?" I asked. Okay, I smiled at

him, consciously trying to make him like me enough to want to help me. "My elderly roommate is in Room 101. She called and asked me to come get her."

"If she's your roommate, what's she doing here in the motel? Not working, is she?"

I understood exactly what he meant. The Crown Motel had gone down in more ways than appearance. "Absolutely not," I answered. "She's an old lady."

"That doesn't mean anything, sweetie. These days they have all these specialties. Some johns want 'em real skinny; some want 'em fat, and I don't mean chubby. I mean bigger than obese. Some want women that look like little girls and some of the peds want little girls that look like women. There are probably johns looking for old ladies, too."

"Well, my friend isn't 'working.' She's just here because the exterminator was coming, and he said it would be better for someone elderly not to be there," I lied.

"Makes sense to me. Let me check for you and see if it's safe to bring her out now." He turned and I stepped behind him. "Wait here," he said.

He went to the registration office, looked inside the door, and then came right back. "You'll need to wait a little longer," he told me. "Your friend's room is close to the lobby where he is. They think he's subdued now, and they're going to try to bring him out."

"Who?" I smiled again, even bigger.

"The night clerk. He apparently went off his rocker during the night. Trashed the place, ripped it apart. The ambulance has already taken the day clerk to the hospital. When he tried to go inside to go on duty, the crazy man attacked him. What they're trying to do now is get that madman out of there. Your friend is safer in her room and you need to stay here with me, sweetie."

"He seemed fine last night when we checked Glory in," I commented. "Little round man with a white beard? Looked like Santa Claus."

"I was one of the first ones in when we got here. Sounds like the same man. He had what's left of a white beard when I saw him."

"What happened? Who cut off his beard?"

"Nobody. My lieutenant said the man had pulled out some of his hair and most of his beard. When I saw him, they were trying to cuff him. He was bucking like a wild horse. I can't see how he was even standing up with his legs twitching like they were. Sweetie, your friend is safer in her room than she'd be if she comes out before we get that crazy bastard locked in the paddy wagon or that ambulance." He pointed.

"He's inside," I said, "all she'd have to do is get in my c . . . " I was going to say, "car," but the door of the office flew open and last night's sweet Santa charged out, dragging policemen behind him as they tried to hold him back. Some of them grasped the tail of his shirt, but, already shredded, the garment tore right off. "Monster," he cackled. "Monster!" His arms and legs jerked and his head snapped around as he screamed and wrenched against the robust officers trying to restrain him. "Monster," he screeched. "Don't let the monster get you!"

No doubt about what had happened to change his Santa beard to a scraggly few hairs. He grasped what was left of it and yanked hairs from his face bringing blood to his skin. Several men managed to force him to the ground and attempted to cuff his wrists while two more tried to grab his legs, but he kicked so violently that they couldn't hold on.

Sirens announced another ambulance. EMTs leaped from the vehicle and dashed to the struggling man. They arrived as he began clawing his eyes with twisted hands. Blood spurted from one eye as the policemen finally managed to control him and one of the medical attendants jammed a hypodermic needle into his bare forearm. Hardly any effect at all.

"What did they give him?" I asked as another hypodermic was forced into the night clerk's other arm.

"Some kind of tranq, sweetie. See? It's not safe until he's locked away. He could get loose and there's no telling what he'd do. I'll go get your friend for you when that crazy man is secured."

Whatever they had injected, the man quieted and stopped jerking around after the second shot. Instead of screaming, he now whimpered, but it was the same thing over and over: "Monster. Don't let the monster get you." The men strapped the night clerk to a body board, loaded him into one of the ambulances, and drove away.

"Why didn't the police use a stun gun on him?" I asked. "They have them, don't they?"

"Lieutenant said not to taser him. The man's crazy and the way he was jumping around, his heart was probably pumping a mile a minute. Don't want to see on television that law enforcement killed a poor old sick man." He looked back toward the motel. "Sweetie, what room did you say your friend is in?"

"Room 101."

"That's right. You said the one closest to the lobby. I'll go get her."

A few minutes later, he escorted Glory to me.

"What was wrong?" she asked as we walked to the Focus.

"The night clerk went berserk."

She didn't question that, but she said, "I don't want to spend the night there again," as I drove back to the house.

WHEN WE arrived home, Glory went immediately to the front room and lay down on the sofa. "I'm going to take a nap," she said. "There was a lot of noise at that motel, and I didn't get much sleep. Someone even knocked on my door around midnight and asked if I wanted company."

"You nap and I'll make us a nice lunch when you wake up," I said and closed her door. I had no intention of explaining what kind of "company" she'd been offered.

I scrambled some eggs and ate them in a sandwich. What I wanted was a long, hot, soaking bath. As I gathered my towel and clean clothes, I remembered my tonic. As nasty as it tasted and without Glory even standing there insisting I take it, I swallowed down four big spoons full of that nasty stuff.

Submerged under hot water with only my face above the smooth, peach-scented bubbles, I tried to think pleasant thoughts, but I felt like I would explode from fear and worry. *What's happening to me? How did Glory have that wonderful medicine? She told me it was an old recipe handed down for generations. If that's true, why hasn't someone marketed it?* My angst swelled along with dread that I'd fall apart, go crazy like the Santa-looking night clerk at the Crown Motel.

After my bath, I dressed and went back to my room. Trying to work on a manuscript that I was supposed to proofread, I couldn't concentrate. I've never been a smoker, but at that moment, I wondered if a cigarette would calm my nerves. I'd never been much of a drinker either, even as a college student, but at that moment, I wanted a drink. Would alcohol make me feel better? I wondered if Glory had some magic potion to chase away worry. I couldn't concentrate. Couldn't proof-read. I exited out of the book I was reading on the computer and stepped to the back porch.

I looked over at the charred remains of my house. Nate had told me I couldn't have the lot cleared until the investigation was completed, but I never saw anyone over at the house until then. A four-legged creature stood where my kitchen had been.

My first thought was some kind of albino German Shepherd mix, but this didn't look like any dog I'd ever seen before.

A more careful look revealed that this creature looked more like a wolf than a dog. If that's what it was, I thought it must have escaped from the zoo. *Wolves don't live in cities, do they?* The animal stood erect, legs stiffened and firmly planted in a stance familiar from photos of wolves I'd seen. Head cocked back like many of the pictures, the animal had its mouth spread open like a lonesome howl should be coming out of it, but there was no sound.

Slowly the creature turned and stared directly at me. The cold hate in those eyes terrified me. I felt like running back into the house, but, as sometimes happened recently, I froze, unable to lift a foot or to make a sound. Was this a daytime hallucination? Did I think I saw a wolf because of my werewolf hallucination? And had a werewolf visited me in my dream because Doug Kappa had mentioned werewolves? I know the power of suggestion is strong.

Bizarrely, my mind went to one of the *Seinfeld* reruns when Elaine faked a ridiculous Australian accent and said, "Maybe a dingo ate your baby." Of course, she mangled pronunciations and dingo came out "dango" while baby was "bauhbee." That was funny when the show was filmed, but since then, evidence was found proving it really happened. The mother who had insisted her baby had been taken by an animal was in jail for murdering the infant when her child's torn and bloody clothing was discovered in a dingo den.

Don't be ridiculous, I told myself. There were no dingoes around the city. *Unless it escaped from the zoo.* Did they even have dingoes on display there? If that's what it was, I wasn't a baby. I was a full-grown woman, and not a tiny one at that. A bear could carry me off, but not an animal that size. *Who says it would have to carry you anywhere? It could chew you up right here.*

I didn't scream; I whimpered.

The animal just stood there watching me.

"Don't move," a familiar voice said. Before, I couldn't have made myself budge if I'd wanted to. Now I couldn't keep myself from looking toward the other side of the porch.

Richard Arthur stood there. "Be very still," he

whispered, "and it will go away, but if you try to run, it will chase you."

The animal looked down, breaking that petrifying stare. It carefully stepped over the charred clutter left from the fire and walked toward the street.

I couldn't help it. I collapsed in Richard's arms. He held me while I sobbed with relief. As usual, his clothing and the unshaved week or so of beard made him look homeless, but he smelled fresh and clean.

"What was that?" I asked when I caught my breath and pulled away.

"Coyote."

"I thought coyotes lived out west. Could it have been a ghost?"

"It was too solid. To be that dense a spirit would need to have a part of its body—like nail clippings, skin, or hair. It was a real coyote. Now they're all over the United States. They're not uncommon around here, but we usually see them at night."

"My first thought was dingo, but I've never seen one to know what it would look like." I turned toward the door. "Would you like something to drink?"

"Sure, a cup of coffee would be great." He followed me inside and sat at the table while I reheated two cups of that morning's brew and started another pot.

Richard grinned. "You thought maybe the dingo ate your baby?" His accent was an exact duplicate of how Elaine said it on *Seinfeld.*

"Nope." I actually laughed. "I never had a baby."

"I'll bet you will one day. You'll settle down and raise a happy family."

"Not if things keep going the way they are."

"What do you mean?"

"I swear sometimes I think I'm living in one of the horror novels and movies I used to enjoy so much."

"Used to?"

"They aren't so entertaining these days, and I'm trying to read only humorous books now. Seeing that strange animal made me think dingo, but it also made me think jackal. Mom and I watched this old movie *The Omen* years ago. They dug up a grave and found a jackal in the coffin where a boy's mother was supposed to be buried."

"Your thoughts weren't so far off. The coyote is sometimes called 'the American jackal.' What does your cop friend say about all this?"

"Nate thinks I'm having dreams and hallucinations brought on by the stress of my mother's death, ending of my engagement, moving down here, finding my friend's body, and my house burning down."

"That's enough to stress anybody. When you say it like that, I can understand why you'd be distraught to the point of nightmares and delusions, but I don't believe that's what's happening. I think something is actually going on in your life. Did you call Doug Kappa to check out your house?"

"That's exactly what I did. He came but none of his equipment worked. He wants me to have the house wiring examined by an electrician. He says that sometimes problems in the electrical system will cause the meters not to work."

"Then he didn't find anything? Any voices or changes or . . ."

"I just told you his equipment didn't work," I snapped. Immediately I regretted this out-of-character response. My tone softened as I added, "He's coming back later."

"When I was working on my paranormal book, I went on a couple of trips with ghost hunters. We went to an old jail and to a mental institution in Charleston."

"Did you see or hear anything?"

"I'm not sure if I did or not, but we split up and went in pairs after we got there. Some of the partners claimed to have recorded voices on their machines, but when they played them back, I couldn't make out any words. I think most of the creepiness I felt was from knowing what had been there years before. Those institutions weren't known for humane treatment in the past."

"Why'd you stop writing your paranormal book?"

"The truth?" I nodded at him and he continued,

"I started believing in too much of what I read and what people told me. It seemed like an interesting topic, but the deeper I got into it, the less I wanted to write about those things."

"In other words, you were scared."

Richard nodded.

"I'm frightened all the time now," I said.

"What's the meaning of this?" Glory's voice preceded her entrance to the kitchen. I might have thought seeing Richard surprised her, but she'd put her wig on, so she knew someone was in the house.

"Miss Glory, this is my friend, Richard Arthur," I said. "We're having a cup of coffee. Would you like some?"

I fully expected Glory to explode. Instead, she smiled and sat down. "Yes, that would be nice."

When we each had stirred in sweetener or sugar and cream, Glory asked, "What were you two talking about when I interrupted?" She sounded conversational, not confrontational.

"We saw a coyote next door," Richard responded.

"A coyote?" Glory questioned.

"Yes, a silver or white coyote," I said.

"Coyotes are brown," Glory stated. "Wonder where it came from?" She turned toward Richard.

"No telling, but I've seen coyotes in the city occasionally though it's usually at night and someone told me he'd seen an albino coyote in this area."

"Are they nocturnal?" I interrupted their

exchange.

"They are now," Richard said, "but I've read that being nocturnal is an adaptation to living around humans. They aren't nocturnal when living in the wild."

Glory grinned at him. "You're very knowledgeable."

"Comes from reading a lot." He drained his cup, stood, and put it in the sink. "I'll leave you lovely ladies to talk about me," he said. He was standing at the back door when he turned and said, "Don't forget to call an electrician, Julie."

Glory frowned and asked, "Why do we need an electrician?" She didn't give me time to answer that. As soon as the door closed behind him, she had another question, "Where do you find these men?"

"I met him the morning my house burned," I answered without supplying any additional facts. I'd never discussed finding Jerry Patterson's corpse with Glory.

"Would you pour me a fresh cup?" she asked and handed me her coffee mug. "He looks like an old hobo, but I like him better than that cop you're seeing."

"Nate and I not *seeing* each other," I protested. "We're just friends."

Glory stood. "I'll be watching television if you need me," she said. "I guess I can assume that the medicine worked if you're feeling well enough to be flirting with that man."

After she closed her door, I grabbed my cell phone and stepped out onto the back porch. There was no sign of the coyote or dog or whatever we'd seen earlier. I called Gates Electrical Service and placed an order to have the wiring checked out. The lady said she'd send someone Monday. Then I phoned Apparition Investigations and left a voice mail for Doug Kappa to please call me.

16

THE MINUTE Richard walked away from the house, he regretted leaving. He had no reason to get out of there. He'd actually been fairly comfortable around the old lady with her straight gray hair sticking out from beneath her curly white wig.

Julie had acted before as though Glory would be furious if she invited him into their home, but the elderly woman had been friendly enough.

His mind wandered back to that moment when Julie had screamed and fallen into his arms on the porch. He knew that holding her that way was nothing more than comforting her in her fear, but, damn! It felt good pulling her close to him. Her breasts were firm, but her overall sensation was soft and cuddly.

His thoughts moved to wondering how she'd feel if he held her like that when she was unclothed. What would she have done if he'd had the nerve to pat her behind while she was in his arms?

Probably would have slapped me, he thought. *She doesn't think of me that way. Is it because I'm playing the role of a homeless man or is it just me? What would she say if she knew how often I watch her house from that laundry-dry cleaner across the street? How often I'm behind her when she goes somewhere? That car she bought is going to make watching her into a big problem to me, but it's not like I stalk her. Or is it?*

Sometimes a man needed some privacy, and this had turned into one of those times for Richard. He went across the street and locked himself into the men's room at the laundromat.

17

NATE SMILED. "No, I don't think you're crazy, and I don't believe something evil is after you. Just think about what all you've been through. It's enough to mess with anyone's mind." He patted my hand — something he did with increasing frequency lately.

"Are you saying my brain's messed up, but I'm not crazy?" Without conscious thought, I moved over in my seat toward the car door, as far away from him as the seat belt allowed. He'd asked me to see him and insinuated he had news about the investigation into Jerry Patterson's death. He did. Jerry's autopsy report was back. He'd had no drugs or alcohol in his system, but cause of death was inconclusive. No signs of trauma, no knife or gun wounds. Nate told me it appeared Jerry had simply stopped breathing, almost like he'd been strangled, but with none of the usual signs of choking such as a broken hyoid bone in his throat. No sign of heart damage either.

When I pressed the issue, Nate said the police department had some new leads, but he wouldn't tell me what they were and he didn't sound optimistic about them. I had the feeling he had just wanted to see me and used Jerry Patterson as an excuse.

"I've been investigating these delusions of yours, too," Nate said. "All the strange things that you think have happened to you are based on real places here in Columbia, but with sick twists," Nate said. "The unreal parts are the time frames and the monsters you think you see—someone follows you to a hotel where a woman shot her cheating husband in the twenties. You see a vampire in a building that still exists, but you see it in the structure as it was over seventy-five years ago. You see a mysterious dog that look like a small wolf but is probably a coyote. You believe a werewolf chased you." He frowned and added, "From what you told me about that dream, you saw the werewolf before 1959, which was the last year the Carolina-Clemson football game was played on Thursday of the week of the South Carolina State Fair. I know because I checked it out."

"It sounds silly when you talk about it."

"No, I don't believe it's silly. You believe these things either happened or you dreamed about them, but you also told me you've always loved scary books. Maybe your reading feeds your brain with fears of creatures. Your mind is rebelling against the tragedies of your life by escaping into distorted versions of books you've read."

"But I never studied about old hotels and nightclubs in this town, and I certainly don't have any connection to what you insist is a dog. I never had pets. We couldn't afford food for an animal or vet care, but if we had owned anything, it would have been a cat, not a dog."

"You didn't ever have a pet of any kind?"

"No, never. I thought about getting a kitten when I moved to New York, but then I met Greg, and he took up my time."

"Did you ever go to the State Museum when you lived here before?"

"Of course! Our classes went to the museum almost every year, and sometimes when Mama had the day off in the summertime, they had 'free days' there. We'd go spend the whole day inside where it was cool. We'd even carry our lunch with us."

"Perhaps some of the places in your dreams are coming from those long-ago days at the museum."

"I remember a lot of things, but nothing about the places in my nightmares. Your theory doesn't explain why you found me outside of The Big Apple that morning. If it's all in my mind, I should have been in my bed dreaming."

"Tell you what. I'm off tomorrow. Let's go to the museum and see if there's anything in the permanent exhibits that could be hiding in the back of your mind and popping up when you sleep."

"I'd love to go with you, but I don't think we'll see anything. What I remember about the museum is the shark hanging from the ceiling and the Hunley submarine that sank off the Charleston coast during the Civil War. I did a report on it in middle school."

"What about the section with the old store and classroom? The part that shows life in South Carolina in the 1800s and early 1900s?"

"Not really. Guess that didn't interest me much back then."

"I'm off all day tomorrow. Go to church with me, and then we'll have lunch and go to the museum."

"I can't go to church. I don't even *own* a dress."

"I attend a church that's nondenominational and casual. You could wear jeans, but if you want to dress up, those black slacks of yours will be perfect."

We ended the discussion with my agreeing to be ready for church when he picked me up at ten-thirty the next morning for the eleven o'clock service.

SINCE GLORY had taken care of me so well after my cystitis, I realized that my occasional shortness with her was just another manifestation of the lack of patience that had developed since I returned to South Carolina. We spent the evening chatting and watching television together, and I made a conscious effort to be more gentle, more my old self, with her. We'd been getting along really well, so I was surprised when she objected to my going to church with Nate the next day.

We were sitting on the couch watching television, and the minute I told her about it, her expression changed — not so much to irritation as to fear.

"You'd better be careful," she said, "those churches turn people into fanatics. Before you know it, you'll be spending all your time there."

"I don't think so, Miss Glory. Nate Adams goes to church regularly, and he's not a fanatic. "

"Is this church Buddhist or Hindu or something like that?"

"No, ma'am. It's a Christian church, just not a particular denomination like Baptist or Catholic or Greek Orthodox."

"There are a lot more denominations," she said in an arrogant tone and named off, "AME, Episcopalian, Lutheran, Methodist, Presbyterian, and others." She grinned and added, "See? I may be old but I'm still sharp mentally. I automatically alphabetized them."

"You sure did, but don't worry about me. I think people who become fanatic about religion or anything else have addictive personalities to begin with. I don't, and I certainly don't think going to church will hurt me. Mama and Daddy took me sometimes when I was a little girl."

Glory looked up with an innocent expression. "Oh, I forgot to tell you. UPS delivered a box for you yesterday."

Annoyance swept over me at the thought she'd kept the parcel a secret on purpose. After all, those packages with manuscripts to be proofed were my income, and to my knowledge, she had no idea how much insurance money I'd received. But I quickly considered her age and decided she'd genuinely forgotten the delivery. She'd probably set it down after the man left and thought no more about it.

Glory laughed and nudged me in the ribs. "You're a working girl now. Gonna be too busy to go traipsing around with that cop all the time."

"I promise you, Miss Glory, I have no real interest in Nate. He's just my friend."

"Thank you, Jesus!" Glory shouted.

We made popcorn in the microwave and watched television late into the night. After my bath, I was too tired to even read—for work or pleasure. My next thought was puzzling. *Why was Richard on my porch? Did he see the animal and come over to get a closer look? That didn't make much sense because he could've seen it better from the street.* I didn't stay puzzled for long. I'd grown to trust Richard and figured he had a good reason to be on Glory's back porch. I pulled the covers up to my chin and went to sleep.

The next thing I knew I was dancing—not the Big Apple—slow dancing. I looked down and saw that I wore a slinky metallic silver dress that clung everywhere it touched. My partner, classically masculine with a chiseled face, obsidian eyes, and dark brown hair, sported a tuxedo, but I felt his muscular physique through the fabric. I realized I wore nothing beneath my dress. Where the man's hands touched blazed beneath the crimson silk — on fire in a wonderful way.

No words necessary. I knew where this dance would lead. It was supreme foreplay. Heat surged through my body to places the man's hands weren't touching, but I knew he would caress me all over before the night ended. Not only did I know it, but the idea wasn't at all repulsive.

Instantaneously, the dance ended and we were lying on my bed, wrapped in each other's arms. I sizzled. After being abstinent for so long, I couldn't get enough of this man. Both of our bodies were bare though I wasn't conscious of having disrobed.

"Stop!" The word boomed through my mind like an explosion.

"Stop! Stop that right now!" This time I recognized the feminine voice. I opened my eyes and looked up into the face above me.

Jerry Patterson — but not the Jerry Patterson from high school and not the pale face I'd seen on Assembly Street a few days ago. This was Jerry as he probably looked now if he was still in the morgue. No, not even that Jerry. He'd be refrigerated in a body cooler. This was Jerry Patterson as he'd look if he'd been left out dead for a long time.

His body wasn't the lean, hard form I'd been

feeling. Now it was bloated—pudgy and soft. His skin was greenish with touches of deep purple in spots and eyes that bulged, but appeared sightless behind the thin gray film covering them. He seemed to be trying to flick his tongue in and out, or maybe even speak, but it was swollen and no longer fit in his mouth.

"Wake up!" The voice wasn't Jerry Patterson's. It was the same one that had said, "Stop, stop that now."

When I sat up, Jerry disappeared. A woman stood at the foot of my bed. Her figure was vague, just a shadowy outline of a female. She reached toward me and then disappeared. Right before she faded away, I saw her face and recognized my mother.

I jumped up and twirled around, looking to see where she'd gone. "Mama," I screamed for her, wanting my mom to come back to me.

Glory ran in wearing her green flannel nightgown. "What's wrong?"

"Bad dream," I answered. "The worst part of it was that my mother appeared at the end and disappeared before I could talk with her."

"I know it's hard, but you're still in denial. Your mother's gone. Nothing we can do will bring her back." She paused, and then asked, "Are you okay?" she stepped back into her room before returning with her robe and wig in her hand.

"It was just a dream," I assured her and fell back on the bed.

"Are you ready for breakfast?" Glory asked.

"No, thank you, the only thing I want right now is a bath. I feel dirty."

As I scrubbed my body while Glory made coffee, I convinced myself that the dead Jerry and my mother were a nightmare. Glory called through the bathroom door, "Are you all right? The coffee's ready. Want me to bring you a cup?"

I assured her that I was fine. "I'll wait until I've finished my bath before I have my coffee." I knew there would be nothing wrong with Glory coming in the room while I was in the tub, but I didn't want anyone to look at me, not even the old lady who helped me so much. The dream had made me ashamed of my nakedness.

WHEN NATE and I pulled up to his church, I was surprised that it was in a building that had been a discount shoe store when I lived in Columbia before moving to New York. A man stood on the steps. I understood why Nate had said I could wear whatever I wanted.

This man was young, maybe under thirty, wearing sandals with jeans and a dark blue zippered hoodie. A wooden cross on a leather lanyard banged against his chest on top of the sweat shirt when he rushed over to the car after Nate slowed down.

"Good morning," he said in an energetic voice. "Sorry, but I have to cancel our services today." He waved an arm toward the front door. "We've got some kind of sewage backup, and there's no way you'd want to go inside."

"Have the toilets overflowed?" Nate asked him.

"I don't really know. The stench in there is so bad that I couldn't get back to the restrooms. I called a plumber."

"You need to call the city. This building's on city sewer. It's probably their problem, not one the church would have to hire a private plumber to handle."

"I should have thought of that," the man said and then motioned toward me. "Who's this pretty lady?"

"This is my friend Julie Bates."

The young man grasped my hand and shook it firmly.

"And your name?" I asked.

"Excuse me," Nate said, "this is our preacher, Ron Corbett."

"Everyone calls me Preacher Ron."

We shook hands and exchanged a few more pleasantries, interrupted regularly by parishioners arriving and being told the service was cancelled.

"How deep is the water?" Nate asked Preacher Ron.

"I didn't go in far enough to see any water. When I opened the door and smelled it, I came back out."

"Let me park and I'll check and see how much flooding there is. I've got some fishing waders in the back of my car."

Nate parked and asked me to stay there and wait on him. I agreed, certainly not willing to go inside with him. He put on a pair of wading boots from the trunk of his car and walked up to Preacher Ron. They spoke a few minutes, and then Nate went inside while I watched the preacher send people away.

It seemed like Nate was gone forever. I grew bored, got out of the car, and walked to Preacher Ron. Even with the doors closed, a hint of stench filled the porch area and steps. I couldn't understand how the man could bear standing there.

"Tired of waiting?" he asked.

"Thought I'd like to ask you a few questions."

"Go right ahead."

"Preacher Ron, do you believe in ghosts?"

"I believe in the Holy Ghost, but I've never personally encountered a ghost of any other kind. I would say that I'd have to see it to believe it, but I don't have to see God to believe in Him."

"Then why do you believe?"

"I see God through His creations and His works. I also feel His spirit within me. How about you? Do you believe in the Holy Ghost?"

I almost lied to him, but a little fib to a preacher seemed bigger than bald-face lying to other people. I told the truth. "Sometimes I do, but sometimes I doubt. My mother was brutally murdered. She was a sweet lady who worked hard her entire life and would never hurt anyone. Why would God let that happen?"

Preacher Ron looked deep into my eyes, and I was glad I'd told the truth. I thought that if I'd lied to him, he would have known.

"Ms. Bates, I can't answer that for you."

"Just call me Julie," I said.

"Why the ghost questions? Do you think you've seen one?"

"I don't know. Strange things keep happening."

"Would you like to meet sometime and talk with me about these things ?" His smile lit up his face.

Before I could answer, Nate opened the door, and the stink swept out like it was blown by a hurricane. I gagged. Bile surged up into my throat. I ran around the building—retching and choking—unable to hold back vomit.

Nate followed me, embarrassing me that he saw me throw up. Even worse was that some of the puke landed on my blouse. He pulled a handkerchief from his pocket and wiped my mouth, then the spots on my clothes. I didn't even know men still carried cloth handkerchiefs, but I was glad he had one.

"Let's go back to your house so you can get cleaned up and change clothes," he suggested.

"Don't you need to talk to the pastor?"

"I told him to call the city and tell them it's an

emergency. There's no water on the floors, not even in the restrooms. The smell must be sewer gas, which could explode under the wrong circumstances."

As we got into the car, Nate handed me a business card. "Preacher Ron said to give you this and ask you to call him. I assume you told him what's been happening to you." I put the card in my purse without a word.

I dreaded having to explain the throw-up on me to Glory, but she wasn't home. I didn't feel comfortable having Nate sit in the living room, which was technically now Glory's bedroom, nor on my bed, so I asked him to sit at the kitchen table while I took a quick bath and changed.

When I returned to the kitchen, fully dressed with hair combed and fresh makeup, Glory and Nate sat at the table together, drinking coffee, and talking about sewer gas. As we left, Nate asked, "Miss Glory, would you like to go to the museum with us?"

"Not me," she said. "All that old stuff is depressing. Besides, I hear that museum is haunted."

18

SOUTH CAROLINA State Museum was different from the way I remembered it when Mom and I went there years ago. Expansion had increased the size of the exhibition areas as well as adding a state-of-the-art planetarium and probably more that I didn't know about.

When we stopped to pay, the young man behind the counter asked, "Do you want only general admission or would you like King Tut exhibit tickets as well? There's an additional charge for that."

Nate turned to me. "Would you like to see the Tut display? I saw it the last time it was here, but I won't mind doing it again if you want."

"I've never seen it, but with all these creatures in my dreams, I don't think I want to look at a real mummy. I've seen too many mummy movies."

The admissions clerk interrupted, "Ma'am, the real mummy of the Egyptian pharaoh isn't here.

These are less expensive duplicates of beautiful artifacts found in his tomb and replicas of the mummy, its caskets, and sarcophagus."

"Caskets?" I asked with an emphasis on the "s" at the end, feeling stupid that I'd thought it was all real.

"Yes, King Tut's face was covered with a gold mask, and then the body was placed in three coffins, each one inside a slighter bigger one. The sarcophagus was the outer casing."

"But you're sure it's not the real mummy?" I asked.

"No, ma'am, it's not, and I think you'd enjoy the amazing Egyptian jewelry on display as much as the statues and replicas like the golden chariot from Tut's tomb."

"Okay." I smiled and turned toward Nate. "Let's go visit King Tut." I opened my purse and took out my wallet.

"No, no," Nate said. "Put your money up. I'm paying."

"It was more than enough for you to buy things for me before I got access to my money and then not let me repay you, but I'm not destitute," I protested. "Why don't you let me treat this time?"

"Because I was hoping that instead of this being one of those times that I rescue you, which is pretty much my job—to serve and protect—this could be a date."

Was Glory right about Nate's intentions? I wasn't

interested in romance or any kind of relationship with anyone. A red flag popped up, but I didn't let it show.

"At least let me pay my own way. Lots of people go 'Dutch' on dates."

"Maybe you and your ex-boyfriend, but not this good ole boy." He smiled, but his tone was serious, so I put my money back and thought I might buy him a present sometime to show my appreciation.

We took our tickets and rode the elevator to the third floor. When the doors opened, a gigantic Egyptian mural in front of us led to a door where a man, who may or may not have been Egyptian, accepted our tickets, and gave us a brochure. He pointed out signs that forbid taking photos in the exhibit though we could pay to have our pictures made with a sham casket.

The first room was filled with ancient Egyptian artifacts not from King Tut's tomb. I was amazed not only at the beauty of the items, but also at the strong resemblance between the necklaces and earrings and their modern counterparts. Inexpensive copies of these genuine gold and gemstone creations would sell like wildfire in today's market.

Nate noticed my expression. "Still beautiful, aren't they?" he asked.

"Absolutely."

Two replicas of life-size wooden statues of the pharaoh stood on the sides of the entrance to the actual Tut exhibit, just as the two authentic statues had guarded the entrance to the burial chamber for over three thousand years before British archaeologist Howard Carter opened the grave in 1922. I knew that because it was printed on a poster by the door.

Nate and I took turns reading aloud the informative signs by each exhibit, but I suspected that he remembered a lot from having seen the display before. He explained, "Tutankhamun ascended to the throne when he was only nine years old and died before he reached his twentieth birthday."

I was more interested in the alabaster, bronze, and gold items buried with Tut for his future life than a history lesson.

Most macabre to me were the canopic urns. During the seventy-day process of ancient Egyptian mummification, internal organs were removed from bodies and placed in these ornamental containers.

Actually looking at the fake mummy of King Tut wasn't scary at all, probably because I knew it was a dummy. It was also small. The framed write-up stated the boy king had been less than five feet, five inches tall. In those chilling movies, the mummies are giants lurching along with outstretched arms. This mummy looked like a small Halloween skeleton wrapped in thin strips of cloth. I knew he was like a doll or mannequin and couldn't stand, but I also felt that if he could, I'd be able to knock him over with no problem. The duplicate face looked like pictures I'd seen of King Tut in magazines — a bony mask of dark, leathery-looking skin.

"Kind of pathetic, isn't it?" Nate asked. "He had all that wealth but died so young."

"I think it's tragic when anyone dies in their teens," I answered. "What happened to him?"

"There's no definite answer to that. Scientists used to think he died of an infection, but a later hypothesis was that he was murdered. CT scans of his mummy exposed a hole in the back of his head. Arguments against that propose that the hole was caused during the mummification process or that Carter's people damaged Tut's head in their eagerness to find all the riches and amulets in the linen wrappings. There's even a theory that his death was a result of a chariot crash."

"Sad either way." I trembled. Mention of murder automatically brought my mother to mind. "Ready to go look at the other exhibits?" I asked.

"Do you have any favorites?"

"Not really."

"Then our next stop will be the good old days."

On the elevator, Nate seemed to stare a hole through me.

I shook my head a little self-consciously. "What's on your mind?" I asked wondering if he was picturing me as I'd looked before lunch when he took me home to get out of vomit-spattered clothing

"Just wondering. Do you feel at all strange? Is there anything spooky in your mind?"

"No. Why?"

"Because this part of the old mill that became the museum is one of the areas where Bubba hangs out."

"Who's Bubba?"

"You grew up in Columbia and never heard of Bubba at the museum?"

"Oh, I've known a few Bubbas around here, but not at the museum," I laughed.

"Bubba is the resident ghost in this building, and his favorite spot is the elevator. He wears coveralls and disappears quickly after you see him. I thought that if any of what's going on in your life is because you have ESP, perhaps you'd see Bubba here in the elevator."

"Nothing strange at all."

I couldn't resist taking pictures when we reached the area devoted to the 1800s. I snapped photos with my telephone camera as I stood behind the barrier staring at the classroom with its old-fashioned desks and ink pots. I remembered when I was a girl, standing here with my mother while she explained what the ink pots were and how they were used.

From there, we moved to the life-size model of a general store. One section represented the outside complete with old pumps that stored gasoline in glass tanks. There was a well, too, but I liked the exhibit showing the inside best. Displayed merchandise included oil lamps as well as clothing. The old-fashioned men's neckties and ladies button-up shoes fascinated me. Two mannequins, a man and woman, sat at the back while another form stood behind the counter.

"I could stay here forever looking at all the things for sale," I told Nate. "Life must have been so much simpler then."

"Yes, simpler, but harder with no televisions, microwaves, Internet, or cell phones."

"I could live without all that."

"What about your job? Don't you depend on computers sometimes?"

"Yes," I grinned. "I'd just have to have someone deliver typewritten manuscripts by Pony Express instead of Federal Express or UPS."

"I think your time frame is a little off."

We moved on to see the horse-drawn hearse along with an antique embalming table and morticians' tools. When I was a child, the funeral coach had made me think of fairy princesses even though it was black and I thought of Cinderella's transformed pumpkin as white or gold. I could picture a fancy-dressed man on the seat driving Cinderella to the extravagant dress ball. The biggest difference between a fairytale coach and the old hearse was that the back of the undertaker's wagon was elongated and had glass panels on all four sides.

This area wasn't very well lit, which lent an air of eeriness to the display cases. I began photographing the hearse and old mortuary tools.

"Does anything about this display cause you strange feelings?" Nate asked.

"No, but it's interesting."

"I would think if you're psychic, you'd get some kind of spirit feeling from this. These items aren't replicas." He pointed to a slanted, rectangular metal table. "That hearse has hauled hundreds of bodies who were embalmed on that tin board using the tools right beside it. All of this was donated by a man whose grandfather ran a funeral home."

"Nothing." I laughed. "I don't see any ghosties flying around in here."

Nate moved over to several glass display cases lined up beside the wall. "Come look at this."

He pointed toward a wreath inside. It had intricate, delicate flowers woven from strands of pale yellows, white, grays, and brown. It was pretty, yet it didn't appeal to me at all. "Do you know what that is?" he asked with a sheepish grin.

"Something old morticians used to put on the doors of the deceased's home, like they put white silk flowers on houses of death in modern times?" I said, remembering those fake white flowers on my mother's door when I came home for her funeral. I'd told the police which funeral home to use when they called and said she was dead. They'd managed to get a wreath on the door even though the house was roped off with yellow crime scene tape. From that thought, an unwanted scene popped into my brain: a fancy-dressed man holding a bouquet of white roses.

"Nope. This is an example of Victorian era hair art. It was a type of memorial. When a family member died, some hair was taken from the corpse and formed into a flower or ornate shape to be added to a wreath with hair designs from other deceased relatives. Another way to create hair art in memory of dead people was to use the hair as thread in an embroidered piece."

"Euuuuuh!" I sounded like a thirteen-year-old. "Why would they want to do that?"

"Why did Roy Rogers have his horse Trigger stuffed by a taxidermist?"

"To display in his museum for money."

We both laughed.

"I prefer to think," Nate said, "that he loved the horse and couldn't bear to part with it and that making art from the hair of a dead relative was done out of respect and caring."

"Maybe," I murmered. "Let's move on. This is creepy."

We wound up at the H. L. Hunley display, which had been a part of the museum even before the Civil War submarine was brought up from the ocean floor and went on display in Charleston. As a little girl, the Hunley model had fascinated me. At that time, the real submarine was still missing. I'd been morbidly attracted to the mannequins of sailors in the exhibit, somehow getting them confused with the stories my teacher had told the class that the Hunley sank three times, killing her crew each time. When Mama brought me to the museum, I'd stand staring at the mock-up, thinking those figures inside were the bodies of the dead sailors. Never crossed my mind that if the eight men on the sub when it sank the last time were dead and the vessel itself was lost, those weren't corpses.

I snapped several photos of the Hunley from different angles.

"Do you remember when they found the Hunley back in the nineties?" Nate asked.

"Yep," I said. "I did a social studies report on it."

WHEN WE grew tired of walking around, Nate asked a security man where the café had been moved.

"It's being remodeled," the guard said. "Best you can do is go back down to the side entrance. There are soda and snack machines near the classroom and birthday party areas."

We followed his advice and were soon sitting on a bench in the hall outside an educational area drinking grape soda and eating peanut butter on cheese crackers.

As I snapped several more pictures, Nate asked to see the photos I'd taken. I handed the cell phone to him and he slid his finger down, scrolling through them. "Isn't it amazing?" he asked. "These new cell phones take better pics than my expensive cameras. The world's changing fast."

I agreed. "Digital is the way to go."

Nate slid his finger across the cell phone screen looking at my photos. Then he inhaled sharply and reversed the direction he scrolled.

"Look at this," he said. "There's someone in the back of the hearse in this picture, but not in the one before it. Didn't you snap these one right after the other?"

"I like to take several shots of each subject in case one doesn't look right. So yes, they were taken one right after the other."

Nate handed the phone back to me. The glass-enclosed back of the hearse was completely empty in the first shot, but the second picture showed a body right in the spot that was empty only seconds before. The woman was lying flat with arms crossed over her bosom in the classic death pose. She wore a white dress and held a white flower in her hands.

The strange thing was that there was no coffin. Apparently she'd been positioned directly on the floor of the hearse. I strained to get a better look and then remembered I could zoom in on the photo. A touch of my finger on the control brought the face of a woman into full view. I'd expected it to be my mother, but she was not anyone I'd ever seen before.

"Look at this." I handed the phone back to Nate.

"Let's go look at that display again," he said. We

dropped the remains of our snacks into the trash can and took the elevator up to the funeral display. We both leaned across to get a better view. Neither of us could see anything, so I climbed over the barrier ropes and pressed my face against the glass to see inside the hearse. It was empty.

On the ride down in the elevator, I felt woozy. I must have looked like I might faint because Nate kept asking, "Are you all right?"

I nodded yes, but I wasn't breathing well and my throat felt like it was closing. Was I allergic to something I'd touched or even to the grape soda and crackers? When we stepped out of the elevator, breathing became a little easier, but my neck hurt. Nate leaned over and took a close look at my face.

"What's this?" he asked.

"What?" I managed to answer.

"You have some marks on your neck," he said.

I took a hand mirror from my purse and looked carefully. The red discolorations around my neck were shaped like fingers. I wanted to scream or cry, but I didn't.

"Guess maybe Bubba struck again," I said.

"There have never been any reports of Bubba harming anyone," Nate said. "It's more likely you're so upset that your body responded."

"You think I intentionally choked myself? How? You were right beside me. I didn't touch my throat."

"I don't mean intentionally and I don't mean with

your hands. The marks could have made themselves in response to all that's happened to you."

Now, I liked Nate, and I appreciated all he'd done for me, but at that moment, he just seemed way too smug and know-it-all for me.

"So you think everything is all in my mind?" He didn't answer. "Then, explain that picture with a corpse that isn't there," I snapped.

Instead, he suggested, "I'd planned a better lunch before we had to go back for you to change. Let me take you somewhere nice for dinner."

"Why don't you just take me *home?*"

The words were hardly out of my mouth before the thought that I really had no home made me sad. From feeling irritated at Nate and sadness, my emotions jumped to guilt about Glory. I thought I should spend some time with her. If it weren't for her, I'd probably be staying in a rented room somewhere, though certainly not at the Crown Motel.

Just as I opened my mouth to apologize to Nate for my shortness, he received a phone call. His mother was sick and needed him to go to the drugstore.

I LOADED my museum photos onto the Mac and was very pleased with the sharpness and detail. My new printer was equal to the camera. The finished pics looked professional.

Sad that the museum hadn't allowed photos in the Tut exhibit, though that probably was a restriction from the people who owned the artifacts, I was more than happy to have the ones from other displays.

"Miss Glory," I called, "come in here and look at my photographs from the museum."

She came from the front room and sat on the edge of the bed. I handed her the prints and she went through them one by one, examining each closely. I wanted to know if she would see the woman's body that Nate and I had seen in one of them.

"What's this?" she asked and handed me one of the empty funeral coach.

"It's an old horse-drawn hearse," I answered and gave it back to her.

"Who put the corpse in it or maybe I should say who took it out?" she said.

"There's no body in there."

"There's not one here." She held out a picture. "But there's definitely someone dead in this print." She thrust the photos at me with as much conviction as she showed in her words.

I looked. I saw. A human being, eyes closed, arms crossed over the chest, lay in the back of the hearse in one picture, but this one wasn't a woman. Obviously dead, the figure wasn't in a casket. It lay there in a black suit and a top hat. Was it the man who'd taken me to Potter's Field? In all other pictures of the glass-sided vehicle, the back was empty—

completely vacant. Where was the woman Nate and I had seen and why hadn't we seen the man?

"Look at the rest of them," I told Glory. "See if there's anything weird about the others."

After a few minutes of fanning through the prints, she handed me two of the H. L. Hunley submarine. I looked at them but saw nothing unusual.

"Look at the man at the very back," Glory said.

I didn't notice anything strange about him.

"Put them beside each other and look," Glory added.

Doing it that way, the inexplicable became obvious to me. The mannequin was in a different position. It was obviously the same form, but in the second picture he was turned slightly more toward the camera, more toward me, and his expression had changed from serious to a grin.

"Do those figures move electronically?" I asked.

"How should I know? But I'll tell you this: What he's doing in this one isn't something the museum would do in that historical exhibit." She handed me another snap of the Hunley. The man in the very back still looked toward the camera, but he was no longer in a rowing position. He was waving one hand and flipping the bird with the other.

Maybe Bubba wasn't the only ghost at the museum.

19

THE ELECTRICIAN showed up Monday morning before Glory was up. I heard a knock on the front door and Glory shouted, "Who is it?"

"Gates Electrical Service. I've come to check your wiring," I heard through the outside door as I ran into the front room.

"I didn't call no electrician," Glory yelled at the door. She grabbed her robe and ran to the kitchen.

"It's okay, Miss Glory; I called him," I said and opened the door for the serviceman.

"What's the problem?" he asked.

I hardly knew what to tell him. I didn't want to say, "My ghost hunter said to get the wiring checked."

"This house is so old," I began, "that someone told me I should be sure the wiring is safe and working properly."

"Are you buying or selling the house?"

"Neither. I just want it checked out."

"Your money," he quipped. "Where's the electrical panel?" Then, apparently assuming I wouldn't know what an electrical panel was, he added, "You know. That metal box with circuit breakers in it. Do you have to reset the breakers very often."

"Not since I've been here."

He found the breaker box on the back porch wall and burst into laughter when he opened it. "Lady, this house still has a fuse box and you've got the smallest electrical service I've seen on a house."

"What does that mean?"

"The service on a building is determined in amps. The more amps in your electrical service, the more electricity you can use. This house was wired for very few appliances. Most houses like this have had their fuse boxes replaced with circuit breaker boxes when they increased the amperage of the electrical service. What you've got is probably exactly what was put in when the house was built years ago."

He puttered around some more in the fuse box and used a pronged device to check out all the receptacles while Glory and I sat at the kitchen table drinking orange juice while waiting for the coffee to brew. When he'd finished, he handed me a bill and I wrote him a check.

"I don't like to take checks," he said. "I'd rather have a credit or debit card."

"Then I'll have to go to the bank to get money. I don't have that much cash. When will you tell me what you found?" I asked.

Glory glared at him and left the kitchen.

"As soon as you pay me," he told me.

Glory returned and counted out the exact amount of money onto the table but refused to hand it to him until he wrote her a receipt.

"Now, what did you find?" I asked.

"The electrical service and wiring are both totally out-of-date. It's a wonder you're able to use any of these appliances with the amps you've got and surprising that the wiring hasn't set this house on fire with these adapters you've put on the receptacles so you can plug in four things. For safety, you need to install grounded outlets instead of using adapters to plug in modern three-pronged things, too. I suggest having the whole house rewired and the service increased."

"Can you give me an estimate for doing that?" I asked.

"My boss would have to look at it," he said. "Just call the office and make an appointment for him to come out."

"We'll do that," Glory said as she stepped closer and closer to him, forcing him to back up until he was at the front door.

When she had closed the door behind him, Glory said, "You should have checked with me before you call someone into my house."

"Miss Glory, I just wanted to be sure you're safe here. If the wiring in Mom's house was like yours, it could have caused the fire."

"That man your mother married after your daddy died had her entire electrical system replaced."

"How do you know that? Mom divorced him before you moved here."

She looked at me like I was addled. "Julie," she said, "you know how close Juliana and I were. We spent so much time together that she told me everything."

I left the house before Glory did because I was eager to get away to call Doug Kappa without her hearing me. He wasn't available, so I left another message.

THE HOUSE was empty when I returned home and carried the grocery bags inside. I didn't know where Glory had gone, but the idea of cooking without her leaning over my shoulder pleased me. I was trying harder to be patient with her, but her obsessive attention got on my nerves—a lot. I washed the ingredients for my stew before sitting down at the table with a cutting board and sharp knife.

Mama used to invite Glory over for supper when she made what she called "Brunswick Stew." It was her own version made with one-half pound each of chicken, beef, and pork. The broth, tomatoes, okra, and onion remained the original Brunswick Stew recipe, but Mom substituted green beans, cabbage, and celery for the usual starchy vegetables. This time, I didn't bother to substitute for the starchy vegetables. I bought little red new potatoes, fresh corn, and tiny green butter beans. I loved those things, and I wasn't as conscientious about eating healthy as I sometimes had been. I'd also bought fresh garlic. Anytime I cooked, I added a lot of garlic to the recipe. I figured it couldn't hurt even if the vampire I'd encountered lived only in my mind.

Chopping the meats and vegetables, I realized I had way too much to fit into the cast-iron Dutch oven that Glory kept on the back of the stove. I opened the cabinet beneath the sink to look for a bigger pot. Kneeling, I reached to the back for the largest one. That's when I saw a box shoved far against the wall under the drain pipes. I could see Mama's name in her handwriting on it — *Juliana* written in what looked like black Sharpie, Mama's favorite way of labeling anything. The box was heavy, but I managed to move it to the floor in front of the cabinet.

The box flaps were taped shut with gray duct tape, so I cut them with a knife. Flipping open the tabs revealed a carton packed full of Bell canning jars — most empty, but a few with lids. I lifted one and saw that it was home-canned tomatoes. Mama had written the date on the jar's label, and they should still be good. Smiling at the thought of using Mom's instead of the canned ones I'd bought, I remembered Mama in the kitchen when I was a little girl. She went to the Farmer's Market and bought fresh produce in bushel baskets, then canned them — singing "Love Me Tender" and "Are You Lonesome Tonight?" all afternoon as she preserved our vegetables for the winter. In the fall, Mama made fig preserves. I hoped to find a jar of them, but no luck.

One container near the center had a red string tied around the top. I lifted it out. No label. When I held it up to the light, it appeared to be nails, pins, and needles. Maybe this didn't belong to Mom. Daddy kept nails and screws in jars when I was a child. I wiggled the jar and saw liquid slopping around in there with long red hairs swirling around. That didn't fit. I didn't recall Daddy ever soaking nails in any kind of fluid, and there certainly wouldn't be any reason for Mom's hair to be in it. I was attempting to pry the lid off when Glory entered the back door.

"What are you doing?" she asked in a monotone that was neither friendly nor aggressive.

"I decided to cook for you tonight. Remember Mom's Brunswick Stew. I bought everything to make it, but I needed a bigger pot. I found this box of Mom's preserved goods under the sink. It has some home-canned tomatoes that aren't out of date, but this jar doesn't make sense." I held it out toward her. She took it, looked at it, and set it on the table.

"Oh, Julie, I'd hoped I'd never have to tell you this. Sit down here and let's talk." Her eyes sparkled with tears.

I sat down where I'd been before. She brought out another cutting board and knife, then sat across from me, and began pulling the strings off the celery.

"What didn't you want to tell me?" I asked.

"One reason I try so hard to protect you is that I'm worried about these dreams and delusions you've been having. Juliana wasn't well before she died. She began complaining about nightmares and hallucinations. Convinced there was a witch near here who had put a spell on her, she was really out of her head at times."

"Oh, come now, Miss Glory. Mama didn't believe all those old wives' tales about luck. She'd walk under a ladder carrying a black cat if it suited her."

"But, toward the end, she became very superstitious. She made this bottle by directions she found on the Internet, thinking it would protect her. It's called a witch bottle. You can have it or throw it away." She shoved the jar over closer to me. "Everything that belonged to your mother belongs to you now."

"Why is it here at your house? Did Mom give it to you?" I laid my knife on the table and picked up the jar again, more interested in this conversation than peeling potatoes.

"No, I brought the box to my place after I found Juliana that morning. I didn't want the cops to find it and, heaven forbid, have some nosy reporter printing your mother was involved in witchcraft or devil worship."

"Is that what this is? Witchcraft?"

"I don't really know. Whatever it is, it's over now. Let's get these things chopped and put the stew on. You know Juliana used to let it simmer a couple of hours."

I set the jar on the counter, but it made me feel creepy. *Mom doing witchcraft? Even protective magic doesn't seem possible.*

"Excuse me, Miss Glory, I'm going to put this away." I went to the bedroom, placed the jar on a shelf in the wardrobe and closed the door. I felt a little better with it out of sight.

As I headed back to the kitchen, I glanced at the bedside table, unconsciously expecting sight of Mom's beautiful picture to improve my spirits. It wasn't there. I looked behind the table in case it had been accidentally knocked to the floor. Nothing.

"Miss Glory," I called. "Did you move my mom's portrait?"

"No," she called and came into my room to help me look for it. We couldn't find it. The mystery was solved that night when we went into Miss Glory's room to watch television. Perched on top of the TV was the framed photo. Glory accused me of moving it, but I knew she'd done it herself. Glory carried it back to my room.

A rainstorm woke me from sleep before midnight. I felt like the witch jar was calling me. Fear engulfed me. Had my mother been a sorceress? Did that piece of witchcraft have anything to do with my horrible dreams and hallucinations?

Richard—maybe he could help me, at least tell me if there was a special way to get rid of that spine-chilling jar without bringing more trouble on me. I dressed, grabbed the witch bottle, and dashed through the bitter, sheeting rain out to my car.

Surely he wasn't sleeping in the cemetery during this storm. I drove to the Columbia Men's Mission. Did I dare walk up to that door and ask for him in the middle of the night? Did I even want to hear what he might know about this jar? He claimed to have learned what he knew from research, but was that true? What if Richard himself was evil?

20

THE SMELL was strong that night. A year ago, Richard never would have believed there could ever come a time when he'd prefer sleeping curled up on the ground in a graveyard to a bed, but if not for the rain, he'd prefer to be outside instead if in this room crowded with bunk beds. Nothing like a bucketing storm to drive most of the area's homeless to seek somewhere indoors to stay for the night.

Richard chose the Men's Mission for nights like this because in addition to hot meals and semi-comfortable beds, they provided showers to anyone willing to wait in line. Richard scrunched down under his blanket and wished whoever was perfuming this part of the room with a first-class case of BO had taken advantage of the showers like he had.

When the weather was really terrible, the shelter filled quickly. Homeless men could stay there for up to thirty days at a time if they followed the rules. Richard rarely spent more than one or two nights before returning to the cemetery. When he did go to the mission, he always managed to arrive early enough to be assigned a bed, not offered a mat on the floor, which was how they handled an overflow crowd.

Richard chose to sleep at the mission when weather was bad and the graveyard when it was good. He'd never slept in the caves down by the canal though he'd visited there. The tunnels and caves made him feel weird and though he'd met many homeless people he liked, he felt safer from the few truly evil or deranged ones at the mission.

He never had any trouble with the restrictions because he didn't drink when doing research and he'd finally kicked his cigarette addiction three years ago. He hadn't been on the streets through winter yet and wondered if he'd be forced to seek shelter more often then. He inhaled and almost gagged. Really — one of the supervisors should make whoever smelled that bad either shower or leave.

Richard pulled the blanket up over his nose and tried to sleep. His mind drifted to the redhead. He'd been physically attracted to her from the first time he saw her, but their occasional encounters since then had created an even stronger fascination. He whispered, "Julie." Her name was delicious on his tongue. He yawned and fell into deep slumber.

Sleep didn't slow Richard's reactions. When someone touched his arm, he shot up like a jack-in-the-box. He'd been dreaming about watching Julie walk down the street with that little jiggle her behind made, especially when she wore workout clothes, but he'd wakened immediately when touched, well aware he was in the shelter, the *men's* shelter, which admitted no women and had no female volunteers working at night.

"Mr. Arthur? Are you Richard Arthur?"

"Yes, I am," Richard answered, wondering, *What the hell? I was assigned this bed. Are they going to move me to one of the mats?*

"There's a woman at the door insisting she see you *right now*." The attendant sounded annoyed.

Puzzled, Richard slid his feet into his shoes. So far as he knew, no one in his family was aware of where he was, what city, or what he was working on. Even if someone knew about the project, there were several shelters in the area. How would anyone know where to look for him?

At the door, Richard drew in a long breath of surprise. The red-haired Julie stood there holding a plastic bag. She wore a raincoat, but water puddled at her feet. It only took a moment for him to realize that as much of the water on her face came from tears as from the rain.

"I *have* to talk to you," Julie said. "Why can't I come in?"

Richard didn't have time to answer before the attendant spoke. "This is a shelter for men only. No women are allowed inside during evening and sleeping hours. You can come back after nine in the morning."

The pleading in those deep blue eyes melted Richard's heart when Julie begged, "Please help me. I need to talk to you."

"Let me get my jacket and I'll go with you," he said.

"Richard, if you leave, you can't come back here until tomorrow," the attendant warned.

"I know." He turned toward Julie. "The closest place we can talk is the all-night coffee shop. Do you have an umbrella?"

"Yes," she sniffled, "but better than that, I have my car."

21

I'D PARKED less than half a block from the mission. I unlocked the doors, and we climbed in with me in the driver's seat, but I didn't start the engine. I turned on the overhead light and opened the plastic bag I held.

"Oh, shit!" Richard said when he saw what I had.

"From your expression, this must be bad," I told him. "I've been told it's a witch bottle."

"That's what it is—a witch bottle. He paused, then added, "Though in this case, I think it's more of a witch *jar*. Did you make it?"

"No, I found it."

"Where?"

"I discovered it packed in a box of canned goods under Glory's sink. She says that Mom thought someone had put a spell on her and made this jar to protect herself."

"That makes sense, but if it were to protect your

mother, it should have been hidden in *her* house, not in Glory's."

"Glory said she moved it after Mom's death." I wiped my eyes with the back of my hand. "How does it work?"

"It's supposed to have sharp items in it. It looks like some of them have rusted. I can't really tell much about that through the liquid. The nails, razor blades, needles—whatever is in it—are to deflect bad luck and spells from the jar. Then it should have sea salt for purification. The liquid could be one of several things. Some people use wine, but they spit in the wine before sealing it. That's to mark the bottle as belonging to the maker. I see red hair in there, too. Is it yours? If so, this could have been to protect you."

"No, Mom couldn't have gotten my hair while I was in New York." I leaned over, looked more closely, and then told him about the hair flowers in the wreaths at the museum.

"That would be mighty handy for voodoo practitioners when they needed some hair or fingernails. Convenient, too, for ghosts who want to fully materialize and need a part of their physical bodies to do it." He stared at the jar. "Aside from that, if it's your mother's hair, it's another way to make the jar as protection for her."

"I think that's white wine," I commented, watching my mother's hair float .

"Could be, but it might be your mother's urine."

"Ugh."

"Urine of the person needing protection makes it stronger to keep the spell away. Kind of like pissing in every corner." He held the jar up to the light.

"Don't shake it. I don't want it spilled in my car."

"It won't spill. See the edge." He pointed to the lid and pulled the red string from around it. "The top was sealed with black candle wax before the cord was tied around it."

"What's the significance of tying it if it's already sealed?"

"It brings additional protection. Whoever made it knew exactly how to do this."

"Glory said Mama looked it up on the Internet."

"Then she would have known that it could be buried far away from her to keep the spell away or hidden in her house for protection. She chose to keep it near her."

"That's weird."

"Yes, it seems those are opposite of each other, but that's how witch bottles work."

I smiled. "I thought you'd know about this, and I couldn't wait 'til morning to talk to you. I remembered you told me that when you went to a shelter, you went to the Men's Mission. I'm better, but now I feel guilty that you have nowhere to sleep."

"Don't worry about me." Richard spoke to me in a condescending tone, but I was so grateful for the explanation of the bottle that I didn't react.

"What are we going to do about a place for you to sleep tonight? I can't invite you to spend the rest of the night on the couch at Glory's. That's where she sleeps, and she's already threatened me if I tried to bring a man back into the house. She was nice to you the day we saw the coyote, but I think it would be a different story in the middle of the night."

"Threatened you with what?"

"She didn't say, but I'll rent you a room at a motel." I turned the car on and pulled out of the parking space.

"A rented room with a private bathroom and television sounds good," Richard said, "but I want to stay near you. Letting you pay for a place for me when the night is almost over is out of the question."

"It wouldn't be if you were truly homeless," I said, thinking, *He must be telling the truth. He's really a writer living his research.*

"I can't let you do that," Richard said, and the tone of his voice left no room for questioning. "Way more than half of the night is gone. Could I just sleep a few more hours in your car?"

"Whatever floats your boat." *Why did I say that? It's such a trite cliché, and I've never used it before.*

"In this rain, anything will float."

The downpour stopped on our drive back. "Why do you park in front of your house instead of Glory's?" Richard asked.

"Don't ask," I muttered. "She doesn't like me to

park in front of her place."

He climbed in the back seat while I ran inside the house for a blanket and pillow. When I handed them to him, I said, "I'll bring some breakfast out to you in the morning."

"Or we can go to IHOP," he said.

Richard gazed at me with an expression of longing. I hoped it didn't go any further than a look, and it didn't. He turned sideways, bent his legs, and covered himself with the blanket.

MY STOMACH ached, not inside, but on the skin outside. I lifted my nightgown and looked down. I must have scratched myself during the night because bright red marks striped across my abdomen. They hurt, but not nearly like the gut-wrenching pain I'd felt before.

I lay there for a moment, pleased that there had been no nightmares after I returned to my bed, pleased that I wasn't suffering the torment of cystitis. I heard rain on the rooftop. I looked at the bedside table. There was something eerie about my mother's picture being beside her witch bottle. I leisurely got out of bed and put the jar behind the closed door of the wardrobe before heading toward the kitchen to make coffee.

That's when I remembered I'd left Richard Arthur asleep in my car with promises of breakfast this

morning. There was food in the kitchen to cook, but I
didn't want the smells to wake Glory. I dressed
quickly, grabbed my umbrella, and ran out the back
door and around to the street.

The first thing I noticed was that the Focus sat
lower than it should have. A closer look revealed
why. I walked around my car and discovered that all
four tires had been flattened. I peeked into the back
seat. No Richard. Had he done this? If so, why? If
Richard hadn't ruined my tires, had whoever sliced
them confronted him and made him run off? Or
worse, yet, taken him with them?

I did what I'd always been told to do when
there's trouble. I called the police. Not 911 and not
the precinct. I called Nate personally.

"Go back inside and wait for me," he answered
when I asked what I should do. "I'm on the way."

I watched from the window as Nate pulled over
to the curb behind my pretty new Focus that wouldn't
be taking me anywhere right away. He got out of his
car and walked slowly around mine, squatting down
at each tire and examining it. When he'd been around
the car twice, he took out his phone and made a call,
and then headed toward the back of Glory's house. I
met him on the porch.

"Did they slash the tires or just let the air out?" I
asked.

"Neither. It's hard to describe. The tires are
destroyed. They'll have to be replaced, but they

weren't exactly cut. I called my garage and they'll tow your car in and replace the tires. I'll also make a police report on it."

"How were they flattened?"

"Each tire has a shredded spot on it as though it's been gnawed or chewed."

"I IMAGINE you saw lots of Broadway plays when you lived in New York." Nate reached across the IHOP table and patted my hand. He did that a lot those days. I wasn't paying full attention to him. I'd eaten a complete pancake breakfast, a full order. In the past, I'd always chosen the sugar-free syrup while other people could pick from maple, blueberry, strawberry, boysenberry, or honey-cinnamon. This day I'd tried some of every flavor.

"Why are you asking me about the theater when you know I'm upset that someone slashed my tires last night?" I asked. I didn't dare tell him that the "homeless" man who'd been with me when I found Jerry Patterson's body had probably been in my car when it happened.

"Your car's being repaired. I asked because I want to know if you enjoy live productions."

"Sure, but I saw more off-Broadway than on."

"How about a play here in Columbia? Would you go to the theater with me?"

"What's playing and where is it?"

"A Tennessee Williams piece—*A Streetcar Named Desire* – are you familiar with it?"

"Of course I've heard of it. I even saw the old movie, but I've never seen a live production of it."

"You'll enjoy it, I guarantee."

"Is it at Town Theatre?"

"No, it's playing at the Longstreet Theatre on the University of South Carolina campus."

I couldn't help laughing at him. "Still trying to find some psychic ability in me?" I asked. "I'm not psychic, but I'm starting to think I may be psycho."

Nate looked surprised. "I don't think you're mentally ill, but you could have some psychic abilities. What have you heard about Longstreet?"

"More what I've read than what I've heard, but I went to the University of South Carolina and remember being told about ghosts there. After all this started, I Googled haunted places in South Carolina, and Longstreet Theatre was one of the locations I searched."

"And what did you find?"

"Longstreet served as a hospital during the Civil War in the 1860s. The basement was used as a morgue, and the stories are that ghosts haunt that part of the building, which is now used as a 'green room' for stage productions."

"That's pretty much it, but did you know that in the mid-sixties, the building was used as a gym? Female students had basketball and modern dance

236

classes there."

"I didn't read that."

"I didn't either. My uncle told me about it."

I burst into laughter. "He took girls' basketball and modern dance?"

"No, he was with a group of football players who snuck into the building and hid in the balcony to watch the girls in their dance tights. Back then, girls weren't allowed to wear jeans on campus. They had to wear skirts or dresses, and not mini-length either, so seeing them jumping around in leotards was exciting."

"No jeans?"

"Nope."

"What happened? They just looked?"

"No, the teacher caught them hiding up there and made five of them go down and join the class. My uncle said the girl dance students laughed like hell when the teacher called out, 'Ladies, you're not leaping,' at the football players while they tried to do what the girls had been doing."

"I'd rather have seen that than a play or a ghost."

"What about it? Want to see A Streetcar Named Desire?"

"Sure."

"You'll be impressed. That beautiful old building was originally an auditorium and chapel before its use as a hospital and morgue during the Civil War. Now that it's used as a theater again, they have a huge hydraulic lift stage."

"I'm game."

I'D READ that years ago, in the South, going to a live theater production meant wearing what we called "Sunday clothes," but in today's society, many people don't dress up for much of anything. I took the middle road and wore tan wool slacks, a soft amber sweater, and new taupe shoes with a matching clutch purse. I gave myself a manicure and polished my nails tawny, golden ochre. Nate showed up wearing his police uniform. I immediately assumed he'd come to cancel our plans.

"Was your schedule changed? Do you have to work?" I asked.

"No, I thought we might want to take a peek at some of the areas closed to the public." He patted his chest. "This uniform opens locked doors a lot quicker than just showing my badge."

Both the South Carolina State Capitol building and Longstreet Theatre appear to be plunked down smack in the middle of a street. Main Street dead-ends into the Capitol, a massive building that seems to end Main, but on the other side, the street begins again. One block over, Sumter Street does the same thing at Longstreet Theatre on the corner of Greene Street, and then resumes on the other side of the theater.

A Streetcar Named Desire was performed in the round that night with the audience sitting on all four sides of the stage. It was difficult to think that this building was over a hundred and fifty years old and that it had been used as both a hospital and a morgue. Then my mind drifted to the story Nate had told me about female P.E. classes there during the 1960s.

With my thoughts darting around, it was hard to concentrate on the play, and I felt relieved when it was over. Nate and I stood, but when I stepped into the crowd headed for the exit, he touched my arm and held me back.

"Wait, and we'll look around," he said.

I knew where we'd go—to the green room. Sure enough, we went downstairs. I recognized the three barrel-vaulted alcoves with old brick walls from descriptions I'd read. Expecting an area furnished for performers, I was completely surprised there were no comfortable couches or tables with magazines. The area was apparently no longer used as a green room. It was crowded with dusty old chairs stacked on top of one another.

Stepping through the entrance, what felt like a solid sheet of ice slammed me. The wall of cold air stabbed icicles through my body and made my teeth chatter.

"Are you okay? What's happening? Do you see something?" Nate's words penetrated my mind, but I couldn't speak.

The room darkened to only a tiny amount of light from an antique oil lamp on a rickety table. Makeshift stretchers topped with low, bumpy mounds covered with dingy gray and brown cloths crowded the space. Nate disappeared just as the room flooded with an unbelievable stench.

I stepped to one of the gurneys—closer but not too near. I watched my right arm, covered in the cashmere-like sweater sleeve, reach toward the discolored fabric but I couldn't feel the movement. Tentatively, fingers tipped with tawny, golden ochre polish touched the cloth. That's when I realized it covered a body.

If what happened next had been a jump scare in a horror movie, I would have laughed, but this wasn't a movie. This was real.

From beneath the shroud, white skeletal fingers reached up and grasped my wrist. Immediately, the numbness disappeared and sensitivity returned to my hand and arm. The bones gripped like a vise even though most of the flesh had sloughed off and what little muscle remained was dark and squishy.

I went silent with shock.

Still clutching my wrist, the figure sat up and the cloth fell away. Much of the skin and flesh were gone—exposing bones. What skin remained varied from a dark, almost black color to mottled purple. The eyes bulged although I couldn't tell if they really protruded that much or if the skin had withered so far back that it made the eyes look like they were sticking out of their sockets. The eyeballs themselves moved and seemed to look at me though they were shriveled and covered with an opaque film.

The lower half of the face consisted of an open mouth with the lower jaw hanging. The dark tongue, oozing disgusting slime from fissures and cracks, was too swollen to fit all the way in the mouth cavity.

Torn, ragged clothing exposed a midriff of broken ribs and decaying flesh with moss growing in random patches. An area of skin on the lower left abdomen had ruptured, spilling out partially rotted bowels.

I wanted to run, but not a muscle in my body responded to my demands. The thing—that's how I thought of it—began shaking violently. The bony hand released me, but I still couldn't move. Its eyes jerked back and forth and the tongue rolled around. The thing was trying to speak.

In that horrible moment, I had one thought—I hoped this was a dream or a delusion. Then thinking became impossible. My brain felt like it was a child's balloon being pumped full of helium. What was happening to me? Would my head explode? Just as I expected death at any minute, the decaying thing changed. I wondered if this creature was from the North or the South, but as the body filled out and putrefaction reversed itself, I saw that he wore neither blue nor gray.

In what could have been a minute or an hour, the

monstrosity that sat before me turned into a young man who looked about sixteen or seventeen. Sandy hair fell across his bruised forehead over clear hazel eyes that fit neatly into their sockets. The only damage must have been a chest wound because blood oozed through his shirt.

He opened his mouth, and it looked normal inside except for several missing teeth. His lips moved, but no sound came from them. He shook his head and wiped his hand across his eyebrows.

My head felt the swelling again.

"Home." The voice was young and masculine with a strong southern drawl. The boy's mouth didn't move, yet now I could hear him in my head. "Ah wa-unt to go ho-um."

"Where's your home?" I could speak again.

"Val-dausta. Val-dausta, Gaw-gah."

"Is there any way I can help you?"

"Just stop this dambed wa-uh and send me ho-um."

Before I could answer, he collapsed back onto the cot. Right before my eyes, the young man's wound stopped bleeding, leaving dark stains on the raggedy garment. He began decomposing again like a scary fast-forward video on YouTube. Fluid spilled out of his mouth and nose. Scattered blisters popped up on greenish skin as it sloughed off, baring bones in places.

The disgusting odor that filled the room reeked

like nothing I'd ever smelled before, almost sweet —
sickening in the most horrible, nauseating stench. As
the body bloated, his clothes burst revealing more
marbled and blackened flesh.

The lower left part of his abdomen undulated like
the skin was stretched over a roller coaster. Flesh
wrinkled and split. His innards spilled out increasing
the stink. Skin shriveled around his eyes and mouth,
making his film-coated eyes bulge as his tongue
swelled so big it protruded between his splitting lips
again. The entire body ballooned.

Noises — sounds of escaping gases. The body
deflated quickly and returned to the exact condition it
had been when I first saw it. I lifted the crumpled
cloth from the floor intending to cover the soldier.

His bony hand reached for me again.

I escaped into darkness.

22

FROM TOTAL nothingness to glaring brightness—opening my eyes was painful. I closed them.

"Do it again, Julie!" Nate's excited voice. "Open your eyes for me." His breath felt hot on my face when he spoke.

I risked one eye, but not both.

Nate stood on one side of me—bending close to my face. Another man stood on the other side. He looked familiar but I didn't recognize him until I saw the wooden cross suspended from a leather lanyard on his chest.

"Did you give me last rites?" I asked Preacher Ron.

"No, because you're not dying and I'm not Catholic."

My mind began to clear and I realized I was in a hospital setting, but I asked anyway. "Where am I?"

"You're in a holding area at the Palmetto

Hospital. We're waiting for them to assign you a room. You've already been admitted." Nate sounded worried.

"Why? What happened?"

"I should never have taken you to Longstreet Theatre. When we arrived at the green room, you stopped at the door and froze. Couldn't move or speak. I realize now I've been pushing you too hard," Nate apologized.

"Don't go blaming yourself," Preacher Ron interrupted. "Nate, we still don't know. Just because the MRI looks negative doesn't mean there's not a perfectly good medical reason for this."

"What did happen?" I asked.

"We don't know," Nate responded. "They've run a lot of tests, but nothing's shown up."

"Not yet." Preacher Ron added the discouraging words.

"How long have I been here?"

Nate looked at his watch. "About five hours. It's 3:00 A.M."

"Were you so worried that you called for the preacher to come?"

"Damned straight, I was worried. In fact, I'm still worried, but Preacher Ron had been visiting a sick parishioner here. He was leaving the hospital when the ambulance brought you in. He saw me and came over to see what was wrong."

"I was afraid his mother had fallen or had a heart

attack," Preacher Ron said. "You know Mrs. Adams is in her seventies. When Nate told me why he was here, I stayed with him the whole time. He's been mighty upset." He paused. "And, of course, I was concerned about you, too." He paused. "I care about all of God's children."

"Excuse me," Nate interrupted when his cell phone signaled a message. "I need to step outside and take this call."

"I'll be right here," I answered.

While Nate was out, a doctor came in. I'd never seen him before, but he seemed elated that I was awake. After a quick look in my eyes and throat with his little flashlight, he said, "Young lady, we're happy you're out of your catatonic state, but I have some questions for you."

"Yes, sir."

"The officer who came in with you said that you hadn't been drinking or using any drugs. Is that correct?"

"Yes, sir."

"Have you ever been treated for any mental disturbance like schizophrenia, paranoia, or bi-polar condition?"

"No. Is that what you think is wrong with me?"

"I don't believe so. Catatonic episodes with schizophrenia usually last much longer than what you've experienced. We're more sure of what's not wrong than what caused your condition. You were catatonic when you came in. That means you were in a state of inertia, an apparent stupor, unable to move or speak. We've run a lot of tests and may do some more tomorrow. Your policeman friend has also told me about some delusions you've had. Meanwhile, I've admitted you for tonight."

"I'd rather go home."

The doctor laughed. "I'm sure you would, but you need to be checked regularly for a while after the condition you were in."

Nate came in as the doctor finished speaking. The physician turned to him.

"Officer Adams, I'm going to keep Ms. Bates overnight."

"I was right outside, so I heard." Nate turned to me. "I've got to go on a call. I'll be back as soon as I'm finished." He stepped out the door, then came right back inside. "I forgot to tell you. I called Glory and told her you were here. I assured her she didn't need to come."

"I'm a grown woman. I'll be fine with the nurses taking care of me. You go on home and get some rest when you finish working." I wanted to add, "And take care of your mother," but I didn't. Why was I considering such a rude comment? Nate Adams had been more than kind to me, and his mother was none of my business.

"I'll stay with Julie 'til she's settled," Preacher Ron assured him and was still with me when they moved me to a room.

"Sixth floor, neurology," the hospital attendant answered me when I asked where we were. Preacher Ron stepped out while the technicians transferred me from the ER gurney to a regular hospital bed and showed me how to work the electronics to call the nurse, lower or raise parts of the bed, and control the television.

The preacher returned when the attendants left.

"Did Nate give you my card?" Preacher Ron asked as he sat down in the visitor chair.

"Yes, I've been meaning to call you."

"How do you feel? Are you especially tired?"

"Not really."

He pulled the chair up closer to the bed. "Then let's talk now. What's causing you to doubt? What are these 'events' that are making you question the Lord and suspect the existence of ghosts?"

"Did you know my mother died earlier this year and my house burned less than a month ago?"

"Yes, I did. Nate gave me some background, and what you're experiencing may be grief over both of those losses."

"But I'm having sleep paralysis and horrible nightmares that seem so real that they're more like hallucinations. I've dreamed about vampires and werewolves. I keep seeing my mother."

"Where do you see her?"

"I see her in the mirror when I should be seeing

myself. I see her in dreams."

"Does she ever speak to you?"

"I wish she would. I'm not scared of my mother's ghost. I just wish she would materialize and talk to me. I wish I could hug and kiss her, but I don't think it's possible."

"Have you prayed about this?"

Again, I was tempted to lie, but I told the truth. "No."

"Why not?"

"To be honest, I never thought about it, but there's another reason. I found a witch jar that Glory said my mother made. She said Mom was disturbed before her death, thought she was under a spell, and made the witch bottle to protect herself. Maybe my mother was suffering something like paranoia."

. "Why would that make you afraid to pray?"

"It scares me." I coughed and Preacher Ron held my water bottle straw to my lips. I took a sip and continued, "Maybe my mother dabbled in something evil, and the spell could be on me now. Nate thinks I'm psychic, but I don't *feel* psychic, and I never see things from the future, only the past."

"What happened tonight? Nate told me you completely froze when he took you downstairs at the Longstreet Theatre. He tried to bring you around. He said you remained standing but were totally nonresponsive."

"I don't know. I was looking at a bunch of stored

furniture, and I went back in time and talked to a Confederate soldier. The next thing I knew, I woke up here at the hospital."

"You know Longstreet was used as a morgue during the Civil War and some USC students have reported seeing dark, shadowy figures there."

"Think about that," I commented. People die in hospitals all the time. If everyone who ever passed away here haunted this place, there wouldn't be room to move, and when I see Mom, it's not where she died. That house burned."

"Your mother didn't commit suicide, did she?"

"I thought you said Nate briefed you about me."

"He told me you lost your mother. He didn't say how."

"My mother was murdered after she was brutally raped."

"Oh, Julie," he said softly. "I had no idea. I wish Nate had told me."

"It's hard, so hard to deal with, and I didn't tell you about my old high school friend I found dead on Assembly Street."

"You poor child."

A nurse stepped in with a cup of water. "These will help you sleep," she said and held two pills out to me. She turned toward Preacher Ron. "Sir, you should probably leave now and let these work. We want her to sleep, but we can't give her anything very powerful."

"May we pray first?" Preacher Ron asked.

"Certainly," the nurse replied and left.

Preacher Ron took my hand and prayed, "Heavenly Father, please be with Julie tonight. Bless her, make her well, and help her through this difficult time. Amen."

"Amen," I repeated after him as he made the sign of the cross on my forehead.

"I'll come back and we'll talk some more," he said as he left.

The medicine might not have been strong, but it worked. I slept.

Peacefully. No bad dreams. No good dreams. No dreams at all.

NOISE WOKE me. It had been so long since I'd heard a landline ring that it took a minute for me to realize it was the bedside telephone. I grabbed the receiver and said, "Hello," but no one answered. That made me wonder about my cell phone. Where was my purse? Did the hospital have it or did Nate take it with him for safe keeping?

I pressed the intercom for the nurse.

"How may I help you?" The answer came from the speaker above the head of my bed.

"Can you check to see if my purse is here at the hospital?"

"Yes, ma'am. I'll find out and get right back to

you."

"Thank you."

She didn't get right back to me. I grabbed the remote control and turned on the television—nothing interesting.

The assistant came in with breakfast. He adjusted my bed so that I was in a sitting position and placed the tray on a table across my lap. I'd chewed the last bite when the nurse rushed in saying, "I asked about your belongings. The only items that came in with you are the clothing you were wearing. I noticed your ears are pierced, but you weren't wearing earrings."

"No purse or cell phone?"

"No."

"What about a ring with a heart-shaped ruby?"

"No jewelry at all."

It didn't take long for the mystery of my belongings to be solved. Nate arrived carrying a large vase of mixed flowers. I smiled and thanked him before asking, "Do you know where my purse is?"

Shocked is the best way to describe his expression.

"Your purse? Your purse?" He said it twice, and his expression was self-disgust. "I don't remember bringing it. I saw it on the floor in the green room when I called the ambulance. I put the jewelry you were wearing in my pocket, but I forgot your handbag when the EMTs arrived." He rubbed his eyes and gave me an apologetic look. "I'm betting your purse is still in the green room at Longstreet."

"You'll have to get it for me. I'm not going back to that place. I can't remember all of it, but something terrible happened to me there."

"Of course I'll get it for you, and you don't ever need to go back there. I wish I'd never taken you to that place." He looked at his watch. "I can't stay. I'm on duty, but I'll be back as soon as I can."

"When do you finish? I'm hoping the doctor will release me this morning."

"If that happens, call my cell."

When he left, memories of dead bodies in the basement at Longstreet Theatre flooded my mind. I almost passed out again.

I WAITED patiently—well, kind of—for the doctor. I felt like I was going out of my mind for real. The whole hospital experience offended my sense of privacy. I didn't like the Certified Nursing Assistant insisting she help me bathe. What I wanted most at that moment was to be left alone, but she demanded that I go into the bathroom and that she go with me. I did what I used to do in school. I escaped into concentrated thought, but that was daunting. *Was what I remembered from Longstreet something that happened or that I imagined?* I wanted to know, yet, deep inside, I was terrified of the answer.

"Who got hold of you?" the CNA barged into my meditation.

"What do you mean?"

"Was it your husband?"

"I'm not married. What are you talking about?"

"I figured you were in here because some man beat you up."

"Nobody beat me. I was admitted because I had a spell and passed out."

"Then where did all those scratches and bruises on your spine come from?" She touched my back gently with the wash cloth. Unbearable pain. "Sorry," she continued, "I know it hurts when I touch all those wounds."

I've never been an exhibitionist, and I'd become almost obsessively modest since the nightmares began. Now, knowing that my body bore marks, I felt even more reticent about anyone looking at me. I was grateful when the woman finished, helped me back to the bed, and left. I pulled the sheet up to my chin.

"Good morning, how are you feeling? May I come in?" Preacher Ron stood at the door holding a small paper bag.

"Of course," I said, and I meant it. Some of my thoughts before the CNA interrupted to tell me about my injuries had been questions I wanted to ask the man of God.

He set the bag at the foot of the bed and pulled

the visitor chair up close beside the bed. "How are you feeling?" He sounded sincerely concerned.

"Better. I'm hoping to go home this morning, but I want to ask you about something."

"What is it?"

"Tell me about demons. Are they real?"

"If you believe in a literal translation of the Bible, demons are real. They're mentioned in several books of the Holy Gospel, including Matthew, Mark, and Luke."

"What does the Bible say about demons?" I sat up straighter.

"Jesus cast them out of people who were called demoniacs, individuals who were possessed by unclean spirits, which translates to demons."

"Did Jesus kill them?"

"No, the Bible says he 'cast out demons.' There are many examples of Jesus healing demoniacs by calling out the unclean spirits."

Preacher Ron reached into his pocket and took out a small New Testament. "Let me read you the best known example from the New Revised Standard Version of the Bible." He flipped through the pages and found the place. "This is from the Book of Mark, Chapter Five," he said and read:

> When he (Jesus) had stepped out of the boat, immediately a man out of the tombs with an unclean spirit met him. He lived among the

tombs, and no one could restrain him anymore,
even with a chain, for he had often been
restrained with shackles and chains, but the
chains he wrenched apart, and the shackles
he broke in pieces, and no one had the strength
to subdue him. Night and day among the tombs
and on the mountains, he was always howling
and bruising himself with stones. When he saw
Jesus from a distance, he ran and bowed down
before him, and he shouted at the top of his
voice, "What have you to do with me, Jesus,
Son of the most high God? I abjure you by God
do not torment me." For he had said to him,
"Come out of the man, you unclean spirit!"
Then Jesus asked him, "What is your name?"
He replied, "My name is Legion, for we are
many." He begged him earnestly not to send
them out of the country. Now there on the
hillside a great herd of swine was feeding;
and the unclean spirits begged him, "Send us
into the swine; let us enter them." So he gave
them permission, and the unclean spirits came
out and entered the swine, and the herd,
numbering about two thousand, rushed down
the steep bank into the sea, and were drowned
in the sea.

"What happened after that?" I asked. "Did that
man become one of Jesus's twelve apostles?"

"No, the swineherds ran off and told everyone.

People came to find out what had happened and asked Jesus to leave their neighborhood. The cured demoniac begged to go with Jesus when he left, but the Savior told him to go home and tell everyone what the Lord had done for him."

Preacher Ron looked at his watch. "I have a previous appointment, but we'll talk again soon."

"If there *is* a demon involved, can you do an exorcism?" I felt compelled to ask that question.

His face went through a contortion that would best be described as a combination of shock and fear. "No, I can't do that," he said. "I'm a lay preacher, but if I'd been to seminary, I'd still not be who you would need. Catholicism is the only denomination I know that deals with exorcism."

"Oh." I sounded as disappointed as I felt.

"But," he continued, "I have a friend who is a priest. I'll see if I can arrange a meeting for the three of us." He looked at his watch again. "I need to leave, but I'll help you however I can." He handed me the bag from the foot of the bed. "This is a gift for you," he said and handed it to me.

I peeked inside and thanked Preacher Ron for the black, hard-backed book. It was a Holy Bible. "May we pray?" he asked and reached for my hand.

"Heavenly father, we thank you for all the blessings you have bestowed upon us and for making Julie feel better. Please be with her today and every day and help her escape the delusions and turmoil she's experiencing. We pray in the name of the Father, the Son, and the Holy Ghost. Amen."

I repeated, "Amen" after him, and he left. I doubt he meant for me to catch it, but he'd pretty much expressed his opinion of what was happening to me by praying for me to be freed from my "delusions." Preacher Ron was a good fellow, and he might contact his priest friend, but he didn't believe the nightmares I experienced were real.

I waited another hour for my doctor. He seemed rushed when he arrived. "So, your tests didn't show anything significant," he said. "I'm going to dismiss you, but if this happens again, you need to come back here to the ER. I also want you to see a psycho-neurologist." He handed me a business card for the other physician. "My office will schedule the appointment and notify you of the time and date. You can go ahead and call someone to pick you up."

I opened my mouth to ask a question, but he was out the door. A few minutes later, a nurse came in with dismissal papers and removed my IV. I called a taxi.

That plan went smoothly until the cab pulled up in front of Glory's house, and I realized that without my purse, I didn't have any money to pay him. I didn't think he'd take my new Bible in trade for the ride. I ran up the steps and knocked on the front door. No answer. I banged and banged on the door and shouted for Glory. Still no answer. I looked over toward where my house had been and saw my car parked, sitting high and proud on new tires, but that didn't help at all. I didn't have any money in the car.

What could I do? Without my purse, I had no house key or car key. If I'd had identification, I could have had the cab take me to the bank, but all of my identification was in my purse.

I was almost crying when someone touched my shoulder.

23

RICHARD WATCHED Glory's house from the laundromat window. He knew Julie had been gone overnight, almost twenty-four hours, with the cop. Jealousy ate at him when Glory left an hour earlier. Was she headed to wherever Julie was? If so, he'd follow her, but Glory had taken her reusable grocery bags in her cart, so she'd apparently gone shopping.

Julie's arrival in a cab was puzzling. Her beating on the door and crying was more disturbing. She'd left with the cop. Why hadn't he brought her home and why couldn't she get into the house? Jealousy faded to a feeling of protection. Right now he had nothing to offer this woman without quitting the writing project he was researching, and Richard was convinced that this would be his best seller. The hell with the "Great American Novel." Well-written nonfiction might get him in with one of the big publishers. Until then, he didn't dare approach Julie for more than friendship.

A damsel in distress? Richard thought when he stepped onto the porch and touched her shoulder, *Well, your knight in shining armor is here in rags.*

Julie had yelled for Glory; now she screeched in obvious fear until she turned around and saw Richard. The taxi driver jumped out and bounded up the steps. He grabbed Richard and pulled him away from Julie.

"Leave him alone," Julie gasped. "It's okay. He's a friend of mine. I know him."

"Then pay me and let me get outta here."

It was hard to tell who was more surprised — the cabbie or Julie — when the shabby homeless man pulled a roll of paper money from his pocket, counted out the fare plus a generous tip to the driver, and said, "Thanks for coming to her rescue. If it had been someone else who looked like me, she may have needed help."

"Thank you," Julie said to Richard as the cab pulled away from the curb.

"What's happening? Did Glory lock you out?"

"No, I spent the night in the hospital and misplaced my purse. I don't have my keys or money. I'd expected Glory to be home and lend me the fare as well as letting me in, but she must be gone somewhere."

"I was out for a walk earlier," Richard lied, "and I saw her. She was going shopping with her cart." He would never confess he spied on Julie.

"Would you like to go somewhere for coffee?"

"Right now, all I want is to get into this house."

Richard looked around and then stepped closer to the door. In a matter of minutes, he'd picked the lock. The door swung open.

"How'd you do that?" Julie asked.

"I'm a 'jack of all trades,'" he answered.

"I thought you were a writer," Julie said, and Richard recognized a tiny bit of tease or flirtation. He wasn't sure what it was. Hell, it could have been suspicion.

"That's how I learned to do so many things — the key to good writing is research, and I prefer mine to be through living it, not just looking up topics on the Internet."

Julie ignored that comment and invited him, "Come on back to the kitchen. I'll make fresh coffee. I don't think you'd want to drink Glory's leftover anyway. She makes it so strong that it walks even when it's fresh."

24

SITTING AT the kitchen table, sipping hot brew, Richard asked, "What happened?"

"Nate and I went to see *A Streetcar Named Desire* and then went downstairs when it was over. I passed out, and he called an ambulance."

"I don't think they would admit you overnight if all you did was faint."

"It was a little more than that. I was out for five hours."

"What did the doctors say?"

"All the tests were negative, but they want me to see a shrink."

"A few sessions of therapy might help you, but I still believe the things happening to you are real, not delusions. He emptied his cup, got up, and poured himself a refill. "What did you do with the witch bottle?" he asked, and it took me a few seconds to remember.

"It's in my room. I had it by the bed, but I moved it back inside the wardrobe."

"Good. My gut feeling is still that your mother was seeking protection, not trying to work evil."

"I don't think Mom would ever do anything wicked."

"Wish my mother had been like that." He sighed before he continued, "Can I do anything for you?" he asked.

"Make all this craziness go away."

"I would if I could, but I have no idea how to do that. You should call Doug Kappa again." He drained his cup and advised, "Call him *today*." I didn't bother to tell Richard that I'd been calling Kappa, but he wasn't returning my calls.

When Richard left, I washed our mugs and went to my room. The picture of my mother was still where I'd put it on the nightstand. I lay across the bed and didn't even pick up a book to read.

Glory and Nate arrived at the same time. She came in the back door. He was right behind her carrying her two reusable grocery bags that he set on the counter.

"How'd you get home?" Nate demanded.

"I called a cab. Didn't want to bother you at work."

"You know I would have made arrangements to pick you up."

"How did you two wind up together?"

Glory giggled as she began unloading the food and putting it away in the refrigerator and cabinet. "I was walking down the street, and this fine officer of the law picked me up and gave me a ride home in his police car. I'd never ridden in one before."

"That doesn't surprise me," I said. "Did you ride in back behind the metal divider?"

"Certainly not," Nate answered for her. "I'm driving a cage car today, but she rode in the front with me." He reached in his coat pocket, said, "This is for you," and handed me the clutch purse we'd left at Longstreet. "I hope nothing's been stolen, but I didn't check because I don't know what you had in there."

As I opened the clasp, the cell ringtone sounded. I grabbed it out and answered, but no one was there. I shook it.

"I'm going to take this thing back and make them exchange it," I said. "I'm tired of it going off like that when it's not a real call."

"Not a real call?" Nate asked. "Who do you think it is?"

"I think it's a defective telephone," I responded, but I remembered the landline at the hospital had done did the same one-ring thing that morning.

"Check to see if anything is missing," Glory said and nodded toward my purse.

I dumped the pocketbook onto the table. Keys, lipstick, a comb, pen, tissues, and my wallet. "It's all here," I said.

"Check your billfold and see if your money's still there," Nate suggested.

My money, identification, and plastic flip holder were in my wallet, but the pictures of my mother were missing. I shook the open purse over the table again, but it was empty.

"What are you doing?" Glory asked.

"My pictures are missing."

"Whose photos did you have in there?" Nate asked.

"Just a few snapshots of Mom that I found in a box Glory saved for me."

"I'll go back to Longstreet and look for them," Nate promised.

The room dimmed. A whiff of foul air, and then everything was normal again.

As soon as Nate left, I discreetly took my cell phone with me to the bathroom. I felt paranoid as I locked the door and stuffed a towel under the door trying to keep Glory from hearing me.

"Doug?" I whispered to Apparition Investigations' voice mail. "This is Julie Bates, and I need to talk with you desperately just as soon as possible. Please, please call me back." I gave my number and didn't expect it to be Doug when the phone rang immediately. I figured it would be another hang-up call.

"Hello, Julie, this is Doug Kappa. You happened to catch me between extermination jobs. Did you get the wiring in the house checked out?"

"Yes, he didn't find anything specifically wrong except that it's very old, but I need to talk to you. Now these things are bothering me when I'm not asleep and not in this house. Could it be me that's haunted instead of the house?"

"It could be, but I'm not coming back to your home until a licensed repairman has fixed anything wrong with the electrical system."

"Please," I pleaded. "I'm scared out of my mind. I'll get the electricity updated. I'll call today. I'm sorry I didn't just tell them to fix it when the electrician was here. I don't seem able to deal with anything."

"That could be part of what's wrong. Whatever is causing the problems may be making you lethargic, keeping you from dealing with it. It's a known fact that a person's personality changes when a demon tries to take possession. May make you fussy and irritable, too."

"That might explain why I'm so angry some of the time and cussing. The way I've been behaving isn't like I usually am, but I'd rather think it's anything but a demon causing me to act this way. I really want you to come to the house again. I know you don't charge, but I'll be glad to pay you."

"I know that, but I'm not getting near you or that place again until I know there's not a problem in the electrical system."

"Why?"

"I didn't want to tell you, but when Aeden checked my equipment, he found the circuits and insides of every piece of equipment are fried, melted together. I want to know it's not a physical problem there before I risk my new recorders and cameras." He coughed. "If there's no problem with wiring, you may need a priest instead of an investigator." He coughed again, but this one sounded faked. "I've got to get back to work. Call me after the electrician comes."

"I had Gates come out. Do you know if that's a good company?"

"I don't want to be involved in that. Check the Internet."

"I'm not helpless," I complained to Glory. "I've got cabin fever. I need to go out. The doctor didn't tell me to act like an invalid."

She'd told me she didn't want Gates Electrical to come back because she didn't like their serviceman. I had found the number for another electrical contractor, Clyde Electric, but Glory wasn't satisfied with that suggestion either. She followed me around. She even questioned why I'd stayed in the bathroom so long. I had no intention of telling her that I'd hired a ghost hunter.

We'd just finished lunch. I'd offered to wash the dishes, but Glory had insisted on doing them herself. I was still sitting at the table when I told her I was going out. Glory took on her sullen expression.

"Well, I'm worried about you and that passing out. Nate said the doctor said you were catatonic. That's more than just fainting. What if it happens again?" Add whiny to Glory's poutiness.

"Then I'll go back to the ER. The tests didn't show anything. The doctor said it may have been a freak occurrence that never happens again."

Glory's expression changed to joyful, and she cried out, "Thank you, Jesus!" She smiled at me and said, "I know what we can do!"

"I don't want to watch any more daytime television. I got enough of that in the hospital. I don't see how you stand it."

"I wasn't going to suggest TV. Last Christmas, Juliana gave me a little CD player and bought me some of her favorite CDs. Let's listen to music."

If Mom had bought Glory duplicates of some of her favorite CDs, I knew what most of them would be — Elvis. My mother was a big fan. Her own mother had loved Elvis Presley and collected his memorabilia. Not the collectibles on eBay, but any little junky thing with his picture on it. That obsession had lasted only one additional generation. I didn't *dislike* his music. I just preferred more current recordings.

I gave in. "Okay, but after that, I'm going for a walk."

Glory dropped the dishcloth into the water and

hurried out of the kitchen. When she returned, she'd taken off her wig and her shoes. She brought a portable CD player and a cute, miniature suitcase full of CDs .

While she plugged in an extension cord behind the kitchen counter and spread it to the table where she placed the player, I looked through the recordings. Sure enough, lots of Elvis.

I selected the *Early Elvis* album, volumes I and II, and we sat silently as we listened to them. Not to be disrespectful to The King, but by the time he'd given us over an hour's worth of instructions not to step on his "Blue Suede Shoes," "Don't Be Cruel," and to come on and do "The Jailhouse Rock," I was ready for a change.

Elvis Sings Gospel had lots of songs I remembered my mother and Granny singing when I was little. I handed that one to Glory.

"No, not this," she said and put it back into the case. She handed me the two-disc *Aloha from Hawaii*.

"Put this on, and I'll make us some iced tea."

I did and she did. Finally, Elvis reached the closing song of that concert: "The American Trilogy." This one had been one of Mom's favorites, a medley that started with "Dixie," segued into "Battle Hymn of the Republic," then to "Hush, Little Baby, Don't You Cry."

Elvis had finished "Dixie" and crooned "Look away, look away, look away, Dixieland." The music crescendoed for the "Battle Hymn of the Republic" part, which should have begun with a mighty, "Glory, glory, hallelujah." Instead the music built to a loud, powerful, stuttering screech.

"The disc must be dirty," Glory said as she removed it from the player and wiped it with a cloth. She put it back in and forwarded to the final cut. Again, the music played until it reached the Battle Hymn and then squealed and skidded even worse than before.

I grabbed my purse, snatched the CD, shoved it into the pocketbook and headed for the door.

"Don't you want me to go with you?" Glory asked. "What if you blank out again?"

"Then someone will call an ambulance." I went out the back door as fast as I could before she had time to put on her wig and shoes.

Everything seemed normal as I walked from the back porch, but when I reached the front yard, I saw that my universe was altered again—this time in the bright sunlight of afternoon.

Assembly Street was unpaved. I turned onto Gervais, which had also become a dirt road. These were thoroughfares I was used to being on every day, but they were no longer paved. The South Carolina State Capitol building sat on Gervais—a big, Greek Revival-style building with ten columns and a lot of steps in front as well as a dome on top.

The statues and memorials that I knew decorated

the grounds of the State House had disappeared, and instead of the neatly trimmed green grass, the surrounding fields were filled with rows of corn plants, tall and ready to be harvested. How was I on a dirt road that I knew had been paved for years one minute and in bed the next? Realizing I couldn't possibly be awake, I rolled over and escaped into the world of nightmares.

I fought with all my strength—pushing and shoving the man off me. He laughed and continued thrusting and pounding himself into me, brutally and viciously. The assault felt like forever, and I gave up. Stopped fighting him, knowing that when he finished, he'd probably kill me. Was this the same savage rapist who'd murdered my mother?

Naked and covered with sweat, I awoke. My nightgown lay on the floor beside the bed. Had I taken it off and dropped it to the floor myself? No— not all the wetness on my body was perspiration. Some of it felt slimy. I called out for Glory, but she didn't answer.

Pulling the blanket around me, I went into the bathroom and filled the tub with steamy water, as hot as I could stand. I scrubbed my body with soap— sudsing and rinsing, sudsing and rinsing. When the bath cooled off, I added more hot water and repeated my cleansing ritual. That's what it had become—a ritual of trying to make myself clean after these hallucinations. But were they delusions? The substance on my body had been real, and I hadn't been a virgin for a long time. I knew exactly what that goo had been, and I knew that this had been happening to me night after night during my sleep.

I called out to Glory again, but still no answer. I hadn't brought any clothes into the bathroom, but I didn't even consider wrapping myself in the blanket. I couldn't bear to touch it or have it near me. There was probably *stuff* on it, but how could a nightmare leave a substance? I didn't want to even think about it.

With a towel wrapped around my body, I went through the kitchen to my room where I dressed and then slipped out the back door. I had to get out of there, away from the horror.

Walking down Assembly Street, now paved again, I wished that Richard would appear like he sometimes did or that Nate Adams would just show up. I didn't want to be alone, but, on the other hand, I didn't want to see any of the sinister beings who'd entered my life recently.

I turned onto Gervais Street, and across from the Capitol building, I noticed a drugstore—not a CVS, Walgreens, or new Rite Aid—but an old-fashioned apothecary shop. The hanging bulbs were bright, and I could see a harmless looking man wearing a white pharmacist's jacket behind the counter with rows of jars on shelves behind him. He seemed vaguely familiar and nodded at me when I stepped inside. At the rear of the room, several tiny tables and chairs like I'd seen in pictures of old-fashioned soda shops sat in front of a counter with glass banana split dishes and ice cream dippers.

Taking a seat at the nearest table, I reached into my pocket to see if I had any change with me. I didn't.

An older woman, so petite that her feet didn't reach the floor, sat at one of the tables. She smiled at me from across the way. We were the only two customers in the store. "Good morning," she said.

"Good morning," I answered, though I wasn't sure about the time of day.

"Robert," she addressed the pharmacist. "Please bring this young lady a chocolate fudge sundae. My treat. She looks like she needs energy." The pharmacist moved from behind the drug counter to the soda area.

"Oh, no," I protested, "I couldn't let you do that."

She grinned. "I just saw you check your pockets and find no money. I own this building, and I have a running charge account. Robert is very happy for me to take some of the rent out in treats for myself and my guests."

"I would accept a Diet Coke if you let me meet you here later and pay you back," I conceded.

"Diet Coke?" The lady and Robert said it together. "What's that?" he added.

"If you don't have it, I could drink Diet Pepsi."

"Pepsi?" the soda jerk/pharmacist questioned. "I've heard of Pepsi Cola, but I don't carry that drink, and there's no such thing as diet any kind of soda."

"Make her an Ammonia Coke, Robert. She looks tired and confused. That will perk her right up." She turned toward me. "Come sit here with me, dearie. My name is Alma Estes."

"I'm Julie," I answered and moved to her table.

Robert set a tall, old-fashioned soda glass in front of me.

"You said this was an Ammonia Coke?" I questioned, "Isn't ammonia poison?" Was I in yet another crazy hallucination? Were these people real? If they were, would the drink poison me?

Robert laughed. "Drinking household ammonia, the cleaning substance, would be fatal, but this is Pharmaceutical Aromatic Spirits of Ammonia. It's used to revive fainting spells as well as to create a delightful drink that, like Mrs. Estes says, will probably make you feel better. You do look a little peaked."

I sipped the drink and found it amazingly refreshing.

"Where are you from?" Mrs. Estes asked. I realized that her drink was a float—ice cream with some kind of liquid over it, probably Coca Cola since that seemed to be the only soda Robert carried.

"I grew up in a house down toward the mill, but it burned recently, and now I'm staying with my next-door neighbor until I find a new place."

"Burned? I don't recall anything near the mill burning in a long time, but then," she laughed, "my memory is not as sharp as it once was."

"Where do you live?" I asked.

"Right here. Would you like to see?" She stood.

I gulped down the rest of my drink and followed Mrs. Estes through a door at the back of the drugstore. Was I crazy to follow a strange lady? At the time, it didn't seem to be odd at all. We passed into a kitchen, a very vintage room with linoleum instead of Formica or granite on the countertops and a wooden floor painted dark brown. An old-fashioned white range and refrigerator stood beside a black, cast-iron, wood-burning stove.

The pedestal-based large, round mahogany table was surrounded by six ladder-back chairs pulled up neatly to an embroidered table cloth. A painted stairway in the corner of the room led upstairs. I wondered if this place had been redecorated to achieve the antique appearance or if it had looked like this for years.

"Would you like to see the parlor?" Mrs. Estes asked.

Come into my parlor, said the spider to the fly. I couldn't help thinking of that old line from some story my mother had read or told me as a child.

"I really need to be on my way." I shivered.

"Just for a minute. It's upstairs, and I'm so proud

of my home, but especially the parlor."

I wasn't under a spell, or at least I didn't think that I was, but I felt compelled to follow Mrs. Estes up the steps to a long corridor. The doors were open, and I saw that two of them led to neat rooms with carefully made beds covered with chenille bedspreads and pillows. A third gaped wide to a bathroom with a claw-footed tub. Mrs. Estes led me to the end of the hall, and I followed her into what was certainly a parlor, not a den or living room.

Floral wallpaper in shades of burgundy and rose covered the walls, and wooden floors peeked out around a thick, faded Oriental rug with the same colors. The settee and chairs were ornate and upholstered in brocades and needlepoint. A beautiful roll-top desk stood in the corner. Crocheted table doilies with ruffles starched to make them stand up topped the fireplace mantel and tiny mahogany side tables. Fringed shades ornamented each lamp except one which had a Tiffany-glass cover. Little what-nots and small figurines on every surface glistened without a hint of dust. The room was exquisite, but I shivered again.

"We're over the drugstore now," Mrs. Estes said. "Isn't this room beautiful?"

I nodded, and she continued, "This was my mother's favorite room when the weather was too hot or cold. Come with me, and I'll show you where she sat when the weather was perfect."

Her talk of her mother made me feel safe. We passed through a set of French doors beside the fireplace, and I found myself on a balcony with a waist-high railing. The old-fashioned wicker chairs showed a lot of use, and I imagined that Mrs. Estes still spent a lot of time there.

"Have a seat." We both sat.

The view was toward the corner of the State House grounds.

"I dreamed about this," I said softly.

"My house?"

"No, in my dream, I was looking out at the State House. The view was from this angle, but I don't remember being elevated like this, and . . . " I chuckled, "in my silly dream, the land around the State House was covered with corn."

"Shucked corn?" She looked interested. "Or corn in the husks loaded on wagons?"

"No, corn plants growing, planted in rows like on farms."

"You probably read about that in school. During the Civil War era, corn was actually grown on the State House grounds. My grandparents told me about it."

"Did they live here then?"

"Oh, no, this house is old, but not that old." She leaned closer to me. "Was the dream scary?"

My reaction must have shown on my face. "I asked if your dreams frighten you," she said a little louder.

I remained silent.

"Well, do they?" she questioned.

"Yes," and I told her about the dreams and about my mother's death. Mrs. Estes was so easy to talk to that I told her the other things that had been happening — unreal events and people.

Mrs. Estes said hardly a word as I described the vampire at The Big Apple and the shooting at the Owens Hotel. I hadn't even told Glory about these things, but for some reason, I was relaxed telling Mrs. Estes.

"There's a good chance that your dreams are coming from your mental health and your unresolved feelings about your mother being killed, but it wouldn't hurt to take out some 'insurance.'"

"What do you mean?"

"There are defenses against vampires — such things as holy water, crosses, garlic, and the most deadly of all, a stake through the heart."

"I think they were dreams. Do you think I might be haunted?" *If they were dreams, is this a dream?* I wondered.

"I don't know, but I do know that you've described an old hotel I went to as a child. It was torn down a long time ago, but I recall my mother telling me that a woman named Billie Long caught her husband in there with another woman. Everyone laughed and said Johnny was lucky Billie was such a bad shot. Otherwise, he would never have had children."

The man in my dream or vision had been shot in the knee.

"Perhaps you're psychic. Have you had any reason before to think you might have the 'sight' or extrasensory abilities?" Mrs. Estes said.

"No, but I've had other horrible dreams, too." I told her about waking drenched and trembling most of the time even though I couldn't remember anything. Telling about it, I realized what I'd been experiencing—nightly rapes. The face of a man rose in my mind. I described it to her.

"Is this man someone you know?"

"No, he's very handsome and muscular but I've never seen him except in the nightmares. He hurts me."

"This could also be coming from stress or you could be suffering from the visits of an incubus."

"What's that?"

"A male demon who seduces women in their sleep, arousing them, and then having intercourse with their sleeping victims."

"I'm never aroused. There's no kind of foreplay or efforts to make it easier for me. The whole thing is brutal. If it's an incubus, will the garlic, holy water, and crosses keep him away? I know he's very strong, so I don't think I'd ever be able to drive a stake through his heart."

"An incubus is a demon, so I don't know about the effectiveness of garlic, but since the holy water and crosses are symbols of good, and a demon is evil, they might help. I'm getting tired, but I have something to give you." She stood. "Come with me."

I followed her back into the parlor where she opened the top of the beautiful roll-top desk. She handed me a heavy cloth sack with a pull string at the top drawn tight and tied into a knot. "Sit here," she said. We sat side by side on the settee.

"What's this?" I asked. I pulled the cord and peeked in at an old-fashioned gun.

"It belonged to Papa, and it's loaded with a solid silver bullet, but it's a single-shot weapon, so don't waste it. My father gave it to me, and I haven't ever needed it for all these years, so I want you to have it. I don't know what it might do to a demon, and I don't think it will kill a vampire, but silver does slow down all things evil and the damage a silver bullet does to a vampire may not kill it, but the wound will take forever to heal."

"How do you know all this?"

"My father was a necromancer."

My eyes must have bugged out. "A what?" I asked.

"Necromancer."

"Isn't that someone who loves on dead people?"

Mrs. Estes laughed. "No, not at all. You're thinking of a necrophiliac. That's someone who is sexually attracted to dead people. My father was a *necromancer*. That means he practiced a kind of magic that involved communicating with the dead, either by calling up their spirits in apparitions or by actually raising the dead."

"Why?"

"He and his cronies thought they could foretell the future from communicating with dead spirits. Sometimes they accidentally called up evil entities, so he kept things that could be used to protect our family. This gun with the silver bullet is something he bought to protect us. Most people who study this stuff know that a silver bullet is supposed to kill a werewolf, but silver has other powers against evil, too. Take the gun, but be careful. Only use that one bullet when you know it's necessary."

We sat silently for several minutes. She seemed to be having trouble keeping her eyes open, so I stood.

"Thank you so much, Mrs. Estes. I feel better just telling someone what's been happening to me. I'll come by tomorrow and pay you for my Ammonia Coke."

"Don't worry about that. Just take care of yourself." She suddenly sat up straighter. "Salt," she said. "Salt. I don't know for sure about an incubus, but salt is known to protect. Pour salt on the floor all around your bed—a steady stream with no breaks in it."

"Regular table salt?"

"I guess that will work, but sea salt is better." My mind immediately thought of going back to Glory's for my wallet and heading to the Publix for several boxes of sea salt.

"Can you let yourself out?" Mrs. Estes asked.

"Yes, ma'am."

"I think I'm going to have a little nap right now. Just go out through the pharmacy."

Unable to resist myself, I leaned over and gave her a little hug. By the time I reached the stairs at the end of the hall, I heard her snoring softly.

25

THE PUBLIX Richard preferred was within walking distance of the area he usually frequented, but that wasn't the only reason he liked the store. Being in the general vicinity of the university, there were always students as well as people of academia there. Richard identified with the professors and liked looking at pretty girls anytime and anyplace.

He was standing in the wine section trying to select an inexpensive wine, not that Richard preferred cheap wine. He was heading down to the caves later, and he'd found that any kind of alcohol loosened tongues and brought good interviews for his book. Sometimes he considered splurging and buying the guys a quality vino, but that could blow his cover.

Julie's red hair caught his eye. Stooped down in front of the spice display looking at the bottom shelf, her position was ladylike. She wasn't bending—more like little kids stoop on their heels. From Richard's view, her behind looked fantastically firm and round. He wanted to reach out and touch it, but he knew better. *Better keep those thoughts under wraps. Plenty of time to try to court her after this book,* he thought.

Richard stepped closer and said, "What'cha looking for?"

Her whole body jerked in surprise.

"Didn't mean to scare you," he said.

"It's okay." She lost her balance as she stood holding two containers and trying to lift her tote. He reached out and took her arm to steady her.

Gotta quit touching her or I'll be wanting to get back to regular life before my research is complete. Aloud, he asked, "What are you getting?"

"Sea salt to put around my bed. Do you think two boxes will be enough?"

"Probably. Depends on how thick you make that protection line. Want me to help you?"

She laughed, and it was a happy, pleasant sound not at all like the anxious woman she seemed to be most of the time.

"I can do it. Glory was civil to you having coffee with us in the kitchen, but I doubt seriously if she would want you in there shaking anything around the bed."

"Can I walk you home?" The words were hardly out of his mouth before they both laughed.

"I sound like a kid," Richard said and then mimicked in a little boy voice, "I'll carry your books if you let me." He grinned.

"I appreciate anything that makes me laugh these days, but the answer is no. You can't walk me home, but step outside with me a minute. I want to show you something."

They both checked out. Julie paid with a twenty.

Staying true to his homeless disguise, Richard counted out ones and coins. When they'd passed through the automatic doors, Julie stepped over to the corner and held open her tote bag. Richard peered into it at an antique hand gun.

"Where'd you get that?" he asked.

"I'll tell you later, but it's loaded with a silver bullet, and I'm going straight home to put out the salt. I feel safer."

"You've been saying you think everything's all nightmares and hallucinations. If that's so, what made you decide to protect yourself this way?"

"Not anymore. Someone gave me the gun in a nightmare. If everything's a delusion, this gun shouldn't be here, but it's real and it didn't go away when the dream ended. Touch it."

He did.

"That proves that it's not all in my mind. See you later."

As she turned to leave, Richard cautioned, "Hide it from Glory."

Julie headed toward her house with her gun and two cylinder-shaped containers of sea salt in her tote bag.   Richard walked off in the opposite direction with two bottles of rotgut in a paper sack.

26

POURING A stream of salt around my bed would surely have looked funny if somebody had been watching, but I was alone. Or at least, I didn't think anyone was there with me. I had that strange feeling I get when I'm being observed, but when I turned around, I saw no one, not even a shadow.

I didn't know where Glory had gone, but I was glad she wasn't home. The salt made me feel like I was finally being proactive to help myself instead of just enduring whatever came my way, but I had no idea how I would explain it to her.

When I finished, it looked fine except that the bag with the gun inside lay on top of the bed. I stepped across the salt, tucked the gun between the bed springs and mattress, then pushed it way back toward the center of the bed.

Thump! Glory had told me that this house had always had strange noises. She thought it could be shifting and settling of the boards, so she'd ignored the clatter. If the house was structurally that unsound, it should be falling in on our heads. I didn't accept Glory's explanation.

The noise came from the direction of my bedside table. I glanced over there and saw that the framed picture of my mother had once again been moved. That happened frequently, and I still thought Glory was responsible. She'd been very close to Mom. I believed she took the picture in her room when I was out and then forgot to put it back before I came home. She didn't tell me because she didn't want to confess that she bothered my belongings. My Bible was missing off the top of the stack of books on that table, too. Had Glory borrowed it? Fine if she had, but I wished she'd tell me when she messed with my things.

When I heard the second *thump*, I was straightening the pillows on the bed. The racket didn't come from a wall. It was the sound of the bedside table moving. Jumping all by itself out of my salt loop around the bed. It looked and sounded as if someone picked up the table and set it right outside the circle, not placing it on the floor, but plopping it down. Even with all I'd been through, I didn't think a piece of furniture could be angry, but that table moved like it was furious that I'd enclosed it in my sodium ring of protection.

I grabbed my purse and ran like hell.

Freaked out, I ran aimlessly. Finally, I sat on a bench at a bus stop to catch my breath. I don't know how long I sat there before I could think at all. How could Mrs. Estes be part of a dream if the gun still existed? It hadn't disappeared. The experience hadn't been scary at all, but everything had been so old-fashioned — far too out of date. The gun was solid. I could touch it, hold it in my hand, and Richard had seen it and touched it, too. I looked up and realized I was in front of the pharmacy and soda shop where I'd met Mrs. Estes.

As before, I could see into the drugstore. Robert stood behind the pharmaceutical counter. When I went up to him, he leaned forward toward me. He looked amazingly like someone I'd seen before, but I still couldn't identify the memory.

"May I help you?" he asked.

"Remember me? I'm Julie. I was in here earlier with you and Mrs. Estes."

"Mrs. Estes?" His expression didn't change.

"Yes, the lady who lives behind and above the store." I motioned toward where the door had been, but the wall appeared solid with no opening.

"I believe you're mistaken. Mrs. Estes has been gone for years. The door between here and her home was sealed when her place was rented out. The only way back there now is through a door on the side."

"How do I get there?"

"Go out front, and you'll see an alley to your

right. Walk down there. The door will be on your left. Knock on it."

I followed his instructions. The alley was narrow and dark, not nearly wide enough for a car or truck. I found a door and knocked, but no one came. More hallucination. When would the gun Mrs. Estes gave me disappear? I knew it would because none of my dreams were real. Nothing was real. I expected the pharmacy and ice cream parlor would be gone when I returned to Gervais Street, but it wasn't. Robert still stood in the same place. I waved, but he didn't acknowledge me. On my way back to Glory's house, I realized who he looked like — the bartender in the original *The Shining* movie when he served Jack Torrance.

I WALKED down Gervais Street and crossed Assembly. Oppression and guilt overpowered me when I realized how much I hated the idea of spending the rest of the day in that house with Glory secretly moving my things around and denying all the noises I heard. *But what if Glory isn't moving things?* I thought. *She damned sure didn't move my table.* If I went home, I'd have to explain the salt, and I no longer believed in its power. An abrupt pain pierced my head just as I experienced a wave of complete and total nausea so severe that I leaned over a nearby litter receptacle and threw up.

I hadn't looked to see what was in the barrel, but it smelled putrid. *Throwing up in it isn't going to improve the aroma,* I thought. Another even fiercer rush of nausea flooded over me and I leaned forward again.

Something was moving down there at the bottom. Between bursts of retching, I saw motion. I leaned further into the container, and a black paw reached up and scratched me. I was too surprised to even scream. It was dark in there, but I thought I saw an animal, possibly a cat. *It has no face,* my mind told me.

I felt a touch on my shoulder and whirled around prepared to run.

"Are you all right?" Richard asked.

"I'm tossing my cookies right out here in public. Do you think I'm all right?"

"Ohhh, you're in a bad mood. Did you eat something that disagreed with you?" He pulled a wad of paper napkins from his jacket pocket and wiped my cheek. When he pulled his hand away, both it and the napkins had streaks of fresh blood on them.

"*Life* disagrees with me right now. Either I'm crazy or the whole world is possessed. My stomach is upset, and there's a cat or something in there that just scratched me." I pointed at the litter receptacle. "And I want to tell you something else. You've got to stop sneaking up behind me and touching me. You scare me when you do that. Speak first."

"Sorry." He hesitated, and then added, "You're not accusing me of stalking you, are you?"

"No, I realize that if you live on the streets, you're out here a lot, but with all that's happening, I'm startled and frightened when you touch me without warning."

"Then I'll stop it because I don't want to make you uncomfortable. Will that make you feel better?"

"Yes."

"Want me to help you get back to the house?"

"No." I thought about it. "What I'd like to do is go back for my car and drive out to my mother's grave. The vandalism I saw last time should be repaired by now. If it hasn't been, I want to have a word with the manager."

"Are you sure you feel up to that? You'll have to drive. I have a license, but I don't have it with me."

"Actually, I want to know what's in that can. If it's some kind of wild animal, I might need to see a doctor about rabies." I thought about it a minute. "Can you catch that from a scratch or does it have to be a bite?"

"I don't know, but I don't think we should take that chance."

Richard walked around the litter barrel. "Checking for a hole," he explained. "Some way for an animal to get in or out of there."

"Did you see anything? Is there an opening on the side?"

"Nope. Whatever's in there went in through the top."

"I don't know any way to force that animal to come to the top."

"I do," he said.

Richard looked both ways. The street wasn't crowded, and there were no law enforcement men or women in sight. He simply lifted the container up and dumped it right on the edge of the road, just beyond the sidewalk.

"Better for people to drive through it than step in it," he said.

Lots of paper trash fell out along with the remnants of what I'd eaten, but no animal.

"Are you certain there wasn't a stick poking up that scratched you?" His question offended me. I *saw* a furry arm reach for me.

"Do you see a stick or anything sharp in that mess?"

"No."

"Maybe it's my imagination again."

"That bloody scratch on your face is not your imagination."

RICHARD AND I walked to Glory's house. The thought of going back in there terrified me. We made it to the car before she opened the front door, stepped on the porch, and called out, "Where are you going?"

"I'm going to see my mother," I answered.

"Can I go?"

"Maybe next time."

I put the car in drive and we pulled away before she had time to turn the question into a long discussion.

When we drove up to the big wrought iron gates with "Resting in Peace" over the top, I felt more at ease than I had since the nightmares began. I knew the physical body in that fancy box six feet below no longer held the real essence or spirit of my mother, but I felt going there would comfort me. We were winding through the road to the Garden of Gethsemane where Mama and Daddy were buried before I thought about flowers.

"I should have stopped and bought a bouquet to put on the grave," I told Richard.

"We'll bring some flowers next time or we can go back to the florist now."

"I feel compelled to go directly to the cemetery," I said. "I'll bring roses next time."

As we rounded the curve into the Garden of Gethsemane section, I noticed a crowd of people up ahead, in the vicinity of my parents' burial places. When we reached them, I saw that some were watching while others worked with shovels.

The grave they were digging was my mother's.

I slammed on the brakes and stopped the Focus right in the middle of the road without even pulling over to the side. I jumped out and ran toward the diggers.

"What are you doing?" I bellowed to no one in particular. The manager I'd seen before rushed over as fast as he could waddle.

"Miss Bates, I'm so sorry for you to see this. I was going to call you when everything's repaired."

"What happened?" Richard asked.

"We found this burial had been tampered with, probably during the night but it could have been later today. Nobody saw it until a couple of hours ago."

"What do you mean—disturbed?" Richard did the questioning. I was speechless.

"It appears that someone has been digging into the earth." He pointed. "Just on Mrs. Epps' side. Her husband's space was untouched. We're filling it back in." He turned toward me. "I've also ordered that the ground be sodded tomorrow."

I finally caught my breath enough to speak. "Did they dig up my mother's coffin?"

"No, it appears they didn't get deep enough to even touch the vault or casket."

"*Appears?*" Richard jumped back into the conversation. "What did you people do? Just fill it in from however you found it? This grave needs to be opened enough to be sure no one has removed her mother's body." He turned toward me and grasped my hand. The next words were to me, not the pony-tailed manager. "I know that's hard to think of, but it's the important thing now. Someone could have gone into the casket and been interrupted before they finished refilling the grave."

Ponytail stared at Richard's shabby clothing. "Sir, I don't know who you are, but this is really none of your business. To dig deeper and open this grave, we would have to get a bunch of legal permits. I'm sure Miss Bates wants her mother's grave restored as quickly as possible."

I looked him straight in the face and said, "*Sir*, I want to see that my mother hasn't been disturbed. It won't take much more digging to do that, but I don't care how many permits you need or how many newspaper reporters have to be standing here watching. If you cover the grave now, I'm going to call my policeman friend, and he'll get things started."

Ponytail mumbled something, then called, "Come here, Gene," summoning an exceptionally tall man who'd been watching, not digging.

"Yes, sir?" Gene answered.

"Have those men clear out the opening down to the casket and move the vault lid. The person buried here is this young lady's mother, and she wants to see that she hasn't been disturbed. Don't try to bring the casket up, just get it where you can lift the top and let her take a peek."

"Are you sure? Don't we have to get legal permission to open after interment?"

"Not if no one sees but the people here right now."

Richard and Ponytail both insisted that I sit in my car until they were ready for me. I'd thought Richard would stay with me, but he stood right by the pit and watched as they dug and then manhandled the vault lid out of the way. Several men climbed down into the earth, out of sight from my view point.

Richard walked to the car and slid into the passenger seat. I'd expected him to come get me, tell me I could go look. He didn't. I thought my biggest dread had been realized. *Someone stole my mother's body.*

"Let's go," he said. "Everything's okay."

"What do you mean everything's okay? Is my mother still in her casket?" I asked.

"Yes. It doesn't seem that whoever opened the grave got as deep as the coffin or the vault."

"I want to see my mother!" I opened my car door. The funeral had been closed casket and I hadn't seen her after her death. Now I wanted to be sure that the body in that grave was Mom.

The last time I'd been there, the skies were cloudy and dumping rain on me. On this day, the sun shone brightly. I probably should have insisted on seeing my mother when I came home after her murder. The funeral director had advised me it would be better to remember her as she was before her death, and I'd followed his suggestion, but I'd doubted and sometimes regretted that decision.

Standing beside her open grave, looking down, I saw that the funeral home had wrapped white gauze around her head. I knelt and leaned in, but I couldn't reach her. The tall man that Ponytail had called Gene asked, "What are you doing?"

"I want the bandage off. I want to see her face to know it's her."

"If that's what you want," he said, "but it's been a year. You need to be prepared that even embalmed bodies change after burial." He stepped into the grave, and bent on his knees on the unopened half of the casket lid, the part that covered my mother from her waist down. He leaned over and carefully lifted her head, unwound the wrappings, and tossed them out of the grave. When he was done, a tumble of red hair framed my mother's face, still beautiful to me though in bright sunlight, I could see that the mortician had tried unsuccessfully to cover bruising and cuts, and reduced swelling that had oozed liquid onto the gauze. I understood why the funeral director hadn't wanted me to see her, but it was obvious that he'd done his best even not expecting anyone to ever view his work. She wore the sage green dress I'd bought when I came home, and her nails were manicured and polished. I felt more peace than I had since that horrible phone call from the police to New York months ago.

27

MY CAR still had that wonderful new-car smell. When I rolled up the windows and locked the doors after I dropped Richard off, I felt safe and secure driving alone. He'd protested when I took him back to Assembly Street and insisted I wanted to be alone after we'd watched them fill in Mom's grave.

I'd told him about some of the places I'd been in the dreams, nightmares, delusions, or whatever — probably hauntings — I'd experienced, but not all. I intended to look for them, and I wasn't afraid to do it by myself. I drove up Hampton Street and parked right in front of the Historic Columbia Foundation's plaque at The Big Apple. The wooden structure and metal gabled roof were the same as where I'd seen the vampire, but to me it was a different place. The neat gray and white building didn't summon any of the emotions I would have had if that shabby old yellow nightclub stood there.

Research had shown me that university students *had* watched the young African Americans dancing in the thirties and spread their moves to New York and the world just as my nightmare had insinuated. Nate's mother had even confirmed that the previous location of the synagogue on Park Street had been called Gates Street years before. But, nowhere in literature or on the Internet was there any mention that the place was haunted, much less housed a vampire.

From there, I drove up to Main Street. The Columbia skyline displays several downtown high-rise buildings, and they're part of the uniqueness of my hometown. Beautiful restored two and three-story southern mansions built in the 1800s coexist with modern construction. The banks, government buildings, art museum, and hotels are as contemporary as they can be, but Main Street shows an attempt, years ago, before I moved to New York, to create a small-town atmosphere. The plan included reducing the street from four lanes and planting small trees along both sides of the street. The trees have grown so large they overpower the two-lane street with its inlaid brick strip running smack down the middle.

I parked on Main directly across from the S. C. State Capitol building. I certainly didn't see any evidence that cornstalks had ever covered the plot of land now filled with numerous old trees, lush green grass, statues, and memorials. In the shadow of the stately Greek Revival structure, an elderly lady sat on a bench with a bag of birdseed. She tossed the seeds to the pigeons with hands twisted and crippled from arthritis. A black metal walking cane leaned against the bench touching the brown paper sack beside her.

The poor old thing was almost a caricature from the top of her hat to the soles of her unlaced brogans. The multicolored stocking cap was pulled down to her eyebrows and touched the top of her eyeglasses, which had been repaired with masking tape on the nosepiece. Frizzy brown hair streaked with gray bushed out on both sides. A black shawl draped her shoulders over a shapeless brown wool dress that barely touched her swollen knees. Rolled-up red and white Pippi Longstocking socks distracted my eyes from the scuffed shoes but not enough to make me miss the fact that there was a hole in the leather over her left big toe allowing the sock to show.

I remembered my class visiting the State House when I was in grammar school. After we looked at the bronze stars marking places where artillery from Sherman's cannons struck the Capitol when he invaded Columbia and set fire to many buildings, including the Capitol, we'd fed the pigeons, too. I didn't remember seeing black pigeons back then. Several of the birds crowded around the woman were black but still looked like pigeons, not blackbirds, ravens, or crows.

My childhood was a time of peace and love. That must be what prompted me to unlock my car doors, get out, slide several quarters into the parking meter, and cross the street. Strange that walking around the building so many years later, looking at stars commemorating war, calmed me into a childlike serenity after what had happened. When I reached the front again, I sat on the bench beside the woman feeding pigeons. She looked at me as though I intruded into her space though there was at least two feet of space between us. I scooted so far to the edge that my fanny was hanging off the seat.

"Beautiful day, isn't it?" I attempted to start a conversation—anything to make me not think about that bedside table or my mother in the coffin.

"Not to me. All the ghosts hanging around here are spoiling it."

Crap! Of all the people downtown, I sit by a kook. Or is she? Maybe she sees in daytime what I've been seeing after midnight.

"What do you mean?" I tried to sound interested, not nosy.

"You probably don't see anything. Most people don't, but I do. The spirits of soldiers from the Civil War run all over this place sometimes. Today, a lot of them are chopping corn."

"What do you mean by chopping corn?" I asked,

"You see it, don't you? There's a crop of cornstalks right over there." She pointed to her left, east of where we sat. "This whole area is full of haunts." She smiled a toothless grin before adding, "My name is Frannie," and thrust out a twisted, liver-spotted hand.

As we shook, I said, "I'm Julie."

"I know." *Strange answer,* I thought. *I've never seen her before.*

She emptied the bag of birdseed on the ground in front of us and stuffed the cellophane bag into the paper grocery sack. "Let's go for a walk, Julie."

I hoped she didn't want to go all the way around the block. I had an idea that those knobby knees and walking cane meant it would be a slow stroll. *But she might be a medium or something like that woman Nate and I saw at the restaurant. She says she sees ghosts. Maybe she can help me understand what's happening in my life.* In the past, I would have thought she was crazy, but not after what I'd gone through since I found Jerry Patterson dead on the sidewalk.

Frannie pointed to the west. "If we walk that way," she said, "we'll reach the Vista, an 'in' section with fake gaslights and shadowy alleyways. Have you seen the Adluh Flour Mill sign on the side of the building?"

I nodded yes.

"A longtime Adluh employee named Jerome Busbee, who they said practiced voodoo, watches over the warehouse. After his death, the cart he'd used to carry materials couldn't be moved, frozen in place by Busbee's spirit. When the living workers tried to move the wagon, it fell over. It's still in there, lying on its side. Some say that's a legend, but I've seen Busbee in that building."

"I've heard lots of ghost stories about Columbia, but I never heard that one."

"Oh, they hear footsteps and doors shutting and all kinds of sounds in the old buildings in the Vista. The difference is that when I go in those buildings, I see what's causing the noises."

"Are you a medium?"

"No, I'm just an old lady who's been seeing spirits since I was a baby."

"Do they frighten you?"

"No, they annoy me." She pointed east. "Come this way, and I'll show you more."

We walked to the end of the block and crossed Sumter Street. It took a while because Frannie limped slowly even with her cane. On the corner of Sumter and Gervais, a black wrought-iron fence enclosed the churchyard around Trinity Episcopal Cathedral. Mom and I had visited there several times, and I used to call it "the pink church," though now the stucco exterior looked more buff-colored than pink.

"Have you ever been in the graveyard?" Frannie asked.

"No, I've been in the church though."

Frannie sensed my hesitation and said, "Just stay with me."

I followed her into the cemetery with more kinds of markers than I'd ever seen in my life. Small stand-up headstones no more than two feet above the foot markers identified the graves of infants and children. Most of them were so old that they were now smooth where the engraving had worn off. Beside them stood towering monuments — some of them twelve to fifteen feet tall. The grounds were crowded with old graves going back to the early 1800s. I was standing by one with a death date of 1825, but I noticed a few modern flat bronze markers.

Drawn to the ones that had slabs of concrete or stone the size of the graves lying flat over them, I thought of unwrinkled heavy blankets protecting the dead. Some were engraved with only a name, dates of birth and death, and maybe family relationships such as Beloved Wife of So and So. Others were filled with as much biography as could be etched in the space available.

The burials that fascinated me even more were elevated grave-size concrete, stone, or brick boxes sitting on top of the ground. Their flat tops were inscribed with names, dates, relationships, and accomplishments. I wondered if the caskets were inside those boxes or below ground. Many of the older ones had cracked and been filled with concrete. A few had fissures and holes that weren't yet patched. I wondered if I'd see an old, deteriorating casket if I peeked in there, but I was scared to try it.

A little sign warned visitors not to sit on walls, graves, or markers and to be careful walking as some of the bricks in the walkways might be loose. I didn't see any of that, but a gigantic oak tree's roots had grown under part of the brick walkway causing it to roll up and down like a miniature roller coaster. On the other side of the tree, roots had shifted one of the above ground boxes so that it tilted against the tree and had an open gap that had obviously already been repaired with concrete but had split again.

Low brick walls separated specific family plots. On the side nearest Gervais Street, more wrought-iron fencing set apart a section filled with graves. Frannie hobbled over to the black gate and opened it.

"Come see this," she called.

We went inside together where she pointed out several old graves and commented, "There are three illustrious Wade Hamptons buried here." She pointed to one of those large boxes. "This one was the first and was a celebrated general during the Revolutionary War. There was a Hampton in the Revolutionary War, the War of 1812, and the Civil War. Their wives, children, and other relatives lie beside and near them."

I stepped around, bending over to read inscriptions.

"Have you ever heard of Jimmy Byrnes?" Frannie asked.

"Name is vaguely familiar."

"In your schoolbooks, he was probably called James F. Byrnes and described as a statesman. He and Henry Timrod, the poet, lie here along with senators, governors, and distinguished generals as well as people you'll never hear of unless you read the inscriptions on their tombstones." I couldn't help wondering if Frannie was a retired history teacher.

She pointed to another grave. "This is the Wade Hampton III who served as a general in the Civil War." She grinned. "It's said that just before World War I, a large ghostly figure was seen on horseback riding around the Capitol. I've seen him. It was General Wade Hampton III wearing his Civil War uniform, arriving to warn citizens that war was coming. Sometimes he still rides in the sky."

"You say you saw him?"

Is Frannie disturbed in her head or is she messing with mine? Or could it be that she's telling the truth?

"Oh, many times," she assured me and wiped her nose on her sleeve. "Some ghost stories are true. I've seen them. Others? I have doubts about them."

She pointed across the street to a skyscraper with a bank name on it. "You'll hear about the fanatical southern lady rebel ghost over there. She supposedly hated the Union soldiers so much that people who wear the blue of their uniforms in that building are likely to be pushed, shoved, or have something thrown at them. I don't believe that tale because I've been in there at all times of the day and night, and

I've never seen her."

"So you believe in the generals haunting this yard and the Capitol but not in the woman across the street?" I asked.

"Yes, some things are real, Julie. Some things are not. Many people have seen the generals buried here rise at night, but what I hear here at night are the children crying and sometimes your mother comes here though her grave's not here. She cries over you, Julie. She cries for you."

"Are *you* real?" I asked.

She laughed and spread her arms out wide beside her. "What do you think?"

Broad daylight. Standing in a small cemetery with the sun outlining the Gothic spires of the church, she *disappeared* right in front of me. Not a wisp of smoke or any other dramatic trappings. Vanished completely.

I realized my actions would have looked bizarre if anyone were watching. I paced around the tree, peering at it from all angles and looking behind gravestones. Frannie was gone. I got out of there myself. Dashed up the street to the bench where I'd met her. I dropped to my knees and examined the ground—no sign of any birdseed. But then, maybe the pigeons had eaten it all while Frannie and I were at the church.

Thinking, hoping, Frannie would re-appear, I parked myself on that bench and waited at least an hour. No sign of her. When a slight drizzle began, I crossed the street and sat in my car—watching the rain and thinking about the unbelievable things that kept happening.

28

WHEN I finally switched on the car, put it in gear, and turned off Main Street onto Gervais, I looked at the big building on the corner of Gervais and Assembly, but whatever had been there — apothecary, pharmacy, drugstore, or ice cream parlor — it no longer existed. No alley either. One of the tallest buildings in Columbia took up the entire corner where I'd sat on the porch of Mrs. Estes' apartment looking across the street at the State House.

Stop being stupid, I told myself. *The gun is real. It didn't disappear when I woke up. I don't know how far back in time I traveled to meet Mrs. Estes, but she exists. Somewhere, somehow, she lives. I don't know where Frannie went, but she's real, too. Something's happening to me. I'm not schizophrenic or psychotic. Evil is causing all this.*

Rather than upset myself even more with my thoughts, I turned on the radio, hoping for some soothing music, but neither country nor rock settled me, and I was in no mood for pop or classical.

My mother! I felt like a little girl who wanted her mommy. Recently, I'd sometimes tried to block memories of my mom because, inevitably, they led to thoughts of her dying which led to mental visions of what Nate had told me — that my sweet mother had been raped and brutalized. She hadn't looked gruesome in her casket, but memories of the bruises and abrasions visible through the mortuary makeup brought tears that stabbed my eyes like needles. I opened my purse for a tissue.

Elvis! The CD was still in there. His photo wearing the fancy white jumpsuit with bell bottom pants on the *Aloha from Hawaii* case in my purse took me back to one of those out-of-body flashbacks. I saw my mother mopping the kitchen floor. She was playing her portable player and singing along with it. Occasionally, she'd stop and do a few dance steps to the music. She had a big smile on her face. Elvis always brought Mama to my mind in a comforting way. She loved that man though she'd never seen him except on television.

Dancing in my seat while I drove probably wasn't any safer than using a cell phone or texting, but it brightened my spirits as I listened to "C C Rider" and "Burning Love." I hit the forward arrow and jumped tracks over to "The American Trilogy." After living in New York, I almost felt guilty that I loved the song "Dixie" so much, but it had been one of my mother's favorites. I fully expected the CD to start skipping and stuttering when Elvis hit the "Battle Hymn of the Republic" part and tried to sing "Glory, glory, hallelujah."

It didn't happen. Elvis sang the whole song without any static at all.

I kept reversing the CD so that Elvis sang "American Trilogy" over and over. The CD wasn't scratched or damaged. There was no problem listening to it in the car. It just wouldn't play at the house. *It's not me; it's the house,* I told myself. *There's something evil in Glory's house. I have to get out of there. Maybe go back to New York, but what about her? I can't just run away and leave Glory to deal with whatever is haunting or possessing her home.*

While I drove around thinking, the CD kept playing Elvis. I smiled when the intro to "Suspicious Minds" played. That had been another one of Mom's favorites. I heard the words in my mind:

> *We're caught in a trap*
> *I can't walk out*
> *Because I love you too much, Baby*

That's how Elvis sang it when he was alive. I knew that for a fact because I grew up listening to that song—over and over. I was stopped at a red light when Elvis' voice blasted out of the car speakers:

You're caught in a trap
You can't walk out
Because it won't let you, Julie

I pulled over and stopped the car on the side of the road. My life had been hell while the attacks were confined to midnights when I slept. Now whoever, *whatever*, produced these horrors was attacking me in broad daylight while I was wide awake.

Reaching for the CD player to turn it off, I found myself unable to move. Whatever had taken over Elvis' voice immobilized me. In my mind, a white car trimmed in blue with the gold logo for city police skidded around me, swerving wildly as it went into a spin that landed it against the concrete abutment beside the road. The crash of the impact was deafening as the front end of the car crumpled like an accordion.

LOOK WHAT YOU DID. YOUR NOSINESS CAUSED THIS.

The words came through my car's sound system, but they were no longer Elvis Presley. Loud yet guttural — filled with hate — they released me from the paralysis. I looked around. There was no accident. People and traffic moved along the street through their lives, unaware of the terror inside my car. *Or is the horror in my mind?* I had to speak to Nate. Had I seen his car in a horrible accident or was it another police car or just a delusion?

I'd put Nate's number on speed dial, but I didn't get an answer when I tried over and over to reach him. I wished I was back in New York—anywhere but here. I wanted to still be engaged to Greg, to be close to him like we'd been a few years back— intimate beyond a physical relationship. I *had* to talk to somebody, tell someone about the horrible fear that overwhelmed me. What would Greg say if I called and told him about the hell I was living through down here? Had he married his new girlfriend yet? Would she let him talk to me? *I really am going nuts,* I told myself, but added, *or I'm just that desperate.*

If Nate didn't answer this time, I'd call Greg at work, hope he'd at least listen. I pressed speed dial for Nate one more time.

"Hello?" A female voice, but young, probably not his mother. I didn't hang up. I couldn't care less if it was someone he was seeing romantically. I wasn't in love with Nate.

"May I speak to Officer Nate Adams?" I asked.

"Ummm, not right now." She sounded hesitant. "Are you his daughter or a relative?"

"No, just a friend," I said. "Could I leave a message?" *His daughter? I didn't know Nate had a child.*

"Well, not really." Another pause. "Who are you?"

"Julie Bates."

"Are you that girl whose mother was murdered last year?"

"Yes, but I'm almost thirty, hardly a girl."

"I'm a forensics tech. I have Lieutenant Adams' phone and other personal effects."

I gasped. Personal effects? That sounded like police talk on television when someone's dead.

"I shouldn't say anything, but he's said so much about you, I don't think he'll mind if I tell you what we know. Officer Adams is in surgery at the county hospital. He was involved in a car accident."

"What happened?"

"I don't think I should tell you anything more, really shouldn't have answered his phone nor told you this much." She disconnected before I could thank her.

The hospital was only a few minutes away. I parked in a no-parking zone and ran through the main entrance to the info desk. The man there wouldn't tell me whether Officer Nate Adams of the city police department was in the hospital or not. Wouldn't tell me if his surgery was over. Something about privacy policies, but he did give me directions to get to the surgical waiting area. Stepping from the elevator, I saw two uniformed policemen standing nearby. I slipped into the chair closest to them and eavesdropped on their conversation.

"Makes no sense, you know what I mean?" the blond man said.

"No, it doesn't," the other one, an African American, answered. "Why in hell would Adams drive straight into the concrete wall under the I-20 highway bridge? It's not as if the traffic was wall-to-wall like it is on I-26 in the mornings and afternoons."

"I wonder if a bee stung him or something like that, you know what I mean? Something triggered that crash, and the doctors have already said there's no sign that he had a heart attack or stroke."

"Didn't one witness say she thought she saw someone in the car with him?"

"Yes, she said that, but Adams was alone when they finally got him out of the cruiser with the Hurst Jaws of Life. That vehicle is way too smashed for anyone to have climbed out before emergency services arrived, you know what I mean?" He looked at his watch. "Guess I'd better get out of here and back on the job."

"Detective Corley should arrive any minute with Adams' mother. Corley interviewed the neighbors when Mrs. Adams wasn't home — tracked her down at the salon having her hair done. The old lady's going to be a basket case."

"Of course, she is. That's how mothers are, you know what I mean?"

"She's very close to her son. When her health began declining, Adams moved his mom into that big, expensive house of his, and it's been just the two of them for several years."

"I didn't know he had a fancy house."

"Adams was an only child. His dad was a police

officer who was killed in the line of duty, so Adams was always attentive to his mother. He married a beautiful woman who was hit by a car when she was out running one morning. They had already begun building their dream home and she'd planned everything—the furniture, curtains—every detail. We all wondered why he didn't sell it, but he furnished it like his wife had planned and stayed there—alone until his mom couldn't live by herself and he moved her in with him."

"Damn! That's a sad life, you know what I mean? I don't even want to think about it. I'm going to the station. You stay and speak to his mom when Corley brings her in."

"Yeah, I'll stay. May as well take a load off for a few minutes." He turned and sat in the chair right beside me as the other officer left.

"How are you today?" the policeman asked me.

"Could be better," I said.

"Most of us could be better, but then again, most days we could be worse, too. Who are you up here with?"

"I believe the same person you are—Sergeant Nate Adams."

"Are you kin to him?"

"No, I'm not related. Just a friend."

"I'm Detective Edward Stack. They won't tell you anything, but stay with me and you'll hear everything I do. Adams is in pretty bad shape.

Broken bones and concussion. The surgery is for a ruptured spleen. His mother is on the way, and I'm going to stay until the doctor comes out when the operation is over."

"Thanks." I stuck out my hand and added, "I'm Julie Bates."

"You're the murdered woman's daughter?"

I nodded yes,

"Adams told me you were back in town and that your house was set on fire. Sorry you're going through so much."

"Nate has become a good friend. This is terrible. I couldn't help overhearing you talk to the other policeman. Did I understand that it was a one-car accident?"

"Yes, it seems he just veered to the right and smashed into the retaining wall under the bridge where I-20 and I-26 intersect, over there at Malfunction Junction."

"What's his prognosis?" I asked.

"Won't know 'til the surgeon comes out." He cracked his knuckles, and then commented, "There's complimentary coffee over there. Would you like some?"

Before I could answer, a woman came in wearing green surgical scrubs. She walked directly to Detective Stack.

"You're waiting for news on the city policeman, Nate Adams, right?"

"That's correct."

"I'm Dr. Benson. The surgery is over. He did well and he's in recovery, but he's not awake yet. Depending on his condition then, I'll probably put him back to sleep, what we call a medically induced coma, for a few days while he begins to heal."

"There weren't any bullets in him or anything like that?" the policeman asked.

"No, all of his injuries appear consistent with results of an automobile crash. Why? Did someone shoot at him?"

"Not that we know of. I'm just looking for a reason for the wreck."

"I didn't find any evidence of that. You can see him in recovery for a few minutes, but don't expect him to respond to you." She pointed toward a door and added, "Go through there and tell the nurse whom you wish to see.

We followed her instructions and then the nurse to an area that was a room with only three walls — all of them covered with medical equipment. The fourth side was partitioned off from the hall with a heavy plastic beige curtain, which the nurse left partially open when we went in. One of the screens above the head of the bed had four separate tracings in different colors. The red one was jumping up and down all around the baseline.

Nate looked twenty-five years older. Not much of his face showed because an oxygen mask covered his mouth and nose. The bandage around his head wrapped over his forehead.

What I could see of his face was pale, not like pale flesh, but gray, an ashy color. He had two IVs and numerous cords and tubes leading from his body.

The nurse must have assumed a much closer relationship than friendship between Nate and me because she said, "You may pat his fingertips if you like, but please don't touch him anywhere else. I realize how bad this looks to you, but it's all part of postsurgical care."

"Thank you," I whispered. Normal volume in this setting seemed disrespectful. I only stroked his thumb, avoiding the monitor clamped on his index finger. I didn't expect any response, and there was none. The policeman touched my elbow, and we left Nate's room. The nurse followed us back to the waiting room, where she said, "He'll stay here until he's ready to move to Intensive Care. When he gets there, you may visit him, one at a time, for ten minutes every . . . "

"Devil woman!" The shriek filled the room, far too loud to be coming from the tall, thin gray-haired woman stepping off the elevator with a uniformed policewoman and pointing her finger at me.

"I know who you are—that wicked bitch who consorts with Satan!" She tried to run at me, but the female cop grabbed her. Detective Stack stepped in front of me.

"My boy told me all about you telling him those stories about vampires and werewolves and ghosts and things to cover whatever evil you're up to. He lies awake at night worrying about you and your made-up delusions. No way you could have known about Gates Street, no way." She yanked her arm, trying to break loose from the policewoman's hold.

"You have no right to be here. Only relatives." Suddenly, she stopped screeching and burst into tears. "Only relatives, and I'm his only one. Nobody else." She turned to the policewoman.

"I'll sit here until the doctor comes out." She pointed to a chair, and I noticed her hands shook.

The lady I assumed was Officer Corley raised her eyebrows at Detective Stack. He stepped forward to Mrs. Adams and said, "The surgeon has already come from the operating room. Her name is Dr. Benson, and she says he did well, but when we saw him, he has a lot of tubes and monitors. The nurse told us they're normal after his kind of surgery."

"How dare that slut go in to see my boy before his own *mother*! I told him the only reason a girl her age would spend so much time with him was to get his house and money." Her voice rose again into a wail with no words.

"I think it might be best if I leave," I said and stepped away.

"I'm positive it's for the best," Officer Corley said with an embarrassed look. "Call me later."

29

THE OLD woman's words sounded over and over in my head as I drove to the church, speeding along downtown streets. I had to let Preacher Ron know about Nate's car wreck. He'd want to go to the hospital and be there when his friend became alert, and because he was a pastor, they'd let him. I had a selfish reason for letting Preacher Ron know about Nate's condition, also. I needed him so he could tell me Nate's condition no matter what Mrs. Adams thought about me. I had an idea that if it was in her power, she'd have me barred from seeing her son.

Just as important, I needed Preacher Ron as a pastor and counselor for me. I was falling apart—full meltdown. Nothing made sense anymore, but that table jumping out of my salt ring had freaked me out.

I pushed the door open and stepped into the church. Remembering the stink that had poured from the door when I was there before, I sniffed the air.

Not even a whiff of stench, but the scent of the room wasn't fragrant like air freshener or cleaning supplies. It didn't have any smell at all.

Rows of metal folding chairs substituted for church pews, and a plain wooden table at the front served as the altar. Fired-gold ceramic candlesticks with unlit white tapers stood on small stands at each side of the altar. The top of a wooden cross made of two trees attached to the wall behind the makeshift worship center towered about fifteen feet. Branches on the boughs had been sawed off, leaving stubs no more than four inches long protruding from the beams and maintaining the minimalism of using trees instead of processed boards.

Unlike The Big Apple's arched windows, no stained glass decorated this place of worship, and the only thing that might be even related to a statue was the figure of Christ on the cross. He was depicted as a man dressed in modern day casual—red and black plaid flannel shirt and jeans. Even as upset as I was, I wasn't surprised that Preacher Ron didn't display a robed, bearded savior of the past. He taught a living God—the Father, the Son, and the Holy Ghost—a God of *now*. What was that figure made of? Preacher Ron or one of his parishioners had probably built it, perhaps from an old store mannequin. Maybe a broken one because the head was bowed forward at an extreme angle. Or maybe the head loosened almost off the dummy when the cross pulled loose from the wall at the top.

Stepping behind the table to get a closer look, I saw an aluminum step ladder lying on the floor. As though my eyes wouldn't focus on the scene that my brain refused to comprehend, I still didn't realize what I saw.

I looked up at Jesus. His arms hung limp by his sides, and his legs must have come unattached from the cross because they dangled awkwardly. His head was bent so far toward the front that most of his face was pressed against the chest of that incongruous plaid shirt. In the pictures and crucifixes I'd seen all my life, Jesus' head slumps forward and his chin touches his shoulder, but never was he depicted in such an extreme, bizarre pose—an impossible position unless the head was detached from the body.

That's when I saw a strap running from his neck to one of those sawed-off stubs on the vertical beam of the cross. I shrieked when my eyes focused on the six-inch wooden cross hanging upside down on a plaited piece of leather suspended from the stump. That's what held the preacher up there—not a rope or cord, but a braided leather lanyard that extended from around his neck to the remnant of a branch.

The sight wasn't movie gruesome—no blood— and the angle of Preacher Ron's head made it impossible to see his face. I *knew* who was hanging there, but it was too horrible to be real.

I ran out the front door. Standing on the step

where I'd talked with Preacher Ron the first time I met him, with tears streaming down my cheeks, I made the call.

"911. What's your emergency?" the dispatcher answered.

"I'm at the nondenominational church on Fern Street," I answered. "There's been an accident. A man is dead."

"What's the . . . " she began, but a sudden wind gusted across me, almost blowing me over while drenching me with a stench more disgusting than a polecat's spray. In a panic, I pressed disconnect on the phone, ran to my car, and sped away.

"MISS GLORY," I called when I entered the back door. I'd come to get her, take her away, but there was no answer. I went through the kitchen and bedroom to the front room, but Glory wasn't there. Just then I heard the toilet flush. *She must be in the bathroom,* I thought.

"Ju-u-u-u-ulie." A voice drew my name out in a soft whisper. I was afraid that Glory had fallen or hurt herself, so I ran to the bathroom. The door was unlocked. I flung it open. The room was empty, but fine white feathers covered the floor and tub. Had Glory torn open a feather pillow in there for some reason? Did Glory even own a feather pillow or was that what down was like? I'd never owned anything filled with down and didn't think Glory could afford it either. I picked up a feather between my fingers. It fluttered away.

Once again, I heard my name. A familiar voice, it was too low to identify. Odor assaulted me, not the smell of defecation or decay. This was the reek of sulfur.

As I closed the bathroom door, the toilet flushed. I didn't look again. Whatever was in there was invisible. I pulled the cloth sack Mrs. Estes had given me from between the mattress and the bed springs. Expecting to find it empty, I was surprised to see the antique weapon still there. I grabbed the witch bottle from the wardrobe.

I glanced at the bedside table, looking for Mom's photo so I could take it with me, too. The picture wasn't there. My mind didn't have time to process that before the framed print flew through the air from the front room right past my head and landed upright on the vanity. Before my eyes, the dress my mother wore in the portrait changed from green to a deep, crimson red. The color of blood wasn't a color I'd ever seen my mother wear.

Another "Ju-u-u-u-u-lie." Soft and low, but vaguely familiar voice, followed by banging—loud, earsplitting knocks from the walls.

Gleaming copper pennies appeared scattered over the floor. They didn't come from anywhere— just materialized. I'd read about this kind of thing.

Poltergeists caused visible and audible disturbances, sometimes associated with adolescents and thought to be related to their hormonal upheavals. There hadn't been any young people in this house for a long time, but had the delusions of rape and my crazy hallucinations screwed up my hormones so bad that I'd attracted a poltergeist? Doug Kappa had suggested there might be a poltergeist, but he hadn't been able to get readings in the house.

I didn't have enough time to give this much consideration. As I clasped my hands over my ears trying to drown out the thudding in the walls, I saw that the ceiling seemed to be closer to my head. I looked up and actually saw it lowering in slow motion. The walls gradually crumpled into accordion folds. Still holding the witch bottle and gun, I rushed to escape through the kitchen.

The door wouldn't open. Stuck or locked. I couldn't tell why, but it wouldn't open. Same with the door to Glory's front room.

I was trapped while the walls hammered out a deafening bass beat as they wrinkled until the ceiling was only inches from the top of my head. The floor was next. The boards rippled, rising and falling, very slowly at first. The rhythm surged, swelling.

I screamed and screamed and screamed as loud as I could. Everything stood still. The kitchen door opened, and Glory stepped in carrying a shopping bag.

"What's wrong, Julie?"

"Don't you see?"

"I see you've thrown pennies all over the room."

"I didn't put them there. We have to get out of here, Miss Glory." I looked around. The floors and ceilings were normal, but I knew now the things I'd experienced weren't hallucinations. I patted the heaviness of the gun in its bag. I wasn't crazy. It was all real.

"Why?" Glory's bewilderment showed in her face and tone.

"We have a poltergeist." I don't know how, but I said it calmly, not expressing my fear and horror.

"Poltergeist. Balderdash! There's no such thing."

"Get your meds. We're going now."

"Where?"

"I'll rent us a room."

"I'm not going back to that Crown Motel," Glory said, and I agreed with her.

30

RICHARD ARRIVED in front of Glory's house just before Julie and Glory stepped out of the front door. He'd come prepared with a wooden stake, a gold crucifix, and a small container of holy water he'd lifted from the Catholic church up the street. He dashed across the street and into the laundromat but stayed near the window — watching for Julie as he had since the first time he saw her. He looked over at her car. The tires were flat again.

He didn't wait long. The two women hurried outside. Glory had a small suitcase, and Julie carried the witch jar and the cloth bag she'd shown him at the grocery store.

Beep. Julie pointed the key fob toward her car. She opened the driver's door and shoved her things inside. After that, she went around and opened the passenger door for Glory.

She hasn't noticed, Richard thought. *Whatever's*

going on, Julie's too upset to see that all four of her tires are flat. He ran from the store and up to Julie's door.

"Stop!" he shouted and slapped the glass.

"What now?" Julie asked and lowered the window.

"Your tires are flat. What's wrong? Where are you going?"

"It's the house, Richard! There's something in this house. Poltergeists or something more evil."

"I don't think it's a poltergeist."

"You don't know what's been happening today."

"I know that poltergeists don't do a lot of what's happened to you. Where are you going?"

"To a motel, but not where Miss Glory stayed when the exterminator came. I'll rent a room for Miss Glory and me until I can get a priest or someone to clean the house of whatever evil is in it."

"Forget about a motel. The City Lights Hotel is close enough to walk. Come on. I'll help you carry your belongings." He reached for the cloth bag, but she handed him the witch bottle instead. Glory gave him her overnight case.

31

THE LADY at the registration desk of the City Lights Hotel wore a name tag that said she was "Patti." As she filled out paperwork, she seemed amazed by the strange group standing before her. She'd apparently never had an old lady, an obviously flustered redhead, and an unkempt, ragged, homeless-looking man register together before. "Please don't put us on the sixth floor," Richard said. "With our luck, we'd get room 666."

"We don't have a room with that number." Patti placed a form on the desk. "I'll need to see your driver's licenses also and please fill in your car's tag number."

I signed "Julie Bates" and handed over my driver's license. Glory scribbled out "Glory Nomed," and said, "I don't drive." I didn't think I'd ever seen or heard her last name before.

Richard stepped up. "I won't be registering

because I'm not staying. I'm just helping them get settled in."

"Don't lie to me," Patti said. "I don't know what kind of *ménage a' trois* you three are up to, but I'm charging for three in the room." She handed the form back to me. "I need your car tag number."

"We didn't bring the car," I answered. "My tires are all flat."

"Credit card?" Patti's voice took on a mechanical, recorded quality. She must have decided to get us to a room or away—whichever would get us out of the lobby as soon as possible.

"I don't have one yet," I began. "You see, my house burned and . . . "

"No card, no room," Patti cut me off and turned away. I slapped a roll of money on the counter and she turned back toward us.

"Will cash work?" I asked.

"If not, we'd like to see the manager," Richard said. "This woman's home burned completely. She needs a room."

"Okay, but I'll have to hold a deposit."

"Take what you need, then give her a receipt and a room key."

"We don't use keys. We use cards with magnetic strips," Patti snarled sarcastically with a matching expression.

"That's a kind of key." Richard picked up the card and asked for a receipt for the money.

Unlike Santa at the Crown Motel, Patti didn't offer to escort us to the room or fetch ice and sodas for us.

ROOM 414 had all the accoutrements of a modern hotel room, yet, somehow, it made me think of the hotel where I'd seen Billie Long take a shot at her husband so many years ago. Maybe any hotel would have brought that memory.

Glory squealed with delight when she opened the doors of an expensive wooden entertainment center and revealed an enormous television. It was huge.

Richard unlocked another cabinet and exposed a mini refrigerator and a stash of snacks.

Tasteful framed signs informed us that we had WiFi, not that we needed it. I hadn't brought my computer and my phone wasn't fancy enough to use WiFi.

The clerk hadn't asked about beds, and I'd assumed we'd have two beds. Granted, we'd told her only two of us would stay, but she'd given us a room with one king-sized bed instead of two doubles.

I turned to Richard. "Will you call down and tell that woman we want a different room—one with two beds?"

"That's okay," Glory interrupted. "This bed's big enough for us both."

"You don't understand," I said. "It has nothing to

do with you, but after those nightmares I've had, I don't want to share a bed with anyone. The linens get wet with sweat and I feel like I'm freezing. I might thrash around. You could get hurt."

Richard didn't join this conversation. He called the desk, asked for a room change, paused, and then told her, "I'll expect the manager to call me here about that."

He turned back toward me. "What did we do to piss her off so bad? She swears they don't have another room, but she says she'll have the manager call when he comes in."

"Balderdash," Glory said.

"Let's don't worry about that right now," Richard continued. "I want to know what happened that made you two get out of your house so fast." He pulled the office chair away from the desk and sat. Glory settled on the edge of the bed. I took the recliner and set the gun bag on the little round table beside it.

While I tried to bring Richard up to date about tables that jumped around by themselves and walls that closed in as well as Frannie and Elvis, Glory turned on the television. She kept turning up the volume until I almost had to shout to tell my story.

"Then I found out that my friend Nate Adams, the policeman, had an accident like the one I saw in my mind. He's in the hospital." I started to tell Glory to turn the TV down, but I didn't really want her to know about everything. She must have been watching a comedy because she giggled softly.

"Did you talk to him?"

"No, he was in surgery and now he's in a medically induced coma, but that's not the worst thing that happened. I went over to Nate's church. His preacher is dead."

"How'd that happen?"

"Apparently, that cross made out of two trees over the altar at his church came loose from the wall. He was on a ladder repairing it when the leather lanyard around his neck caught on a short stump where a limb had been cut off. The end result is that Preacher Ron is hanging there dead. The ladder is on the floor. I don't know if it collapsed from under him causing the accident or if his struggles when the cross he wore around his neck got caught made him kick the ladder out from beneath him by accident. The really weird thing is that the wooden cross he wore on that leather strip is upside down right over his head."

"Julie, you seeing the cop's wreck could mean that you're psychic and the voices and visions might be the result of tension, but I don't believe that. An upside-down cross is a symbol of evil. I think you're being possessed by a demon. What have you been doing about all this?" Richard said.

Totally absorbed in the television, Glory giggled again.

"Preacher Ron said that demons are unclean spirits from hell," I answered. "He planned to talk to a priest friend of his about exorcism. Doug Kappa, the ghost hunter, said he'd come back and try to determine if I had a ghost or poltergeist when the wiring is updated and he gets his equipment fixed."

"At least you're trying to take action, but it may be too late."

"I've got the gun from Mrs. Estes, but Preacher Ron said it's impossible to kill a demon. The only way to get rid of one is to send it back to hell, which is what an exorcism does."

Glory laughed out loud.

Furious, Richard turned toward her. "What's so funny?"

"Just this show I'm watching."

"Yeah? Well, I don't believe that. Maybe you think all of this is humorous because you like to see Julie suffer." If looks could kill, Glory would have ended Richard's life right then.

"No, Richard, she helps me," I objected. "Glory had the medicine to cure my cystitis."

"She cured you medically? Maybe Glory is a witch." Suddenly, Richard ran at Glory, pulled a small container of liquid from his pocket and yelled, "Or a demon. You signed that registration slip downstairs 'Glory Nomed.' I thought it was a strange name. It's 'demon' spelled backwards. I brought holy water and a crucifix. We'll see what you are."

He grabbed Glory's neck. The muscles in his arms knotted as he squeezed. His jaw tightened and his eyes bugged. Glory struggled for release, scrabbling at Richard with her poor arthritic hands and knocking the bottle to the floor.

"Stop!" I shrieked. I didn't think. I grabbed the gun from the bag and pointed it at them. I only meant it as a threat, but it fired with an awful sound and smell. Did I pull the trigger? I didn't know then and don't know now.

Richard released his hands from Glory's neck and fell to the floor.

A small patch of blood blossomed on his shirt, and he lay still, his eyes wide open staring at the ceiling. Horror filled me.

Julie roared big guffaws deep from her belly and turned away from me.

SILLY GIRL. YOU'VE KILLED HIM. The same voice I'd heard in my car came from the corner where Glory stood with her back to me, but it couldn't be her. Too deep. Too loud. Overpowering.

"Miss Glory," I shouted, "get away! Run! It's in that corner."

I AM SHEEAHLZEERAH!

The sound filled the small space—surrounded me, stifled me.

ARE YOU SO STUPID THAT YOU THINK I FEAR HOLY WATER? The voice was so loud that it hurt my ears and reverberated against the walls.

Where was it coming from? Was there a ghost or demon behind Glory? I ran to the elderly lady and attempted to put my arms around her.

Glory turned to face me. **WATCH THIS!** She picked up the vial of water, opened it, and drank from it. When the container was empty, she spit on the bed. Little flames flickered up from each drop, but the bedding didn't catch fire.

Impossible! Glory was my friend, my protector. Even more important, Glory was a female. I'd washed her back in the bath. I'd seen *with my own eyes* that Glory's body was that of an old woman.

Whoever, *whatever*, haunted me, it was male.

Laughter roared from Glory's mouth. So strange. Such a loud, rumbling sound from a little old lady.

GENDER? YOU DARE TO DOUBT ME BECAUSE OF GENDER. I AM SHEEAHLZEERAH. I TRANSCEND GENDER. SEE THE REAL ME.

Glory's face melted. Like molten wax dripping down the side of a burning candle, her cheeks drooped. Eye lids dropped over bulging eyes. Hair disappeared. Arms and fingers elongated, reaching almost to the floor, and diaphanous wings folded into them.

The thing in front of me was no longer a person. I saw a monster. A hideous beast. I backed away until I touched the wall, but there was nowhere to go. I felt the surface behind me move and undulate. The other walls closed in, then backed away. Beneath my feet, the floor rippled.

The thing's belly popped out, swelling so I feared some other creature would burst from it. Feet shriveled into hooves.

A WEREWOLF? A VAMPIRE? THOSE WERE ONLY TO SCARE YOU AND TO MAKE YOU DOUBT YOURSELF IF YOU EVER REMEMBERED ME IN WAKING MOMENTS. MY WINGS ARE PART OF THE REAL ME, BUT ONLY YOU COULD SEE THEM.

I LAUGHED SECRETLY WHEN YOU ADDED GARLIC TO OUR FOOD TO PROTECT US. I AM NOT A VAMPIRE, BUT IF I WERE, NO AMOUNT OF GARLIC WOULD DETER ME— SUPERSTITIONS—ALL OLD SUPERSTITIONS! SHEEAHLZEERAH IS REAL, NOT BOUND BY MYTHS!

"What have you done with Glory?" I gasped.

I AM GLORY. I AM SHEEAHLZEERAH. AND I AM YOUR LOVER.

The hanging jowls drew into finely chiseled masculine features. Thick, lustrous sandy brown hair topped the handsome face. The chest and bulging belly shrank into a firm six-pack of abs. Arms and legs became the muscled limbs of an athlete. A handsome male, the lover in my dreams, stood before me.

I'd known his cruelty.   I'd felt him take my

body brutally with no concern for my agony. I'd been told that the incubus was exceedingly handsome and would allure his victims. This creature, regardless of his human beauty, had made no effort to enchant me.

SORRY ABOUT YOUR MOTHER AND YOUR HIGH SCHOOL FRIEND. Still loud, the words were more feminine—Glory's voice coming from the man's mouth. **THEY HAD TO GO.**

"Why?" I screamed.

I RODE YOUR MOTHER EVERY NIGHT SINCE I CAME HERE, BUT SHE WOKE TOO EARLY ONE MORNING AND AFTER THAT, SHE KNEW ABOUT ME. HER SILLY BOTTLES AND HER INCANTATIONS WERE ATTEMPTS TO ESCAPE ME. I HAD TO DESTROY HER.

"What about Jerry?" I asked.

YOU FOUND HIM ON FACEBOOK. YOU WOULD HAVE ENDED UP LIVING WITH HIM, AND THE ONE TIME I CANNOT HAVE A WOMAN IS WHEN SOMEONE ELSE IS IN BED WITH HER. I COULD NOT LET YOU STAY IN YOUR HOME AND WHORE AROUND WITH YOUR OLD BOYFRIEND. I HAD TO GET RID OF HIM, TOO.

"How?" I asked. "Nate said the autopsy didn't show any cause of death, and how did you get him downtown so early in the morning?"

The incubus opened his mouth and sucked in the air. It sounded like the wind of a typhoon. I was snatched across the room toward him, but he reversed his breath and blew me against the wall.

I INHALED HIS BREATH, SUCKED THE LIFE FROM HIM AFTER I LURED HIM DOWNTOWN. IT WASN'T HARD. I CLAIMED I WOULD PAY AN ENORMOUS SUM FOR HIM TO WORK FOR ME ILLEGALLY, BUT I COULD ONLY MEET HIM AT THAT TIME.

"Did you do that to Preacher Ron, too.

NO, THAT SILLY PIECE OF WOOD CAUGHT IN THE CROSS HE WAS NAILING BACK TO THE WALL. THEN IT TWISTED AND HANGED HIM. A hideous laugh filled the room. **BUT I CONFESS, I MADE IT HAPPEN.**

Glory's face convulsed into more weird, wild laughter.

"I don't understand. How could you go around like an old lady saying, 'Thank you, Jesus,' all the time?"

MOCKERY. WE OF THE LEGION ALWAYS MOCK RELIGION.

"And you wrecked Nate's car, didn't you?"

I DIDN'T FORCE YOUR COP FRIEND TO WRECK HIS CAR. ALL I WANTED WAS TO HAVE A TALK WITH HIM, BUT WHEN I APPEARED IN MY NATURAL FORM, HE FREAKED OUT AND DROVE INTO THE CONCRETE.

"What about my house? Did you set it on fire?"

I began inching backwards toward the door.

HOW ELSE COULD I FORCE YOU TO LIVE WITH ME? I WANTED YOU. I NEEDED TO CONTROL YOU ALL THE TIME.

"You killed Richard, too," I accused.

NO, YOU DID THAT YOURSELF.

The beautiful man laughed—a long, loud, ugly sound of mirth. **YOU WASTED YOUR SILVER BULLET ON HIM.** The monster spat and continued his maniacal giggle. **BUT NO BULLET OF ANY KIND CAN SAVE YOU FROM ME. I WANT YOU TO BE MINE FOREVER, AND I WON'T BE WAITING UNTIL YOU SLEEP WHEN I RIDE YOU FROM NOW ON.** A pause and then: **WHY ARE YOU BACKING TOWARD THE DOOR? YOU CAN'T ESCAPE ME!**

Doom flooded over me, consuming every thought. Eternity as slave to this monster?

The fiend changed rapidly back and forth: from Glory to Monster to Cruel Lover. When I thought of the faceless cat, the dark emptiness transformed to the man in the top hat and then to the white coyote—an endless, hideous parade.

"What did you do to the man at the Crown Motel?" I asked.

Immediately, the demon before me became a beautiful young woman. A voluptuous female with long mahogany hair and a sensual mouth. Her expression was innocence, but the voice remained loud and bragging.

I PLEASURED HIM. The beautiful face broke into a tantalizing smile. **I AM MALE OR FEMALE— INCUBUS OR SUCCUBUS—WHATEVER IS MY OWN PLEASURE. OH, HE LIKED WHAT I DID TO HIM UNTIL I GREW TIRED AND RETURNED TO MY NATURAL FORM.**

This is another nightmare, I told myself. *It can't be real.*

SHEEAHLZEERAH IS A SHAPE-SHIFTER. I CAN BE ANYTHING OR ANYONE. I AM MANY. I AM LEGION.

I grabbed the witch bottle off the bed and held it in front of me.

Just then my cell phone rang. I looked down at it lying there. Only one ring, but there was a word on the caller ID space. Keeping the bottle pointed at the demon, I leaned over the now quiet phone. The word on the ID was "Mama."

THAT STUPID BOTTLE IS NOT GOING TO HELP YOU. I'M NOT A WITCH. I AM SHEEAHLZEERAH.

The handsome young man flickered across the form, and then his monstrous, winged image took control. He grasped the jar from my hand, drew his arm back like a baseball pitcher and flung the vessel against the wall. The glass shattered. Pins, needles, nails, and red hair spun around like a miniature tornado, then shot into all directions like shrapnel while the liquid and other items fell on the carpet.

Richard had told me a ghost could fully materialize if part of the physical body remained. I grabbed my mother's hair from the floor and screamed, "Mama!" I didn't really expect it to do any good, but if I'd ever wanted my mama, this was it.

SHE CAN'T HELP YOU. SHE CAN'T EVEN REACH YOU. SHE'S BEEN TRYING IN HER FEEBLE GHOST WAYS—CREATING PICTURES OF HERSELF, MOVING THINGS, SPREADING FEATHERS AND PENNIES EVERYWHERE—BUT SHE CAN'T MATERIALIZE WITHOUT PART OF HER BODY. I EVEN DUG UP HER GRAVE TO BE SURE SHE HADN'T ESCAPED.

Like a terrified child in the night, I cried, "Mama, Mama, Mama."

The wall behind Sheeahlzeerah opened and formed a dark tunnel. At the end of that cave-like cavity, a woman wearing a flowing crimson gown appeared walking toward us. Not a shadow, my mother reached out a fully materialized arm toward Sheeahlzeerah, who rapidly morphed into Miss Glory.

My mother's voice filled the room. "You'll never have her, Glory. I tried and tried to come to my daughter, but you kept playing your shape-shifting games—making my Julie believe she was visiting the past and seeing creatures or going crazy."

Mama turned to me and touched my shoulder.

"I *have* been trying to reach you, Julie—wanting to warn you. The one rings on the telephone, the face in the mirror, the flushing in the bathroom, the sounds, pennies, feathers—all of that was me, but the other things were Sheeahlzeerah and closing the walls in on you was Glory's doing, not mine. I've been here all along. I even sent Mrs. Estes and Frannie to you, hoping they could help you."

"I couldn't cross over the light at the end of the tunnel because I have unfinished business here," she continued. "Taking care of you, my child, was my responsibility, but the demon's power kept me from you." She laughed softly. "I even made Elvis stutter and refuse to say her name at the house. I'm tired. I need to go on, but I can't. TCB. My business is not yet finished."

AND WHAT UNFINISHED BUSINESS DO YOU HAVE HERE? YOUR DAUGHTER IS MINE.

"No, she's not. I won't let you take her."

HOW DO YOU THINK YOU CAN STOP ME?

"I made a pact with the devil to give me power greater than yours for one hour. That time has come, and I'm taking you with me." She grabbed Glory and dragged her into the tunnel toward the white light.

AT THE END OF THE TUNNEL, THEY WON'T LET ME INTO HEAVEN.

I realized what my mother had done for me as I heard the final words of her sweet voice:

"That's not where we're going."

AFTERWORD FROM THE AUTHOR

AS I said at the beginning, this account was told to me as truth by Julie Bates. She claimed that when the authorities arrived after Patti called them because "the ungodly noise from Room 414" was disturbing the peace, she and the dead Richard were the only two people there. Julie blamed Richard's death on Glory Nomed. The desk clerk verified the old lady had checked into the hotel with them but must have "escaped."

After recovering from his wreck, Nate Adams found Richard Arthur's journals hidden in the cemetery and turned them over to me. I changed what Richard had written to third person, but I kept his words wherever possible. If you meet someone named Julie Bates, please don't assume she is who told me this story. I've used pseudonyms for all of the people names though not the location names in Julie's story. She changed her name several times before I lost touch with her. Nate Adams has resigned from the police force and left Columbia.

PHOTOGRAPHS

The pictures on these pages are of places in Columbia, South Carolina, where Julie Bates experienced the paranormal events described in The HORROR of JULIE BATES.

All photos by

Nathan R. Rizer

unless otherwise noted

Julie Bates approached Fran Rizer at one of Rizer's book-signings for her cozyesque Callie Parrish Mystery Series. Rizer spent many days and nights listening to Julie's story before writing The HORROR of JULIE BATES.

THE BIG
APPLE

2016

Julie awoke in front of this building, but she remembered being in the 1937 structure.

THE BIG
APPLE

1937

*Public
Domain
Photograph*

"Meet me at the rocket" is a familiar announcement at the S.C. State Fair for friends to catch up with each other, but Julie Bates met a horrible creature from the past instead of friends.

Julie saw inanimate objects moving when she visited the SC State Museum to see the King Tut exhibit.

Every USC student has heard or read that Longstreet Theater is haunted, but no others have reported the manifestation Julie experienced there.

Huge letters on giant buildings are trademarks of Adluh Flour which opened for business in the early 1900s.

Frannie described the workers from long ago who still haunt this building in the Vista section of Columbia.

The S.C. State Capitol building, built in the Greek Revival style, encompasses more than 130,000 square feet. Julie saw a corn crop being raised on the state house grounds. Frannie said the ghost of General Wade Hampton III rides his horse in the sky there near the dome.

Trinity Episcopal Cathedral -- The striking twin towers and tan stucco exterior of this Gothic Revival church are distinctive in downtown Columbia and were memorable from Julie's childhood even before she returned there with Frannie.

Trinity Episcopal Church Yard and Cemetery -- With more than three hundred and fifty graves, including burials of generals from the U. S. Revolutionary War, the War of 1812, and the Civil War as well as governors, several presidents of universities and colleges, and the esteemed poet Henry Timrod, a walk through beautiful Trinity Episcopal Cemetery is like a tour through history, but when Frannie took Julie there, it was more like a tour through horror.

Signs caution visitors to step carefully as the roots of a giant live oak in the cemetery have grown under the inlaid brick walk creating a mild roller coaster. effect.

Photos on this page by Aeden Rizer

353

ABOUT THE AUTHOR

FRAN RIZER'S magazine features have been published in *Better Homes & Gardens, South Carolina Magazine, Field & Stream, Southern Gardens, Living Blues, Bluegrass Unlimited, Bluegrass Now,* and others.

After retirement from teaching, she ventured into fiction and was a winner in the Augusta, Georgia, Porter Fleming Fiction Contest. Rizer's fiction has been published in the USA and Canada, and her Callie Parrish mysteries have been nominated for SIBA and Agatha Awards.

The first three Callie Parrish novels were published by Berkley Prime Crime, a division of Penguin Books. Bella Rosa Books released the next three. Odyssey South Publishing brought out Rizer's first thriller, *KUDZU RIVER — A Novel of Abuse, Murder, and Retribution,* as well as the seventh Callie Parrish mystery in 2015 and *Southern Swamps and Ruins,* a ghost story anthology with Richard D. Laudenslager in 2016.

Rizer is a featured author on the SCETV series, *A Literary Tour of South Carolina,* on *Streamline* which is offered to all South Carolina public schools. Check out www.franrizer.com or see the Internet for links to interviews and reviews. She lives in South Carolina near her two sons, Nathan and Adam, and her grandson Aeden Rizer.